THE LEAF QUEEN

A NOVEL

BY

JANET ROBERTS

Copyright @2016 by Janet Roberts

Cover design and illustration by Svetlana Dragicevic

Author photograph by Ruby Rideout

ISBN: 978-0-9973896-0-9 (Print)
ISBN: 978-0-9973896-1-6 (EPUB)
ISBN: 978-0-9973896-2-3 (MOBI)

To my father, the late Richard S. Roberts,

a really good man, husband, father, and grandfather

Surely it is much more generous to forgive and remember,

Than to forgive and forget

Maria Edgeworth

(Irish writer, 1767-1849)

CHAPTER 1

DINA

I t was wet and forgivingly mild for a February in Ireland. A tender breeze spilled off the Atlantic dancing over the slate rooftops and up the Garavogue River before sifting through the open window to stroke Dina Benet's cheek like a mother's caress. A single leaf wobbled on the tree branch outside, a match to the trembling inside of her.

The smell of frying potatoes, bacon, and eggs drifted through the corridors of the bed and breakfast, reminding Dina the body could feel hunger when the mind could not conceive of eating again. The body chose, of its own volition, to go forward and survive.

They would have let her stay at the cottage outside Sligo for a few more days, but she wanted to walk away from the memories, to work through her sadness alone before taking the train to Dublin where she'd finish her classes and, eventually, head back to the States for good. So she'd rented a room in Sligo for a few nights. Kathleen, good friend that she was, swore she was coming by before noon to spend the day with Dina so she would not be alone. But Dina had no intention of waiting for her. She was here, in Yeats country, beloved birthplace of her grandmother—and now her own child. She would take a walk on the beach after breakfast, perhaps try to write again or release herself into the healing powers of a book of poetry.

Dina could hear the voice of her grandmother, Maeve O'Malley, as if it had rolled in with the gentle wind, riding along the years, cursing God just as Dina wanted to curse heaven and earth today. Maeve's lilting cadence had more often read to Dina from Yeats than spoken blasphemy, making her outburst the day that Dina's mother died shocking. It was a moment that lived in perfect clarity in Dina's memory. She'd watched as Maeve's strong, straight back crumpled inward, her sturdy, white work shoes folding under her as she dropped to the floor and pulled her daughter's lifeless body into her arms. Dina remembered seeing the light trace of white foam lying on her mother's bluish lips and smelling the harsh odor of vomit, dried on her T-shirt, before Maeve motioned to a police officer to take her away. The breeze from Lake Erie, so clean and refreshing, had done little that day to mask the smells of beer, cheap wine, marijuana, and death.

"Justine, how could you do this?" Dina had heard her grandmother whisper just before Maeve began keening for the loss of her only child. Then Dina had gone to find her sister, Celia, the strong, responsible, first-born child, and curled up next to her on the steps outside their small apartment. There they waited together, stoicism intertwined with fragility, for Maeve to rescue them, to walk them the few short blocks from their apartment to her home.

But Dina could not curse God today as her grandmother had done all those years ago, nor could she keen with practiced ease for her own loss, still so fresh and raw. She'd made a sacrifice Maeve and Justine had not, but she felt neither courageous nor relieved. It was, she believed, a curse upon the women in her family that motherhood did not inspire the best within them to rise to the surface. If Dina could navigate a worthier path for herself she hoped, one day, she would be a good mother to some as yet unimagined child.

Sliding her fingers into the pocket of Maeve's old, gray sweater, she gently touched the worn rosary, still laying where her grandmother had always kept it. Although Dina was not a particularly religious person, there was a comfort in talking to God, an expatiation of loneliness that she could not explain, even to herself. Pulling the rosary out, she set it in her lap and began moving her mouth in time with her hands to the rhythmic *click, click* of the worn glass beads. Silently, Dina slipped into the numbing relief of this ritualistic familiarity that moved the memory of her mother further away and wrapped her in her Granny Maeve's arms once again.

Maeve had often pulled young Dina close after Justine died, as if she were trying to fill the space she carried in front of her body like an open pouch connected to her heart, only the sound of wind and dust blowing in and out of it. Celia had been less inclined to allow hugging and touching. She was twelve going on forty when they went to live with Maeve. She'd been caring for and feeding Dina since she was six, as Justine graduated from smoking pot to shooting up heroin in seemingly less time than it took Celia to make peanut butter sandwiches when they were hungry. And they were hungry much of the time.

"Oh, Granny, I wish you were here," Dina whispered to herself as the rustling of the leaves outside her window mixed with the creak of the old stairway to the bed and breakfast's dining room below. But Maeve had been dead over a year now.

Dina was tempted to call Celia, but within her sister's support would come small disapproving remarks amidst overt nurturing that hinted at silent condemnation lurking just beneath the surface. Celia believed Dina was weak and over the short span of her life Dina had come to agree. She would never tell Celia the truth about this past year, or this past week. It wouldn't be the first secret she'd kept from her sister, but it was the biggest, by far.

Click, click, click. Hail Mary, full of grace. Maybe the rosary would pave a road out of her most recent failure. If she turned to look back along the same road for a moment she could be nine years old once more. Dina's memories brought her a vision of Maeve sipping her tea as a cool breeze blew in, rustling the curtains and spiraling the steam from her mug across the room. Early May on the Great Lakes brought sunshine that hinted at a promise of warmth the lake winds would not yet allow. Just outside the window, the leaves on a large oak tree had swished in the wind, some still unfurling, others outstretched reaching for sunlight.

"I guess it's finally warm enough for the actual digging of Justine's grave," Maeve had said.

Dina was sitting on a bed that day, too, next to a sleeping Celia and watching their grandmother pray aloud to the Holy Mother and then to St. Brigid.

"Prayer calms me, Dina," Maeve said. "It gives me a sense of balance, of setting upright that which has tipped over and begun to spill about, here and there, in my life."

As she prayed, Maeve gathered herself and her life into a neat and orderly place. Despite Dina's best efforts, it had never worked as well for her, although she continued to try, as she was doing today, hoping if she kept reaching out she would latch on to the feelings that had steadied her grandmother, finding a way to anchor herself.

"Granny, do you forgive God and Mommy?" Dina had asked Maeve that morning.

"Therefore, I tell you, her many sins have been forgiven—for she loved much. Luke 7:47."

"Your eyes were closed an' you were makin' funny noises when Mommy died," the young Dina had observed.

"I was keening as is the way of the Irish when a loved one dies," Maeve said. "It's sorry I am that it scared you so, but Justine was my daughter."

"Why do you call it 'keening,' Granny?" Celia was awake by then too.

"Ahhh...I'm not sure. My mam and the old Irish called it *ullaloo*."

Dina pulled her mind back to the present. *One day far in the future will I remember Sligo as a sanctuary of healing or a place of utter sorrow?* Dina wondered if she could keen out on the Sligo beach, screaming into the wind coming off the Atlantic with the sound lost to all but her ears and God's. Perhaps Maeve and even Justine would hear her cries from their perch in the heavens and sprinkle her with some sort of comforting fairy dust to help her move forward. Maeve had been a big believer in the magic of fairies, despite her staunch Catholicism. She had also believed Dina carried within her the great Irish writers and that, one day, she would show the world her talent. Maeve had never lost that faith in Dina or stopped supporting her, despite Celia's complaints that Dina was irresponsible, that she needed to earn a living.

Dina put away the rosary and stood up. Running a comb through her short, bobbed hair, she looked at the bare branches tapping the shutters and thanked Maeve for her love of Irish poetry and her belief that, against the odds life sent her way, forgiveness was a cure for all ills.

Sweet, there is nothing left to say,

But this, that love is never lost.

Maeve had loved those lines from C.S. Lewis.

"Someday you and your sister will forgive your mother," Maeve had told her often. "You'll see and understand when you get older."

It had worked for Dina, who could forgive all but herself, but Celia had merely shrugged and looked away. Her gazed always hardened when Maeve talked about Justine. There had never been any forgiveness in her heart for their drug-addicted mother and the life they led with her before going to live with their grandmother.

Dina didn't wait for Kathleen but went to walk along the Sligo beach, sifting cold sand through her bare toes, the sun warming the rest of her as it sat, middling and not yet to noon, in the sky. She liked coming early, when it rose, angling softly over the horizon and spilling across the water in a spectacular burst of brilliance, its carroty, golden-tipped rays crossing over the waves and sand. But today she'd slept late, dreaming of the baby girl she'd just handed over just days ago to a better life than she could provide. Dina had held her child for a full thirty minutes that would have to last a lifetime, while the fear that she was failing this baby by giving her away mixed with the fear that she would somehow end up a failed mother, like Justine. She'd never needed her grandmother's love and reassurance more.

"Will you name her Maeve?" she'd asked as she held her child.

"We're set on naming her Katie," Kathleen's cousin, Colleen, replied.

"It was my granny's name and I thought it would give her strength." Dina could hear her voice faltering.

"Well, perhaps Kathleen Maeve would be a good name for our Katie," Colleen said, patting Dina's shoulder.

The words "our Katie" hurt as much today as they had when she handed her daughter over to Colleen. Dina knew she was not part of "our," and she hoped someone had taught Colleen the secrets to mothering that Justine had never given Dina. Katie deserved better than what Dina could offer. She deserved a mother, a father, and a safe home. So when Kathleen had found a home for the baby with her childless cousin Colleen and her husband, Jack, it had seemed the perfect, selfless solution.

But nothing in the calm of the waves or the quiet of the beach, punctuated only here and there with the cry of a seagull, could remove the anguish of giving Katie away or the overwhelming desire to go back to Colleen's cottage and retrieve her, never letting her go again. Dina dropped to her knees and began rocking against the breeze, face upturned to the sun and sky, but no sound would come. She could not keen for the loss of her only child as Maeve had once done for Justine. She was impotent within her own pain.

CHAPTER 2

Shivering, Dina yanked a sweater over her head, sighing with pleasure and warmth as the Irish wool surrounded her thin frame. It was damp and misty outside today. Beautiful and miserable in the way only possible, it seemed, in Ireland. Dublin was both magical and terribly difficult. She had one room with a hot plate and a tiny refrigerator on the third floor of an older, slightly shabby rooming house on Fownes Street Upper, near the Temple Bar area. The refrigerator—which cooled randomly, schizophrenically chugging to life then dying—was empty. She'd moved here without Liam, without a forwarding address, to finish her final exams and try to put the sadness of Sligo to rest somehow.

Unlike Erie, where she'd held her inner self slightly apart from her high school and college friends, in Ireland she was open and emotional in a way that was both freeing and strange. She'd felt an immediate connection to her new friends Kathleen, John, Connor, and, most of all, to Liam, a poet with a crooked smile, a thatch of curly, dark hair and an incorrigible inability to commit to anything, including Dina. She'd craved him as much emotionally as she had physically.

"John would love for you to just give him a chance," Kathleen had often told her. "But all you want is Liam." Kathleen's head would shake in a tsk-tsk manner that rained sympathy and sorrow from her tangled auburn curls—a kindly mist of understanding and disapproval. "Liam's lust, not love, Dina," she'd say with a smile and a casual lift of the shoulders signifying both disapproval and a purely Irish understanding of the lure of a dark poet in a shadowy old pub, the smell of the bog under his skin and the honey of drink and prose rolling from his tongue.

Liam had excited and pained Dina in a murky, misshapen way back then. Maeve would have kicked him out in less than thirty minutes and forbidden her to go near him again. Dina suspected he was much like her father, who she only remembered in small, mental snapshots and cloudy dreams during which he'd played a guitar for her and sang. But breaking it off with Liam had been easy after she'd caught him with a young waitress they both knew. Hiding her pregnancy from him had seemed an impossible task until he announced, when she was in her third month, that if she didn't take him back, he was moving to London.

"Go ahead and leave, Liam. We're through," Dina had told him, pale from morning sickness and nursing a cup of tea at Bewley's.

He'd sat down, stretching his legs, crossed at the ankles, hands stuffed in the pockets of an old, tweed jacket. "You don't look so good, Dina. You need me, and you'll miss me."

"Every time I look at you, I see that little waitress Deidre, her heading peeking out from the covers on my bed. No, I won't miss you. Go, Liam. Do us both a favor and go."

Liam had signaled for the waiter then.

"He's not staying," Dina told him when he arrived. "He was just leaving."

"You're a fuckin' rude one today, aren't you?"

Dina rolled her eyes. "Watch me be a rude American, Liam. I'm leaving and you can pick up the tab."

After that, Dina had given Liam no more thought than she would a passerby. He had less ability to be a father to another human being than she could ever hope to learn someday about mothering.

Dina had known, from the moment she tried to envision herself in this run-down flat, caring for a baby and turning that baby over to Liam on the weekends, that she would be sentencing her child to a life not much better than her own upbringing. Except this time without a Granny Maeve to come to the rescue. She wanted, for this baby, her own idyllic dream of a safe, loving home with two parents, a big yard to play in, and all the advantages she'd never had. To her relief, Liam went to London. As far as Dina could tell, he had not returned and he knew nothing about Katie.

The phone in the downstairs hallway was ringing. Dina could hear Mr. Lafferty's heavy steps as he walked along the wooden floorboards to answer it. She grabbed a few pounds and shoved them in her backpack. She had no classes or work this morning at Trinity College where she was an administrative assistant and a tutor, as well as a graduate student studying literature and creative writing. She was meeting Kathleen at

Quays Bar for a pint, some lunch, and any news she might have about Katie.

"Dina, lass!" Mr. Lafferty called up the narrow staircase. "Phone's for you. It's long distance from America."

"Okay," Dina answered. She was late so if it had been a local call she would have declined, but it had to be Celia. Dina hadn't called home in almost two months nor answered Celia's letters and she knew her sister was furious. Celia knew nothing of Katie's existence, let alone that she'd been adopted, and Dina meant to keep it that way. Dina would tell her sister that she was coming home very soon. Two classes to finish up and a couple papers to write, then she would be on her way. She wanted to start over in America, but somehow actually doing so made it feel like she'd be truly and totally abandoning Katie. The prospect of leaving her forever increased Dina's belief that she was incapable of being a good mother, that all she could do was run away. But staying wasn't a good solution either. Kathleen promised she would send news of how Katie was doing every year and assured Dina she'd been the best of mothers to give her baby such a loving home. With Katie weighing so heavily on her mind and heart, Dina had avoided Celia to circumvent any possible suspicions. Ever relentless, Celia could easily reach out and reclaim her hold on Dina. She was Dina's rock in hard times, but also a suffocating voice of control and authority.

Dina smiled at Mr. Lafferty as he tipped his cap and handed her the phone. She watched him leave, brown corduroy pants and sturdy work shoes moving slowly, his shoulders hunched a bit in his tan sweater. The only splotch of color was a plaid scarf wrapped around his neck. Dina knew he was heading out for a pint himself.

"Hello?" Dina said.

"Dina, it's me," Celia answered. "Didn't you get my letter?"

"Oh, maybe. I lost some of my mail a week or so ago," Dina said. "It fell out of my backpack, right into the Liffey. Too dark out to see where it went."

"Dina, I left you messages too," Celia said. "Didn't anyone tell you?"

The connection wasn't great but Celia sounded like she was crying. Dina felt a twinge of guilt. "No, no one gave me a message, CeCe," Dina said. "What's going on? What happened?"

The silence was mere seconds but it seemed longer and Dina thought they'd lost the connection. She watched as Bridget opened her first-floor apartment door and dropped a garbage bag outside. It reeked of dirty baby diapers and rotten food, old beer bottles clinking against one another and the floor. Dina turned to face the wall. She didn't want to see the baby, to think about him living with Bridget in squalor much as she had lived with Justine. She would want to hold him and then, well, last time she hadn't wanted to hand the little boy back. Things had been weird between she and Bridget ever since.

"Nothing happened, Dina," Celia sniffed. "I'm just worried. I barely hear from you anymore. Since February, you've been a stranger. Are you still angry about Granny's death?"

"What are you talking about?" Dina heard her voice echoing in the hallway. "CeCe, I'm trying to finish my coursework so I can come home...to Erie. I don't want you expecting me to report to you all the time when I get there."

"Okay, okay," Celia said.

"Granny passed away well over a year ago. I admit, I was angry at first because I didn't make it home in time to say good-bye, but I'm over it CeCe. I shouldn't have blamed you and, for what's it worth, I forgive you."

"Thankfully for me, you're much better at that stuff than I am...forgiveness, I mean."

"Well, don't track me like a dog all the time. It makes me worry about coming back home to live. You have to cut me some slack and quit trying to be my mother."

"I'm not trying to be your mother. I don't think either of us knows much about how to do that."

The pause was as small as a baby's breath and as deep as the ocean that lay between them. "No, no role models for us in that department." Dina's voice had a funny, tinny sound to it. "Look, I have to go. I'm meeting Kathleen. I'll be home in about two months. I'll let you know when exactly after I get the plane tickets."

"Alright, I'll wait to hear from you." Celia sighed. "And quit throwing my letters into the river."

Dina hung up the phone. She wanted to laugh but Celia's comments about their inability to mother hit her in the gut. She rocked on her heels, moaning softly. Once mute and unable to voice her pain, now she could not stop herself from slipping into a semi-trance, and at times made a spectacle of herself in the face of painful thoughts.

"Hey, shut up." Bridget was back in her doorway. "My wee one is sleepin'."

Dina wiped her eyes.

"Keening is for funerals, you know," Bridget said. "You're a right crazy girl."

Dina hurried out to the street and began running. She ran as if the wind were chasing her, as if she could catch Maeve's ghost among the throngs of people in Temple Bar and stop this madness. She arrived at The Quays sweaty, hair disheveled, face tear-stained. She ducked her head as she entered, her eyes adjusting to the dim lighting. The smells of roast lamb, bangers and mash, and beer on tap filled her nose as she scanned the bar.

"Dina, what is it, hon?" Kathleen's long, auburn curls danced around her young, slender frame as she moved quickly toward Dina, putting her arm around her friend as she walked her to a table by the window.

Dina shook her head then hugged Kathleen. "I just talked to Celia." She tried to shrug as if it were nothing.

"Are you sure you want to move back?"

"I need a job and I need to put distance between me and what I've done."

"So you keep telling me," Kathleen said dryly. "But I don't believe it's what you want. And you've done nothing but give the child a better life."

"So you keep telling me." Dina smiled. "But still, I think I've gotta go."

"Well, it's not like you don't have a few bad memories in the States, too. Remember when your granny died? You ignored your sister's letters and calls, and then it was too late…"

"Yes, I know. Liam and the baby here…Granny's death and dealing with CeCe over there…" Dina sighed. "We were right here in Quays after I found out Granny died."

"You'd come looking for Liam and some comfort, but instead you got all the comfort in the world you needed from me." Kathleen's smile caused Dina to give her yet another hug. The waitress appeared and they each ordered a pint and a sandwich.

Celia had called her that day last year, too, upset that Dina had ignored her letters and hadn't returned her calls for a month. Dina been so in love with Liam, but all Celia ever said was that she could do better than a flakey, unemployed poet, so Dina began avoiding her sister. Easy to do with miles of ocean between them.

"Dina, I've been trying to tell you about Granny," Celia had said that day. "She was so sick. She went so quickly. I wanted you to come home and say good-bye."

"Good-bye? What are you saying, CeCe?"

"Dina, Granny died yesterday. Please come home. I'll send you a plane ticket. It'll be waiting at the airport. We won't have the funeral until you get here."

Dina had begun crying, clutching the phone as she slid to the floor.

"Come home, Dina," Celia said. "Come home right now."

Dina had felt as if she couldn't breathe. It wasn't possible that her granny was dead. She'd run to Quays then, too, that time searching for Liam. She'd found him at a corner table, writing with a pint of Guinness in front of him, the glass beaded with condensation that created a ring to match similar, still wet rings on his table. He'd looked up at her, pen poised, and exuded a mixture of irritation and mild curiosity. Dina's mouth opened and closed like a fish banked on dry land, no rhythm to the inhale and exhale. Tears welled up in her eyes.

"Dina?" Liam finally put his pen down.

"Granny." It was all she could say. "Celia called. My granny died. I need to get to the airport. I need to go home."

Kathleen was at the next table with her friends, Connor and John, that day. It was Kathleen who heard her and jumped up, coming over to hug Dina and offer help. John had followed, patting her shoulder while Liam simply sat there, staring at her quizzically. Dina had managed to explain that a plane ticket was waiting for her at the airport and that she'd missed the letter and phone calls from her sister telling her Maeve was sick.

"You remember the night you were drunk and you threw my mail in the river?" she'd said to Liam. "The letter from CeCe about my granny's illness was in there."

"No one's at fault," Liam had said, calmly. Dina could see Kathleen roll her eyes with disgust. "We'll find someone to get you to the airport and get you on a flight."

"No, I'll get her packed and John will take her to the airport," Kathleen had said. "He's the only one among us with a car."

Dina remember how Liam was able to pull her away from Kathleen as if she were a small child, walking her out of The Quays and into the muted afternoon light, gray and soft and cold. He'd wrapped his arms around her, pulling her in to him. All she could think of was Maeve.

"Alright then, Liam." Kathleen had followed them outside with John and Connor in tow, determined to stay in charge of the situation. "You get her home and packed and across the Liffey to where John is parked near the Ha'Penney Café. Dina, hurry. We'll be there to drive you to the airport."

Liam slipped his arm around her shoulder and began to walk her home. "I'm here for you now, in this tragedy of yours."

Quickly, they wound their way through tourists and students, navigating the sidewalks to Dina's place. When they got to her room he lay down on the bed, arms behind his head. Dina began throwing clothing in a duffel bag, random, haphazard, stopping to cry as he watched her. Liam motioned her toward the bed and she lay down next to him, her head on his chest. He started to remove her clothing but she stopped him.

"No, Liam, there's no time," Dina had said.

"You're kidding me." Liam smiled. "There's always time and you need me."

"I need you to keep an eye on this place while I'm gone," she'd said. "And give the landlord the rent money for me." She stood up and crossed the room, picking up an envelope with money inside. "Please, Liam. I'm trusting you to be there for me right now."

"Of course I am," Liam had said. "Put the envelope in the top drawer. I'll pay him when I see him."

"Thanks," Dina had closed her eyes, just for a moment, leaning against the wall, then she put the envelope inside the dresser drawer as Liam watched. "Let's go."

Dina's sneakered feet had tapped rubber to road over the Liffey Bridge as she ran to meet John and Kathleen. She'd thought Liam was right behind her, but when she reached the car and turned, he was nowhere in sight. Just as she'd thrown her duffel bag in the trunk and hopped in the back seat, he appeared at the window, leaning in to give her a kiss.

"You were running faster than I move." He'd smiled. "Come back soon, Dina. I'll miss you."

"Come to the airport with us," Dina had said.

"No, I've got things to do," Liam answered.

Dina had seen Kathleen roll her eyes at John just before John pulled out into traffic, leaving Liam standing on the curb.

"Could you tell my professors and the tutoring coordinator at Trinity what happened?" Dina asked Kathleen.

"Sure, as soon as I see you off, I'll stop by or call to tell everyone," she'd said. "When will you be back?"

"I don't know," Dina had answered. "I don't know what I'm facing, really."

"It's a good sister you have to send the ticket," said John. "And good that you're going right away." Dina could tell he was trying to juggle the traffic and get her to the airport quickly.

Soon, buildings and planes displaying the Aer Lingus name loomed ahead. John pulled up to an entrance.

"Will you be back, Dina?" John's concern had felt palpable and personal.

"Yes," she'd said, firmly. "I'll let you know when I'm ready to leave Ireland. But I'm not ready yet. Maybe not ever."

She'd declined Kathleen's offer to wait with her at the airport that day. She hadn't been alone since Celia called and needed some time to absorb the news about Maeve. A panic had begun to set in. Maeve, her beloved granny, dead. It was incomprehensible. She'd directed her anger at Celia then, telling herself her sister could have tried harder to get in touch with her, to get her home to say good-bye to her grandmother. But even then she'd known it was not Celia's fault. Dina's mind, fogged by the stress of it all, couldn't yet face her inner desire to berate herself. She knew Maeve had been suffering while she indulged in her pursuit of a man and left little of herself for those who truly loved her. Instead, she'd curled as much as was possible into the hard plastic seats in the waiting area, put her head to her knees, and covered her face with her hands. She'd ached with the need to cry out loud, but she couldn't. She'd tried to curse her sister, but it felt false and half-hearted, even then. Frozen, mute, she'd waited.

Eventually she'd pulled three worn books from her bag. Maeve had given her three volumes of Irish poetry: Yeats, Joyce, and Seamus Heaney. They were her own copies handed down to Dina, well-thumbed and worn with tea stains and re-taped bindings. It was the closest bond she could find to her grandmother at that terrible moment, their shared love of literature and the deep sense of Maeve's Irishness. She'd said a prayer for her grandmother's soul, then opened Yeats, hoping the poetry would calm her and help her handle the long flight to Erie.

After Maeve's funeral in Erie, she'd come straight back to Dublin.

So much had happened since those days. She'd let Liam go and good riddance to bad rubbish. She'd given birth to Katie and given her up. She'd gently declined John's advances and worked to keep a friendship there, but it was strained. The only thing that had not changed was Kathleen, her friend, her Irish sister. It truly pained her to think of leaving Kathleen.

"I'll let you know when I'm ready to leave Ireland. But I'm not ready yet. Maybe not ever," she'd told John that day at the airport.

Now, nearly a year later, she thought about the irony of that, as she splashed water on her face in the bathroom of The Quays, attempting to clean up a bit before heading back to the table to share a meal with Kathleen and contemplate leaving Ireland again. Perhaps for good.

CHAPTER 3

I t was a carnival, of all things, where she met Luke. The kind she saw six times or more over the course of every summer growing up in Erie. She'd loved them as a youngster, with their rented kiddie rides and food booths that lined up funnel cake next to pierogies, beer and ouzo next to gyros and cotton candy. Old men sipped beer and played cards, women chatted or played bingo, everyone checked everyone else out. Everyone knew everyone; strangers were rare. The intermingling of families and high school sweethearts and sheer knowledge of one another was nearly incestuous.

Dina had gradually readjusted to being home during the six years since she'd returned to Erie. She'd snagged a full-time job teaching writing at a small community college and moved out of Celia's house into a small efficiency apartment. She still liked it well enough, and even continued to write in her own time, although she'd had no luck selling her poetry or short stories. She thought of Dublin often, of Katie every day, but the city of her birth had settled on Dina's shoulders like a sometimes comfortable, other times weighty woolen mantle. She'd given dating a try here and there since she came home, but she felt older—more worldly, somehow—than the guys she met. Dina wasn't sure if it was the trauma of giving up Katie, which had aged her considerably, or the fact that the hometown boys seemed a bit more stable but not half as poetic and exciting as the Dublin men. But given how things had ended with Liam, perhaps that was a good thing, all in all.

Dina had just turned thirty-three. She felt older than her years, with a battered soul that was as ancient as time. A quaint summer carnival wasn't really her ideal birthday outing anymore, but Celia had muscled her into coming, trying to mother her as usual, thinking of Dina as ten years old, which was probably a more appropriate age for this sort of thing.

"God, get that shit away from me!" Dina laughed, pinching her nostrils shut. "How can you eat that slimy, fried dough in this heat? Just looking at it makes me sick."

Foregoing the oozing funnel cake coiled like a snake on her sister's plate in favor of a nice, cold, dollar draft, she stood in line in the torpid July heat with the old men and the young lovers.

Celia smiled, opening her mouth wide like a baby robin, head tipped back, as she pinched a piece of the carnival delicacy off its soggy, paper plate and dropped it in, snapping her jaw shut and chewing, all the while continuing to grin. She was still eating and smiling as she walked away to plop down at a small picnic table.

"Bring me a beer too!" Celia yelled, legs stretched out straight, ankles crossed, leaning back into the table. "To wash this down!"

Dina shook her head in amused disgust. It was as she turned back toward the beer tent, the line inching its way forward slowly, that she saw him. He was leaning nonchalantly against the counter of the booth belonging to a local Catholic church, a beer in his hand, chatting pleasantly with the old men selling hot sausage sandwiches. He grinned at her each time she glanced his way, so she smiled back. He wasn't her type—ordinary looking, a bit banal, he obviously worked hard to look cool with his expensive Oakley shades. He wore a salt-and-pepper goatee, L.L. Bean shorts, and a short-sleeved, collared shirt so overly pressed it spoke miles about his level of self-consciousness. He was trying too hard to give the impression that he was relaxed within his own skin. And yet, he seemed interesting to Dina in the sticky, sweltering heat of a carnival that bordered on slow and lazy rather than sparkling. She felt a tingle deep inside and she waved, just slightly.

That was all it took. He was beside her in what was probably ten steps but seemed like one effortless leap. The old men at the sausage counter grinned and nudged one another, making it her turn to feel self-conscious.

"Luke Daniels." He was still smiling, hand extended. "Mind if I wait with you? By the time you get up there I'll need another one myself."

"Dina Benet." Watching out of the corner of her eye as Celia gave her a thumbs up, Dina slid her sweaty palm into his cool, dry one. "Oh...sorry."

She quickly pulled her hand away and rubbed it on her faded jean shorts. They were under the awning of the beer tent now, almost to the counter. Luke removed his sunglasses and she saw his eyes were blue, pale, and soft. They seemed lacking in warmth when juxtaposed to his smiling mouth, but she concentrated on them anyway, trying to ignore a sudden impulse to kiss him.

He followed her back to Celia and they sat, talking amiably, drinking beer, and people watching until he casually invited them to a party at his friend's beach house that night. He looked at Dina as he spoke, ignoring Celia. The words of his invitation were inclusive but his eyes, his movements, were not. He scribbled the address on a piece of paper and shoved it across the table toward Dina.

"Of course, I can pick you up," he said to Dina as if they were alone in the world.

"That's okay, I'll drive," Celia said, leaning forward to snatch the address, a hint of sarcasm in her voice.

Luke blinked, eyes revealing nothing. "Sure, sure. I'll see you there?"

She nodded. Celia twined her foot around the bottom of Dina's leg, preventing her from getting up as he stood, picked up his beer, and looked from one sister to the other, "assessing the odds" Celia said later. Dina waved miserably, still wanting to kiss him, as he walked away and she remained seated, her shins in pain as Celia's leg hold twisted and tightened.

"What are you doing?" Dina slapped Celia's bare ankle and pushed her leg away. "He invited us to a party. It could be fun!"

"We're not going," Celia said. "He's a creep. Did you see him pretending to invite me then trying to give me a hint not to go? Why didn't he just ask to speak to you privately and ask you out? He's trying to play all the angles. Why is it optional whether you meet him there or he picks you up? He's got other women showing up too, that's why. He should've asked to take you as a date."

"You're too overprotective and you're being too hard on him. There's something about him that I like."

"I'm a better judge of guys than you. Which one of us gets burned regularly and which is getting married in a few months?"

The remark stung and Dina looked away, drumming her fingers on the picnic table, pretending to think, although she already knew she was going to the party with or without Celia. Her life was not interesting enough to pass up the opportunity. But Celia, practical, cynical, and smart about the ways of the world, had hit on the difference between them. Celia and Dave would be married in September, settle down in a little, white, Cape Cod house on Sunset Drive and, Dina believed, live the happily ever after that she was so desperately seeking for herself. But Celia had made different life choices—going to work for a local insurance company after high school where she met Dave and fell in love. They were stable. They earned more money than Dina ever had in her post-college jobs. Dina thought about Liam. She'd chosen a penniless guy who offered great sex, mediocre poetry, and no future. *What if Celia is right and I just don't know how to pick a decent guy?*

"Not trying isn't the solution."

"This isn't the guy to start trying with, Dina."

Celia thought she knew everything.

"I may have a no-wins, straight-losses score in this area, CeCe, but I've been in the game more often than you have. I'd know bad if I saw it and I don't see it here."

Dina was glad she was heading home to her own place today. She knew Luke would call and she had no intention of telling Celia that she was going to meet him at that party. It was just curiosity, she assured herself. She'd prove Celia wrong this time. No more dating bad boys. This guy was different—in a good way.

CHAPTER 4

LUKE

Water pounded down on his back as steam from the shower rose around him. He could hear the phone ringing in the house somewhere, a woman's voice leaving a message. He didn't want to think about any women right now except Dina Benet and what it would feel like to touch her, to kiss her.

The heat, the boredom, the endless jokes told by old men had been getting to him. He'd been feeling restless, itching for a hunt, a challenge, when he saw her. He'd gone to the carnival for his father's sake, to shake a few hands and give the old guys some support as they tried to raise money, waving customers over with smiles and the lure of traditional Polish and Italian food. Every year at this festival, Norman Daniels and his friends cooked up a storm to raise money for the church, and every year he asked his only son, Luke, to stop by and support their good cause. So Luke humored his father by taking back-slapping and bawdy jokes from Mr. Dombrowski and Mr. Zappolo while downing cold beers that eventually began to feel weighty under the heat of the July sun.

He was more than an hour past the first wave of desire to head home, thinking about calling a girl he'd been seeing for a few months, when he noticed Dina. He had already been debating whether he would head out to Tony's beach party later that evening. He hated being alone. Yet, he hated being trapped. This was the irony of his life, Luke often thought. He'd looked over at his father. Not much advice available there. The mouth would give him a lecture and the eye a wink, just as always. More than anything, Luke hated being bored. Dina looked lovely and more than a little vulnerable standing in that line, beads of sweat on her forehead and above her lip, as she twisted her hair and stared off dreamily at nothing in particular. But she still knew just when to inch forward toward the front of the beer tent. She was paying attention to the line, and he was sure she was paying some attention to him as well.

She had a great body, sweat pasting wide patches of her sleeveless cotton blouse to her breasts and long brown legs extending from ragged jean shorts. Her painted toes were as sexy to Luke as her freckles and shoulder-length, dark hair.

It was noon and the carnival was nowhere near the soft lake breeze or the cool invitation of its undulating waves. Luke leaned against the stand to tip his head under the canopy for a little shade but the smoke and grease of sausages frying closed in on him and he pulled away from the tent again. He wondered if this languidly compelling woman would turn out to be a lot of fun, no strings attached. The last thing he wanted was a serious relationship, something he'd avoided since his divorce from Marianne five years ago. He'd caused all three of them—Marianne, Josh and himself—tremendous pain. Marianne was adamant in her belief that he felt little remorse.

"Dad, I'll bet you ten bucks I can lay her tonight." Luke casually pointed his finger in the girl's direction.

He felt a small twinge of conscience. Perhaps it was his mother's voice dispensing admonishments that still echoed in his mind or the memory of the way this sort of thing had caused him endless trouble in the past. Like the thumping of the nun's ruler on his hand when he stared at Mary Josephine Potenkin's huge breasts rather than the chalkboard in the sixth grade. Growing up, there had been different allowances for Luke than for his six sisters. He was scolded but still entitled to more—a private school education while they attended public schools, later curfews, and fewer requirements. His father winked, and his mother sometimes yelled but other times gave him a "tsk and a shrug," or so his sisters said. He was seven the first time he looked the other way for his father and became his confidant. He was twenty-seven the first time his father returned the favor.

"Oh, you shouldn't be saying such a thing," his father said. "We're here at a church festival after all." Then Norman Daniels turned his head away from his buddies and smiled, winking at Luke. It was an old, familiar movement. The eyelashes were now sparse but, as they dipped down above a saggy cheek in a fleshy face, they were still giving permission. It was an entitlement that he slid forward on as easily as he always had done.

Luke laughed and the girl caught his eye, smiling back with a halting little wave.

"Here I go, Dad," he said and seconds later he was standing next to her.

Her eyes were a deep blue, one minute azure, the next almost bluish green. For just a second he looked back at his father, took off his sunglasses, and winked.

CHAPTER 5

CELIA

Celia slipped her hands into the sink's warm, soapy water, an almost luxurious, sensual feeling. She savored it for a moment before adding the dirty dishes, reducing it to what it was meant to be. She cleaned when she was worried about Dina. She put their Granny Maeve in her mind's eye, dead now almost seven years, and cleaned everything she could get her hands on, all the while talking to Maeve's spirit about what to do with Dina. She and Maeve had always been partners in the business of taking care of Dina. It never occurred to Celia there might be a definite moment in Dina's life when the responsibility Celia had felt for as long as she could remember would end. Even when Maeve took over and began raising them, Celia believed she simply allowed their grandmother to share in that responsibility with her.

The dishes had sloshed and settled slowly to the bottom of their soapy ocean. She had a dishwasher, but washing dishes by hand had been her job for Maeve. She'd solved a lot of problems over the years with her hands in warm dishwater. But right now she had a dark, uneasy feeling about that guy Luke, which the scrubbing and swirling of soap and water wasn't helping her to shake. Dina had terrible taste in men as it was, and usually Celia just lectured or rolled her eyes then waited for the ill-fated relationship to end, knowing it would be tears and heartache but no real lasting damage to her sister. This time she felt "tetched," as Maeve would have said in her light, Americanized brogue with a foreboding. Celia carried a bad feeling inside for Dina who was, as usual, star-struck and floating off willingly into Luke's arms, refusing to listen. Celia gazed out the window, seeing not the burst of color from her carefully tended rose bushes or the busy movement and chirping of the sparrows at her bird feeder, but instead Justine, with her rarely combed, waist-length hair, glazed eyes, and taut, undernourished body. She hated to think of Justine, the mother who could not mother them.

"Hail Mary, full of grace. Blessed art thou among women." Celia moved the dish ragdishrag over a plate in rhythmic, circular motions and recited portions of the rosary out loud, imitating Maeve's accent as though she were soaring and dipping through time with the roll of her voice and tongue. *"Blessed is the fruit of thy womb, Jesus."* It wasn't helping. She wasn't connecting with Maeve. She wasn't feeling better about Dina.

Celia had sacrificed a lot to make sure Dina had a better life. Ever protective of her sister, Celia decided to forego college for a job as a policy typist at Erie Insurance after high school. She'd only asked Maeve for enough money to buy a car from the insurance fund they'd inherited when the father they barely knew died. The rest remained for Dina to use for college.

College had come and gone for Dina, but it had not made a good life for her. Instead, Celia thought now, pulling the stopper to drain the water from the sink and then drying her hands on a dish toweldishtowel, it had been she who met a great guy, bought a wonderful home, and was just a few months from marriage. Dina was still lost and wandering. Celia saw her sister in off moments twisting her hair, rocking her body ever so slightly back and forth, her face carrying the same expression it had when they'd found their mother's dead body or when Dina had stood over Maeve's coffin.

Growing up, Celia had seen that look on Maeve's face too, her eyes taking on the same dreamy quality. Celia, ever practical, had been Maeve's helpmate and friend. But Dina was Maeve's dreamer, her poet and writer, and she could throw her wishes and hopes toward Dina like so much dust in the wind, knowing Celia would take her place as Dina's rock once she was gone. Maeve told Dina stories of Ireland filled with history and memories laced with fairies, banshees, and the lyrical folklore of her people. Dina seemed to hug the words close to her heart, creating a half-lit imaginary world that was, at times, equally as populated with winged creatures and tiny leprechauns as it was with people. All the characters Dina created when she began writing spoke with Maeve's lilting, country brogue and lived on the pretend Isle of Wishes. Dina lived on the Isle with them through most of her childhood with no interference from Maeve but brooking constant complaints from Celia who lived squarely in the reality of the grit, poverty, and freezing winters of their decaying neighborhood.

It was great fodder for Dina's papers in high school as she told story after story from her imaginary world, harvesting consistent grades of A+ with notes to Maeve about the depth of her

language skills and the wonder of her imagination. Maeve would smile and say, "Well, she is of the Clan O'Neill and carries within her the Irish gift of writing so it's to be expected." Then, quickly crossing herself, she would add, "and graced by the Lord Jesus as well." All of that changed when Dina entered college. Her Irish folklore and pretend creatures were deemed "childlike" and "replications of earlier work." One professor even accused her of plagiarizing ancient folklore and told her to grow up and begin writing adult literature. Dina came home stressed and unsure. Maeve remained unperturbed.

"And how is it you can plagiarize the tales of a people?" she asked. "It's the stuff of your ancestors and it lives in you."

"Thinking about Dina again?" Dave's voice startled Celia, bringing her back to the present as his arms wrapped around her from behind, his voice low and comforting. He'd surprised her and come home early from a business trip yesterday. "I know that look."

"Dina and Granny. She just wants a family, Dave." Celia turned to face him, sliding her arms around his waist. "She loves me but I've never been enough. She needs a mother."

"You can't protect her from everything," he chided. "She's a grown woman."

"On the outside maybe." Celia sighed. "Now that we're getting married...well, she thinks she's really on her own."

Celia laid her head on Dave's shoulder. "I think she met a really bad guy today."

CHAPTER 6

DINA

Dina leaned forward onto the rail of the upper deck at Tony Singulari's beach house, a warm wind puffing out her long sundress, and watched the sun slowly setting over Lake Erie. Ships, sailboats, and motorboats idled or moved toward the yacht club to berth for the night. Luke was next to her, so close the hairs on their arms touched and tingled. She wanted him in an aching, painful way. She wanted his seemingly solid, stable little life as much as she wanted him physically—maybe more. It was ridiculous. She'd only met him hours before and yet the afternoon carnival seemed as though it were light years away.

"I've heard of Tony...he has quite the reputation...but I've never been to his house," Dina said. "How do you know him?"

"He's my accountant and I'm his attorney," Luke said, shrugging. "He's quite the partier, but he really only invites me as a courtesy. It's nice to have someone to talk to who has nothing to do with these people."

He gestured toward the crowd behind them. "They get tiresome after a while."

Trish, his law partner, walked out onto the deck to join them. Dina straightened her back and stood stiffly, annoyed that the intimacy of the moment was gone. Something about Trish was amiss, off-kilter. Her proprietary, insistent manner with Luke seemed strangely out of sync with their business relationship. Trish had shown Dina pictures of her husband and sons but she was exuberantly friendly in a way that felt false and made Dina cautious. Perhaps she was becoming more like Celia than she realized. This new, cynical side to Dina's private thoughts surprised her. If Dina had any money she'd have been willing to bet that something, somewhere along the way had happened between Trish and Luke that was not even remotely about friendship or business. Trish treated Dina like she needed to be shown repeatedly where the line in the sand was drawn and that, with one step over, Dina could easily be an intruder on Trish's turf. That turf was obviously Luke.

Fortunately, Luke seemed annoyed too. Dina was sure he had been about to kiss her. It was the third time this evening that she'd felt that way and they'd been interrupted by Trish.

"Luke and I were just going to take a walk on the beach," Dina said, trying not to look at Luke's surprised face. They'd had no such discussion. "Maybe we'll catch you when we get back if you're still here."

Dina started walking down the steps, and Luke followed her.

"So we're taking a walk on the beach?" His smirk broadened into a grin, his face tinted by the reddish-gold light of the setting sun.

"It seemed like the only way to be alone," she fired back, sounding a little more irritated than she intended.

"Hey, Trish is just nosy and protective of me. She doesn't mean anything by it. She just worries about me."

Dina looked at him quizzically. "You two never had a fling of some sort that she's not over?"

Luke laughed easily. "No, I'd tell you if that were the case." He reached for her, pulling her close, bending down until he was within inches of her lips. "But I'd like to get a thing or a fling of some sort going with you."

She thought for a second he looked wicked, still grinning as his mouth closed down on hers. A memory of Liam, just after he'd lied to her yet again, flashed before her eyes. Then she shut out Ireland and her past, losing herself in the kiss, the sunset, and that crazy, needful physical feeling he gave her. Seconds later they were rolling on the beach, kissing and pulling at one another's clothes, hands and lips everywhere. She could feel the gritty sand in her hair, her mouth, on her legs. Luke spit out sand, let go of her, and leaned on his elbow.

"What do you say we go somewhere else?" he asked. "Some place where we won't end up with sand up our butts."

"It's nothing like in the movies where it looks so cool and wild," Dina said, laughing.

"Oh, I promise you wild," Luke said, leaning down to kiss her neck and run his hand along the arch in her back. "Just no sand."

"Let's go." Dina jumped up before he could pull her up.

They walked barefoot, hand in hand and carrying their shoes, through the beach grass and onto the road where white ash and birch trees shot up among red maples and the exotic dense thickets of Morrow's honeysuckle shrubs. Leaves rustled a little now and then as the breeze wafted lightly through the branches. Dina was glad they didn't have to go back through the house, past the prying eyes of Trish and the rest of the party, to get to his car parked along the road. Luke drove a silver Volvo, only about a year old, sleek and successful-looking compared to her ancient Nissan Sentra. He opened the passenger side door and she slid onto the Volvo's soft leather seat, sand cascading here and there onto the carpet, the seat, and the console.

"Sorry about all this sand," she said nervously, surprised that she'd lost the boldness displayed such a short time ago.

"No problem." He smiled, starting the car.

She suddenly felt a shift inside her as he put the car into gear, going from nervous to the oddest feeling of safety and protection, of being cared for. The seat seemed to bend to her and enfold her as Maeve's lap had once done. Just as the car began rolling forward, Dina saw a pair of fireflies dancing in unison near her window and she made a wish.

The car ambled slowly down the access road to the pavement leading out to Peninsula Drive, crunching across sand, small stones, and branches blown there by the wind. Chipmunks scurried up and down the trees and birds called good-night to one another as the sun finally dropped below the horizon.

Twenty minutes later they were driving up a short, slightly winding driveway to a brick, colonial-style home, tall white pillars gracing its elegant front portico. Beautiful, big pine trees lent an air of privacy, partially blocking the road. It was too dark to make out more than the outlines of several large trees in the backyard, shrubs and flowers hugging the perimeter of the house. The automatic garage door opened and the light went on. Dina saw rows of gardening tools, ladders, a lawn mower—everything hung neatly along the walls or set up on shelves. She breathed in the orderliness.

Celia had a nice home now, although not nearly as large or as landscaped as this one, her finished basement waiting in the wings as an option if times got too tough for Dina. But Dina longed for the quiet, open space of a house like this. She envisioned herself coming home here as they entered the kitchen through the garage. It was a dangerous, consuming feeling.

Dina took in the hardwood floors, the beautiful stone fireplace, the beams and rafters above giving a cabin-like feeling. Mounted deer heads stood quiet watch from the great-room wall as she roamed from the kitchen to the dining room to the hallway. She shuddered, feeling as if they were peering out from death to assess her. She would not have taken Luke for a hunter. Most of the hunters she'd known were construction workers, blue-collar shop guys, and the occasional polished executive who wore expensive gear and stayed in a cabin with running water and air conditioning. Maybe Luke was that type of hunter.

He appeared then with two cold beers, his fingerprints etched in the condensation. He saw her eyeing the deer heads and grinned.

"Hope you like hunters," he said, laughing at the look on her face.

"So they are yours." Dina sighed. "No, I don't really like hunters, but maybe you'll change my mind."

"I go once a year with my buddy." Luke juggled the bottles, sliding open the door to what looked like a screened-in back porch. "Why don't you join me out here and let me change your mind about hunters?"

She slipped off her sandals and her bare feet made small, slapping noises on the hardwood floors as she followed his shadowy outline. He lit one small candle. Dina surveyed the porch with surprise. Such a nice home, yet this room was more like an upscale lean-to. Just plank wood, screens, indoor-outdoor carpeting, a picnic table, and some chairs. Not much ambiance. She sat down next to him on the picnic table bench. They were both silent as they sipped beer and listened to the sounds of the night. Fireflies were everywhere, cicadas sang, and locusts screeched. It was a hot night with none of the breeze they'd felt at the beach. The leaves from an enormous tree in the middle of the backyard were still, not even a slight rustle. The cold beer cascaded down the back of Dina's throat and a tingling began there, stretching in tiny waves through her nerve endings out to her extremities. Even her ears felt flushed and warm. The knowledge made her giggle.

"I love summer," Dina whispered, breathing in the scents of freshly mowed grass and night air with the bitter taste of beer.

Luke set his beer down and leaned toward her, kissing her neck while slipping and rolling her sundress up and over her head in one practiced motion. She was naked except for her underwear. Dina felt that craving for him again that was more than physical. She straddled him on the uncomfortable picnic table bench as he leaned back, fully clothed, his hands and mouth roaming all over her, his fingers inside of her until she thought she would faint. It felt like a dream. She looked up at the tiny pinpoints of light in the night sky outside, then shifted her hips upward to let him slide his pants off, pulling his shirt off herself. She ripped her own underwear in half rather than move off of him and in seconds he was inside her. She felt a wild craziness—the sense that what had been missing with all the other men was here, in this porch, with this guy, amid the heat of summer. Luke was the last man she would have thought would turn her inside out. He wrapped her legs around his back and stood up, carrying her into the great room and onto the soft rug in front of the fireplace.

"Picnic table was a little rough on my back," he said, grinning.

Dina pulled him down to her and then lost herself in hours of lovemaking. Off and on, again and again, until they collapsed into an exhausted sleep, legs and arms entwined. She dreamed a dream that night that would haunt her for years.

She was lost in a dark forest. The trees were very tall, old and gnarled but ferocious, brown and defrocked of leaves. She was shivering in the wet mist that was not quite fog yet, her heart pounding as though she had been running. The ground was a carpet of dry, brittle, brown leaves.

Something was hunting her and she could hear it coming. She began running again, looking for a way out. In the dream, she knew she must find the green grass and multi-colored leaves to find safety although that made no sense to her later when she awoke. She heard a branch cracking and crashing as footsteps approached behind her and she began running faster and faster, so fast her hair was leaving her head in chunks and her feet were traveling inches above the ground. But still it drew closer and closer.

The green grass and healthy trees were a mere foot in front of her when she glanced back over her shoulder and saw a gun muzzle aiming straight at her. The gun went off with a loud crack and she awoke, disoriented, heart racing, to realize it was raining outside—a hard summer rain with thunder and lightning loudly splintering the night sky. Luke snored lightly next to her. It had only been a dream. She turned her head toward the sound of the rain and saw the deer heads staring down at her with their vacuous, lifeless glass eyes, and she shivered.

CHAPTER 7

CELIA

Strips of sun whisked through the gothic, lead-paned window of the bridal chamber in St. Patrick's Church to sparkle and dance along Celia's beaded, white wedding dress as it fell softly around her petite five-foot, four-inch frame. Dave's family, the florist, and the photographer were all chattering behind her but she remained focused on a small, lavender dot moving as quickly as a pair of stiletto heels could travel across the church parking lot. She could see the warm, September breeze lifting and lowering shoulder-length, brown hair in rhythm with the motion of the bridesmaid's gown. Dina was alone. Celia scowled. That bastard couldn't even come to the wedding with her.

"What's the matter, Celia?" Dave's sister, Stephanie, asked. "I see Dina. She'll be here in a minute."

Celia glanced into an ornately framed mirror to her left and realized her soft, freckled skin had turned from pale to a red that almost matched the strawberry flecks in her hair. She struggled to control her anger. She wanted to marry Dave and have children, a life of their own, and yet she felt as though she were abandoning Dina in her hour of need. It was a need Dina seemed oblivious to but Celia saw with increasing fear.

She had chosen to marry in September in the church where her grandparents were married. It was a different day than that first, ill-fated wedding in 1943 when Maeve O'Neill, in a borrowed dress, with no father or friends to give her away, had become Maeve O'Malley. There was no one to give Celia away either, but the sheer notion of someone controlling the giving of her to anyone was archaic and laughable. Dina would walk down the aisle with her, arm in arm. She was Celia's only family.

Celia sighed. This church held so many memories. A simple reception would be held after the ceremony in the church basement. Years ago, following Justine's death, Celia and Dina had attended another party there to celebrate their baptism. Maeve insisted, despite Celia's protests. Dina was entranced with the mystery of the baptism and happy to follow Sister Cathleen to the basement for cake and ice cream afterward. Celia pretended to follow then slipped away and returned to the sanctuary, where she lay prone on a pew several rows behind her grandmother, who sat, alone in thought, as the party commenced downstairs. Celia hadn't known then what it was she was angry with Maeve for or why she wanted to spy on her rather than sit near her. The pews were scarred but still smooth oak in places, and when Maeve dropped her kneeler it echoed in the cavernous emptiness.

Maeve held the same rosary beads wrapped around her hands that day as Celia held today, on her wedding day. The rosary beads Maeve had offered Justine, who threw them back in her face with a laugh. Despite

Celia's rough beginnings with religion, she treasured them. They cascaded down the front of her wedding dress like a string of pearls, dancing loosely as she absentmindedly touched them. She wanted to pray but she could not. Perhaps Maeve had experienced the same problem the day they were baptized, for she seemed to give up after ten minutes of concentration, slowly easing her backside up and into the hard pew. Celia lay very still that day and listened. Father John joined her grandmother and they talked about old times and things Celia had never known about her mother.

"Maeve, my child, there was nothing you could do. Justine loved you; she was just too far along a dark path for that love to save her," Celia remembered hearing Father John say to her grandmother.

"So much anger inside a me. I need to make confession, Father, for I was cursing God himself when the drugs took my Justine, God rest her soul." They were quiet for several minutes, with just the sound of Maeve inhaling and exhaling a somewhat ragged breath laced with a small sob now and again. "Once it was drink that was the curse of the Irish...but what Justine was doing...so far beyond that."

It sounded, to Celia, as if Father John were patting Maeve's shoulder, then the click of rosary beads sounded again.

"God forgives you," said Father John.

"Big of him. Think he'd clean Justine up and send her back? No, just sendin' forgiveness, he is, wrapping it up with a nice neat bow and time to get on with life."

"I should order you to confession right now, Maeve O'Malley." Father John chuckled. Obviously Maeve didn't get in as much trouble for blasphemy as Celia was told she would be if she spoke ill of God.

"You do that, straighten me out for those two wee girls eating cake and believing I can make all this right for 'em."

Silence again, the beads tapping against one another, the candles flickering. Celia's back was beginning to hurt but she could not move now without getting caught eavesdropping.

"Father John? It's wishin' I am that those statues'd quit starin' my way."

His roar of laughter echoed off the ancient stone walls in the sanctuary and re-echoed again, making a tiny chorus of laughing priests.

"Well, between the two of us, Maeve, I've wished that many a time myself. Guilty I've felt, them being one-of-a-kind collector's items and all."

Celia smiled remembering, just as she had smiled that day. She wondered if it would feel as if the life-size sculptures, each depicting one of the twelve stations of the cross, were staring at her while she said her vows today, just as they had seemed to come alive, about to reveal her hiding place, back then.

"I've got a second chance with those girls, Father. Celia is so angry. So much she's seen in her twelve years. I'd like her in catechism class soon. And Dina, my wee dreamer, she's a lover not a fighter and she's going to surprise us all someday."

Celia felt a companionable silence settle between them and soon the statues no longer seemed frightening. The candle glow lost its heaviness and became strangely lighter. Then Maeve began speaking of the rolling green beauty of Ireland, of waiting on the dock with Mick for the boat that would take them to America and a new life. She spoke of her mother wrapping Maeve within arms that were hugging her good-bye. Celia was surprised to learn Maeve had experienced a moment of indecision then. A moment when she looked her mother in the eye and saw the fear she felt for her seventeen-year-old daughter, her disapproval of Mick, the hurting in her heart. Maeve believed the years had brought punishment enough for inflicting that hurt.

"Justine would not let Celia or Dina be baptized or saved or even touched by the holy water. It's a miracle they've lived long enough for me to right that wrong." Maeve sighed.

"Arah, still keepin' the superstitions of the old country, Maeve. Our prayers are stronger than any water—holy or not—can be. And those lasses will grow up well and good." Celia heard Father John make the patting sound again.

"Celia'll have none of the rosary or the catechism and with her going to public school, it'll be hard coming by the regularness of God like we had in Ireland."

"Well, suppose you join me downstairs for some cake and ice cream and we'll talk a bit about how to put the girls in a Catholic school?"

"Ah, no, Father. Justine didn't leave any money for that sort of thing and I've two more mouths to feed and precious little to spare."

Celia could hear them stand up. She held her breath, trying not to squirm. She did not want to go to Catholic school any more than she'd wanted to be baptized.

"Well, well, now Maeve. Our Savior did say to do for the least among us and I'll be looking out for those girls with you now." Father John's voice was kind. "So we will see about a few spots up at Sacred Heart Elementary. An easy ride on the city bus."

"Thank you, Father. It's caring you are and good in the heart," Maeve said. "I spent hard hours on my knees on the stone floors of the convent where I was schooled, saying the rosary in punishment for mischievousness, but it's served me well throughout my life. Justine didn't understand that, but with my granddaughters I'll be wiser. I will use the one true religion to help them find their way in life."

Celia felt sick that day, thinking Maeve was old and crazy and pushing her in a direction she didn't want to go. But as she stood here on her wedding day in the same church where so long ago she'd heard her grandmother confess her darkest hurts and fears, Celia knew she had been right. Her faith had taken her to this marriage and it would carry her beyond. It was Maeve's gift to her.

Her gift to Maeve was her continued responsibility for Dina. Celia was grateful that she and Dina were so close now, that they were family again. They'd had their fights but they were inextricably wound around one another like a morning glory and a clematis climbing the sturdy corners of a front porch together, always finding their way back to each other. Celia shook away the memories and came back to the present, turning around as Dina softly called her name from the doorway.

"Oh, CeCe, you look so beautiful," Dina said, tears in her eyes, her windblown hair wildly askew. They hugged lightly, Dina careful not to muss Celia's makeup or hair. "I'm reading from Yeats in Granny's honor," Dina whispered in her sister's ear.

The girl hired to fix Celia's hair came over and began straightening out Dina's wayward tresses. Celia looked out across the room.

"Hey, everybody," she called to the group of Dave's family and friends. "Could you go ahead out into the church? I need to be alone with my sister for a little while."

They mingled slowly, moving through the door as if one entity, waving and blowing her kisses. She was about to become part of a big, loving family and her heart ached for Dina. Caught in the steel jaws of a trap of her own making, she longed to run ahead and join the pack yet she was so afraid she would leave her sister behind, unguarded and unprotected.

"It's not your job to watch over me anymore, CeCe," Dina said softly, reading her sister's thoughts. "Today is the day you get what we've both dreamed of, to become part of a family and to create a family of your own."

"Where is he, Dina?" Celia waived to the hairdresser as she too left behind the tiny family. "Don't tell me he couldn't even come with you to your sister's wedding?"

"Oh, CeCe, he had his son this morning." Dina sighed, accustomed to this line of questioning. "He'll show up for the reception."

"He'll show up alone, as if single and available."

"Stop worrying about it. Stop worrying about me."

"You are my family." Celia's lip trembled in anger, a tear or two sliding down her cheek.

"No crying on your wedding day...at least not about me." Dina wiped Celia's tear and the dark circle of mascara it left under her eye. "I promise if he doesn't commit or at least improve in six to nine months, I'll leave him. Sister's honor. Deal?"

"What about six to nine *weeks*?" Celia said.

"We'll see," Dina said. "Smile. It's just about time to walk down the aisle."

Celia tried to muster a grin.

"It's lucky you are to be marrying a nice Catholic boy today," Dina imitated Maeve's brogue with unflinching perfection, making Celia's face relax with amusement.

"I miss Granny today, Dina."

"I know you do. She was the best thing that ever happened to us. What if Justine had never come home to Erie and we'd never known her?"

"I was fifteen months old before she knew I existed," Celia said. "Think how she must have felt to be called from her job in the hospital cafeteria to the emergency room lobby, only to find Justine there holding me, a dehydrated baby burning up with fever. "How wonderful and awful that must have been for her."

"She's the reason we lived to be adults," Dina said. "It's good to think about her today."

"Celia, it's time." One of Dave's sisters poked her head into the room, all smiles.

"Okay, we'll be right there." Turning to Dina, her face serious again, Celia said, "Dina, if Luke doesn't make sure you end up right where I am now, then he's a bum and you're wasting your time."

Celia wrapped her little sister, her dreamer, her responsibility, in her arms and prayed a quick prayer to the Virgin Mary. Then, gathering her flowers, she walked out of the room and into the church, down the aisle, past the ribbons, candles, and life-size sculptures of the stations of the cross, to the altar where Dave waited for her. Dina held her hand the entire way and, later, as the bride and groom lit a candle together to symbolize becoming one in marriage, Celia could hear Dina reading from Yeats. The candle's flame flickered as she heard the familiar words of one of Maeve's favorite poems. Celia held Dave's hand and looked up. Shadows danced along the ancient, gray stone walls behind the altar and she thought, for a minute, she saw Maeve there, smiling.

CHAPTER 8

DINA

Fingers laced around a chipped stoneware mug, Dina sipped the steaming coffee inside. Clad only in an oversized man's shirt she tucked her feet, encased in warm, rag-wool socks, beneath her and leaned back against the couch, trying to ignore Luke who was happily chatting with his son on the phone in the kitchen. It had been four months since she first entered this house and if she carefully ignored certain things, looked the other way, and didn't ask too many questions, she could inhale permanence and quiet the low ache of need that haunted her so often. She inhaled stability on Tuesday, Thursday, and Saturday nights after five in the evening, when Luke was not exercising visitation rights with his ten-year-old son, Josh. She assumed Josh enjoyed father-son bonding on Monday, Wednesday, Friday, and sometimes Sunday, but she couldn't say for sure how their visits really went. She hadn't been included yet.

Pictures of Josh were everywhere in the house. He was an adorable red-headed boy with a cowlick and freckles, who looked nothing like

Luke. Dina wondered what Josh was like as a person and if she could write about the boy she imagined him to be, the way she used to write about the girl she imagined Katie had become. She hadn't written much since she met Luke. She wished she could say she was unavailable on Tuesday, Thursday, or Saturday because she was with her own daughter. But all she had at home were four pictures of Katie—the most recent several years old—carefully tucked in her nightstand drawer under her Bible and Granny's rosary. Kathleen gave her updates about once a year but she had stopped sending pictures.

"Need a warm-up?" Luke was standing over her, hand outstretched for her coffee mug.

"Sure." Dina smiled, handing it over.

He returned minutes later with two full coffee mugs and an afghan. They slipped beneath it together and settled their thick-socked feet side by side on the square, oak coffee table.

"Look...snow," Dina said, resting her head on his shoulder. Light, lacy flakes danced downward in the early morning sun. She felt full, complete, loved—despite the fact that that word had not yet come up between them. In the warm room, with the magic of snow outside and their bodies aligned and relaxed, she turned to him with a smile of confidence, full of her sheer belief in the fairy tale, and said, "I'd like to meet Josh."

The magic of the moment was over in a split second. His body language changed. He didn't move physically yet he shifted away from her all the same, stiffening, staring into his mug. Invisible fingers had snapped and the universe Dina was floating in dislodged with a loud crack, a hollow limb breaking off to crash into the quiet of the hushed forest and rendering a moment of chaos, a shift in the landscape from the skyscraping treetops to the soft carpet of leaves. There was a gap through which a downdraft burst. It would take another hundred years for a tree to grow tall enough to close the rift.

"He's not ready," Luke said slowly, obviously picking his words carefully. "I'm protective and he's not used to meeting new women in my life. I have to talk to him about you first."

"He doesn't know about me?" The breach widened further, another branch fell. "Are you sure? Because his mother seems to like to park herself across the street for coffee with the neighbor when I'm here. They stare at me when I leave, and I'll bet she goes home and tells him about me."

"She doesn't tell him. She has her own issues, but her one saving grace is she leaves him out of it."

"Are you sure it's not *you* that isn't ready?" Dina put her coffee mug down and crossed her arms over her chest, ready for a serious conversation.

Luke sat his mug down next to hers and stood up. "I'm taking a shower. You can join me or wait to take your own, and then I'll give you a ride home."

The carpet of leaves in Dina's head swirled and scattered as she watched him take the stairs two at a time. Seconds later, the shower started. Dina sat on the couch frozen, dismissed. If Celia were there, she would tell her to walk out, ditch him. Dina looked around, struggling to pull herself back to the quiet, stable feeling she'd had only a few short moments ago. Pained and confused, she knew she didn't want to return to the loneliness she had known before she met him. She wanted her dream; she wanted this home and this man.

At the top of the stairs she peeled off her clothing, then, opening the bathroom door, she waded through the steamy mist and stepped into the shower.

He turned and smiled, leaning toward her, and began washing her with soap, his hands everywhere.

"I'm sorry," Dina whispered in his ear, unsure what she was sorry for but desperate to return things to normal. Luke leaned down and began to kiss her. Dina responded with every inch of her body, willing her mind to stop asking why he said nothing, why he didn't say he was sorry.

Three weeks later, she met Josh on a cold, crisp Friday night. She drove to Luke's house after her afternoon classes, and they ordered pizza and watched movies. It had been a long time since she'd watched Batman and Disney films, but she and Josh hit it off instantly. They both liked books, movies, and watching the Road Runner cartoon on Saturday morning. When it was time for him to go to bed, he begged her to be there in the morning to watch cartoons. Dina was floating in happiness again.

"No way," Luke responded when she mentioned it after Josh was sound asleep in bed.

"Why not? He's obviously okay with it. It was his idea."

"He's not really okay with it and his mother will make a big deal out of it."

"You're divorced," Dina said. "People move on—or at least they should. Something weird is going on here."

Luke pulled her coat out of the closet, handing it to her. "It's time to go. Josh really liked you and it went well. Let's just leave it at that. You'll see him again." She was dismissed, like an employee, sent home, lowered into the ever-widening pool of her own insecurity. Dina slipped her coat on and headed for the door. "Hey, hey," Luke called to her back. "What, no kiss?"

Dina turned to look at him. He leaned against the kitchen counter, arms crossed, a knowing smile on his face. She began to walk toward him, conflicted, everything she grappled with inside showing on her face, she was sure. Then Luke wrapped her in a big hug and kissed her.

"Dina, you've never had children, you've never been divorced," Luke said, attempting to make his voice soothing this time as he rubbed her back. "You need to give it some time. Josh likes you but he still wants his mother and father back together. Go slow."

Dina flinched, trying to ignore his remarks. The soft, rolling green of County Sligo from the window of an Irish cottage flooded her memory as, eyes watery, she pushed it away. He was right, she didn't know what Josh was thinking or going through. She had no experience with ten-year-olds, or really with young children of any age. If she'd kept Katie, rather than let her go, Dina might have been able to fight back at his logic. But arguing about Josh only reminded her of her own private, daily heartache, something she was not ready to share with Luke. But, despite her secrecy about Katie and her lack of experience with children, Dina did know what she, as an adult, wanted from Luke and this relationship.

"I'm just ready for more in this relationship. Are you?"

Luke kissed her lightly on the lips, pulled back, and said, "No." It was blunt honesty. Dina heard the old rock song from The Clash in her head and she wondered *Should I stay or should I go now?* A laugh bubbled up from her throat, incongruous to the gravity of the moment.

Luke misunderstood. "Good, then you're alright with things the way they are. Let's slow down and just enjoy where we are right now."

Minutes later she was trudging out to her car where she cleaned off the snow and drove away. He was in charge, and she'd let that happen. She could not turn things around and they seemed to be cresting at a comfortable plateau which she wasn't sure they would ever move forward from to reach the place where she wanted to be. She wanted to live in that house with him. She wanted a family, people to love and wake up to in the morning. She wanted what Celia had.

"He's got his cake and he's eating it too, and you're letting it happen," Celia had told Dina the day before, clearly frustrated. "He's never going to let you move in or marry you. That's not his style. He made that error once. Dina, you're mistaking your yearning to have a family of your own for love."

"No, I'm not," Dina had snapped back. "I love him and I think he loves me, he's just going a little bit slower because he's been married and burned and he has a child to consider."

"Dina, I'm worried about you. I don't have a good feeling about Luke."

Dina had put up her hand. "No more. Don't bad-mouth him anymore."

But now, driving into the night beneath cathedral-like trees tipped in glittering white powder, past darkened houses where families were nestled together and sound asleep, she wanted to run away. Yet she knew she could not escape from him. She was in love, in need, and addicted to Luke all in one ugly but beautiful ball of hope and desperation with no idea how he felt about her. Luke was the opposite of Liam whose shallow but poetic flirtations kept her on an endless ride of joy and frustration. She was able to read Liam, she just chose not to until there was no alternative. But Luke, so staid and emotionless, so controlling, was impossible to fathom when it came to his feelings for her. *And yet, in many ways, they've both made me feel hopeless and helpless, as if trapped on a train that won't stop in its headlong ride to nowhere.*

"Should I stay or should I go?" she sang to herself in the silence of the car, the crunch of the tires over snow and ice providing a thumping background beat. It could have been the beat of her shoes across the Liffey Bridge or up the alleyways in Temple Bar as she decided to leave Ireland for home. How long would she feel the need to run from something before she felt rooted, before she knew where she belonged?

CHAPTER 9

LUKE

"So, what about your new woman?" Luke could feel the chuckle in Henry's voice and he sensed there was a smirk on his mouth. Luke faced Henry's broad back as he bent over the array of thermal long johns, orange vests, bullets, socks, boots, and camping gear strewn across the dining room table, checking each item. He knew Henry better than anyone.

"So what about her?" Luke answered, a grin spreading across his face. Luke and Henry had been best friends and accomplices since kindergarten. Now that Henry was a happily settled family man with two kids, they didn't see each other as often. But they never gave up their annual hunting trip at the beginning of deer season.

They'd started going to Henry's grandfather's cabin in Tionesta when they were thirteen years old, just a couple of kids tagging along with Henry's father and uncles. At nineteen, they began going alone, and when they hit twenty-one, they were having a wild and crazy time that involved a little bit of hunting and a lot of fun in the local bars in town. Luke would have liked to resurrect those times, but Henry called it quits on the freewheeling part of the deal when he fell in love with Lisa and got married. Rather than lose the trip altogether, Luke surrendered and scaled it down to beer, hunting, and just hanging out with Henry, talking well into the night.

"I think you like her a lot," Henry taunted, laughing out loud now. "I think you're tired of being the lonely single guy. So why are you hiding her from me?"

"I'm not hiding her, you just haven't been around when she's here," Luke shot back, a little irritated. "I'm happy you're happy with Lisa, but marriage doesn't work for everyone."

"Luke, just because Marianne wasn't...you know...because it didn't work out, doesn't mean you can't try again." Henry was serious now, moving around the table to face Luke.

"You're picking up the beer this year, and I'm picking you up and driving to camp. Do you think we need more bullets?"

"Nah...I know I'll get a buck with one shot, the rest are for you, sissy boy. You won't be hitting anything!" Henry smiled and shrugged, putting on his coat and picking up his car keys.

He roared with laughter as Luke grinned and flipped up his middle finger. Luke loved the shared history, the fact that Henry cared about him, wanted him happy. But he liked even more that Henry knew when to drop the line of questioning and move on.

"Going to get the beer?" Luke was still smiling as he followed Henry out into the darkened garage, hitting the garage door opener on the way to let some light in. Henry's truck was out in the driveway collecting snow.

"Yeah, I'll get some beer...and food...on my way home," Henry said, his words floating out on puffs of steamy cold breath.

"Snow will be good for tracking," Luke said, gesturing out at the white flakes falling beyond the garage. "I'll pick you up tomorrow, early, before sunrise."

"So maybe I'll meet this new girl when we get back?" Henry's question crested on a laugh as he tried to get a rise out of Luke.

Luke shrugged and grinned. "I'm not marrying her. She's a great girl, lots of fun, good for however long it lasts. Sure you can meet her. You'll like her!"

"What's her name?"

"Dina Benet. Cool name, huh? She's a writer who works as a teacher. Doesn't make much money. Lives in a little two-by-four apartment."

"Money doesn't matter."

"Yeah, I know." Luke didn't want to go that route. He wanted to think about the hunting trip. "Like I said, she's great, she just has these moments when she's cool and moments when she's...well...not."

Still, Henry didn't move. He stood there, thinking, a big giant of a man having some sort of internal debate within himself.

"Are you sure she's just not enough of a challenge for you?" he asked, plainly curious. "I mean, what is it she wants that's not cool with you?"

"Stability...home, family, dog, cat, kids...stability," Luke said, his voice flat. He liked to think of Dina in the laughing moments, the fun, the sensual, and the companionable moments. He didn't like to think about what she wanted and needed from him. His pride and ego didn't want Henry to know how much, at times, he struggled against just giving it to her, that he'd considered starting down that road a time or two.

"Stability...from you?" Henry's face broke into a wide grin and he roared with laughter again, stomping his feet against the cold and slapping his gloved hands together like some dancing grizzly bear. He gave Luke thumbs up and started walking toward his big, black pickup truck.

Luke could hear him laughing as he started the truck and Luke punched the garage door button, watching the door come down and Henry's headlights disappear. He grinned along with the laughter but once Henry was gone, he felt irritable, cranky. He could provide those things to any woman if he chose to do so, but Dina had a need for some sort of deep, intimacy that entwined and locked a man in. It scared him as much as it turned him on, but he couldn't find a corresponding shallow, selfish side in her that mirrored his own. He couldn't see things in her that he understood. He was intrigued, but he wasn't taking a risk. He didn't see any commitment with a woman—even marriage—as a place where he lost his individual self or rights to become one with another person. He was totally turned on by the intensity of Dina's need but he wondered how long they could last if he couldn't bring her to the point where she viewed the current status of their relationship as something she could be satisfied with, possibly permanently.

Luke began packing the items on the dining room table neatly into a duffel bag and backpack. When he finished, he stood up, stretching and yawning, catching himself in the long wood-framed rectangular mirror on the opposite wall.

"I am a hunter," he said out loud. "I like the chase, the hunt, the capture, the kill."

Dina, he knew with a twinge of conscience, would never provide a decent pursuit. Perhaps he should end it with her now, one quick merciful phone call then off to hunting camp. He cared about her, perhaps a little more than he wanted to, but it felt good, coasting midway down the road of their relationship and feeling her love and warmth. He knew that, over time, he would hurt her. But he wanted her and he had this insatiable desire for her at the oddest times. Luke looked up at the clock. It was only nine thirty. Would she come out to his house if he called? He picked up the phone and dialed. As soon as he heard her voice he wanted to see her naked.

"Hey, baby, I'm leaving for hunting camp tomorrow. I'll be gone for a week. I'll miss you. Want to come over and spend the night before I go?"

He listened, smiled, then hung up the phone. He knew she would do it. She would never let him chase her. Yet, he never seemed to tire of her either. Just her neediness. He tired of that.

CHAPTER 10

DINA

Dina sliced through the thick carpet of leaves pretending to be a cross-country skier while Josh laughed at her, choosing instead to jump into the pile his father had meticulously created on the other side of the yard. Dina watched his carrot-topped head tinged here and there with brown and gold blending with the variegated hues of yellow, orange, red, gold, and brown around him. She felt a moment of pure happiness as his little-boy energy slammed into the neat confines of Luke's raking efforts again and again, leaves exploding violently upward then swirling gracefully down to lay in scattered, messy, and beautiful disarray. Josh lay in the leaf pile, legs and arms spread as though he were about to make a snow angel. His hands grabbed fistfuls of leaves, throwing them wildly into the air as he closed his eyes and waited for them to fall as softly as a prayer upon him.

This life she had led for over a year now was much like a carpet of leaves. Dina knew if she skied through slowly and methodically, it simply drifted upward in an insignificant motion, returning gently to form a new pattern where she could sit safely on the perimeter, but never quite weave into the fabric. If she remained still, her movement never disrupting, she could absorb long moments of tranquility and happiness, living a half-life of sorts within a hushed, hallowed clearing in the woods. But then a harsh wind would blow through, creating spirals of colorful foliage that fell in piles she couldn't see over the tops of, exposing the dirt and browned grass they once covered below.

"Josh, knock it off!" Luke yelled from the back of the yard. "How will we ever get this finished if you keep breaking up the piles of leaves? Hey Dina, want to move that rake a little more?"

Hey, I'm just a volunteer—I don't live here, Dina wanted to yell back at him. Instead, she moved the leaves back into a pile.

"I'm going to start bagging leaves." Dina laid her rake down. "Josh, you want to help?"

He jumped up, his wiry eleven-year-old frame filled to overflowing with energy and looking for a place, any place, to expend it.

"Let's turn this big pile of leaves into a couple bags, okay?" Dina peeled a huge, black plastic bag from the roll in a box neatly lettered "Leaf and Lawn – 20 bags." "How many bags do you think we can fill from each pile?"

"Lots!" Josh said, grinning. "Can I put the leaves in the bag?"

"Well, I have a bigger, more important job for you," Dina answered, smiling back. "You hold the bag and once I get enough leaves in there, then I hold the bag while you step inside and stomp the leaves down. Are you a good stomper?"

Josh, his hair longer now than the close-clipped crew cut he'd had when they met, nodded his head vigorously. Impulsively, Dina scooped up a fistful of leaves and sat down on the ground. She could feel Josh's breath on her neck as he leaned over her shoulder, curious, while she tied a string of leaves together with small pieces of twine she pulled from her pocket and a couple twisty-ties meant for the leaf bags. Once she'd closed the leaves in a circle, Dina stood and placed the somewhat lopsided but colorful circlet on Josh's head.

"You're The Leaf King," she said, laughing at his startled face.

Josh extended his arms to the side, headed tipped upward just enough to face the sky without losing his makeshift crown and yelled, "Hey, World, I'm The Leaf King! Bow down to me!"

Luke appeared behind him and plucked the crown from his head, placing it on his own salt-and-pepper mane. It sat slightly askew, slanting toward his right eye to give him a roguish appearance. Dina hadn't seen him walk over, she and Josh had been laughing so hard.

"I'm the king of this kingdom," Luke crowed merrily. "You, boy, are a prince in waiting. Methinks you need to get to work and earn this crown!"

Josh began laughing all over again, wrapping his arms around his father's waist in a hug as he looked up at Luke standing like a strange, modern-day Poseidon with his rake and crown. *All he needs is a fishtail,*

Dina thought. She began to fashion another crown, this one of all red leaves.

"Is that my prince's crown?" Josh asked.

"No, it's the crown for the queen," Dina said gaily, plopping it on her own head. "Every king needs a queen!"

Her words were the wind that blew the carefully patterned leaves beneath her feet into untidy piles and revealed dirt, rocks, and worms in the openings left by its passing. There was silence for seconds that seemed like hours.

"Let's get back to work." Luke walked away, whistling softly, slightly off-key, his mock crown now nearly hanging from his ear.

Dina stood, frozen, afraid if she exhaled to let out her breath, she would cry in front of Josh who was speechless and unsure what had just happened.

"Dina," Josh said softly. "I think you make a great Leaf Queen."

A small cloud had moved in front of the sun and, for the moment, her crown just looked like a tangle of leaves, the reddish glow of a fantasy now gone. She placed it on Josh's head, forcing a smile in place of the tears that were struggling not to spill from her watery eyes.

"Ahh, it looks so much better on you," Dina said, her voice a little shaky. "My granny used to do this when I was your age. She called me The Leaf Queen. But there's really no such thing."

Dina smiled at Josh, who seemed satisfied with her explanation, as the sun reappeared. Somewhere in County Sligo, she had a daughter just about his age who she hoped was running through the leaves with happy abandon. They calmly went back to bagging leaves, the reality of rakes, black plastic, and tired, sore backs replacing the momentary illusion of a fantasy kingdom.

When Luke took Josh home at five o'clock, she would jump in the shower and get ready to go to a political fundraiser for some lawyer who was running for Commonwealth Court judge. She didn't know what she hated worse, dragging all the stuff she needed to get ready over to his house because he wouldn't let her leave anything there, or spending an entire evening with people she thought were primarily a fake, self-congratulatory lot. She knew she would end up at the bar in a very short time with the other "dates," drinking and trying to put a softer spin on the evening.

CHAPTER 11

LUKE

Luke loved political functions the way small children love Halloween. He loved the noise, confusion, dressing up, and showing off, primarily, the woman on his arm. He loved schmoozing and being part of an inner, circular society that was his reward for being a lawyer. Dina looked great tonight in a backless black cocktail dress. She'd headed straight for the bar with a wink and a wave, looking for some of the other dates. He knew she hated these types of dinners as much as he loved them. She said they were all fake, and he felt a tiny spasm of gratitude that she tolerated it for him and an even smaller sense of wonder that it was the fakeness he loved. It was a big playground for him.

"Hey, Luke." Bob Scott was slapping him on the shoulder with one hand, martini firmly lodged in his other. "Dina looks hot. When are you going back to playing the field so the rest of us can get a shot at her?"

"She wouldn't give you the time of day," Luke said, snorting out a little laugh.

He glanced at Dina, standing at the bar talking to a couple campaign workers and lawyers' wives. He'd slept with the three women behind her, one just a couple months ago on a whim after a birthday party for the very Bob Scott who was babbling in his right ear now. He'd gone solo, telling Dina he had a late business meeting. He wanted to spread his wings a little but there was no way he wanted Bob or any of these guys going after Dina.

"So I heard you got the hospital account," Luke said. "Any offshoot legal work connected with it you want to give me?"

Bob was a sloppy drunk at functions but he ran one of the biggest ad agencies in town and he often tossed his own legal work or that of his clients to Luke, usually small stuff, leaving the big retainers and expensive negotiations for a larger firm. Luke didn't want him to know that business was slow for him and Trish right now. They'd been struggling through a dry spell for about three months. Even the steady bread-and-butter wills and divorces were at an all-time low.

"Trish and I are waiting for Benton to decide whether he wants to purchase a big piece of commercial real estate then we are off and running with a major closing," Luke said, still loving the feeling of casually dropping the name of the real estate tycoon in conversation. "While we're waiting we'll be handling a few smaller cases, maybe take a little time off. I've got some time if you have anything you want to loop me in on."

"I'll see what I've got going and give you a call," Bob said, bored with Luke, his eyes starting to scan the room. "That Benton is a good client, but you need a couple more to keep the ship floating, Luke."

Luke watched him walk away, irritated. One closing or a major contract negotiation for Benton was better than all of Bob's clients rolled together. Out of the corner of his eye he saw that little freelance title searcher, Amber Holden, walking toward him. He didn't know how she managed to get into these functions. He guessed as someone's date, since he doubted she made much doing real estate title searches on her own. She didn't present well at something that required evening wear, either. It forced her to hang up her standard grunge style wardrobe of camouflage pants, jean jacket, T-shirt, and flip-flops for a cocktail dress. He thought she looked fine, but she wore it all so uncomfortably that people around her shifted and twitched in sympathy. Where Dina was hard and trim and sexy, Amber was soft and doughy, with love handles and huge breasts. Where Dina wanted to move in and make a commitment, Amber just wanted to meet him somewhere for hot, quick sex and fun. He had toyed with her but kept her at arm's length so far.

His eyes shot over to Dina again, watching her surreptitiously pull a tissue from her tiny handbag then turn her head away from her companions at the bar to blow her nose. Luke felt a touch of guilt. She had been sick off and on a lot lately, and she was only a month past a bout of walking pneumonia. He shouldn't have had her out there raking leaves today. He thought about walking over to her then Amber touched his elbow and he looked down.

"Hey, Amber. Didn't expect to see you here."

"I thought it'd be fun, but I'm getting bored just talking to people about legal stuff," she said with a sigh. "Want to go out to the parking garage and smoke a joint?"

She was always direct with him like this and, until Dina, he would have just gone and enjoyed whatever fun went with her offer. He felt guilty again but this time the feeling made him more than a little claustrophobic. He could see Trish watching him, always monitoring him. She would figure it out, but she wouldn't tell. As that thought passed through his mind, he knew he would take Amber up on her offer.

"You're on," he said, his face tight and determined. "Meet me by my car."

"I'll just wait for you."

"No, you have to meet me there and it has to be between the two of us."

She followed his glance to Dina and then back. He waited to see if she would back off and retract the offer. Maybe she didn't see herself as easy, the way he did. She was silent for only a second and then she shrugged as if indifferent and said, "Okay," before wandering off to the exit without a backward glance.

Luke walked quickly over to Dina. "Hey, how are you holding up?" he asked.

"I'm fine," she answered, her eyes a little bloodshot. "I hope we're going to eat soon, I'm getting hungry."

"I think they'll seat us in about thirty minutes," he said. "Can you hold out?"

She nodded, happily sipping her wine and flipping her thumb toward the woman and two men next to her. "They'll keep me amused and laughing until we sit down."

"Well, our table is number fifteen, over there." Luke pointed across the room. "You can sit anytime. Listen, I need to run out to my car, get a package for a real estate closing I have next week, and hand it off to a freelance title searcher so she can get started on Monday. I'll just be a few minutes."

Dina nodded lazily, kissing him back softly when he leaned down to peck her lips. She was a little drunk and that was good for him right now. Even better that he'd left a legal file in the back seat of the car. He shot out the side door of the big hotel ballroom to avoid Trish and grabbed the first elevator to the parking garage below. When he stepped off into its cave-like semi-darkness, a netherworld filled with steel and chrome high-end cars, he blinked to adjust his eyes to the dim lighting. His footsteps echoed as he ran down one flight of steps to yet a lower level, away from the security guard and any prying eyes. He saw his car in the middle row, but Amber was nowhere in sight. Quickly, he unlocked it and moved the legal file from the back seat to the trunk.

"Psst, over here." He heard Amber's giggle and turned to see her standing in a corner where the concrete walls met to create a dark shadow. It was an open parking spot at the end of the last row, hidden by other cars. He practically ran down there, smelling the sweet marijuana smoke as he approached.

"Couldn't wait for me, huh?" He laughed and grabbed the joint. Inhaling slowly, he leaned his back against the wall. She moved against him, her hands under his jacket and on his waist, her soft form rubbing against him.

"Is that all you came down here for?" She retrieved the joint and inhaled then sealed her lips on his to blow the smoke into his mouth.

"Depends on what you're offering. I have to go back up there and look presentable in a few minutes, you know."

Amber smiled a slow, dreamy smile and handed him back the joint with one hand while she expertly undid his belt and zipper with the other. In one second his pants and underwear were at his feet, yet he could feel no response to her by his body. She seemed unperturbed by this, simply removing her dress to reveal her large, naked breasts and fleshy body. A Botticelli of sorts, he thought, remembering his freshman art appreciation class in college.

She began to rub herself all over him in a bizarre and grotesque dance that was at once erotic and disturbing, holding him gently against the wall and placing his hand on different parts of her until she felt him respond. Then she dropped to her knees and, more like an experienced streetwalker than an awkward twenty-three-year-old title searcher, she took care of business. Luke felt stoned, decadent, strangely transported to freedom by a body he found both unattractive and addictive, and then he exploded in her mouth and woke up from his haze.

"Thanks, Amber," he mumbled, handing her the joint while pulling up his pants. "That was the greatest high I've had in a while. You're awesome, but I've gotta go."

He waited for her to yell or complain, but she did not. She simply pulled on her dress and waved as he walked away.

"My address is in your pocket," she called. "Stop by sometime for a little more."

Luke felt the euphoria of the forbidden that had turned him on since he was sneaking behind the building in junior high, away from the eagle-eyed nuns, to feel the breasts of any willing girls. He wondered how he would feel when he saw Dina. He hoped it wouldn't be a downer. He felt primed and ready to go home and have wild sex with her. These were the moments, Henry told him, when he should realize he had a problem. Luke just didn't see it. He ducked into the men's room outside the ballroom to check his clothes and hair. He looked normal, just a little flushed. He splashed some water on his face.

Dina was waving to him from the table as he walked in the door. He waved back and trotted over.

"You must have run down the steps and back to get and deliver that package," she said.

"Why? Is my face all red?"

"No...I'm just kidding. I thought you'd be late, but you were only gone about twenty minutes and back on time. You must have run!"

"I took the elevator." Less than a half hour and he'd soared to a weird, erotic place then landed back here, next to Dina, as if nothing had happened. That's what he loved about life, the unexpected and the uncomplicated.

The ride home was quiet. A couple flyers and campaign pins lay across Dina's lap as she tipped her seat back, window open slightly, and breathed in the night air. She had this relaxed, faraway look on her face that made him smile.

"Whatcha thinking about?"

"I love you and I want us to make this permanent."

His body stiffened in shock, anger, and frustration. She couldn't just enjoy things the way they were. He pulled into the driveway of his home, one hand on the wheel, the other on the garage door opener. She was still staring at him, waiting.

"It's the wine talking," he said. She looked ready to cry.

Luke knew then that he had to end it with her. She would never just enjoy the ride with him and he would never want more than they had now. He was ticked off at her. He didn't like to be pushed to do these things until he moved beyond caring about doing them at all. He was even angrier because he couldn't bring himself to cut the tie right now, at this very instant. Some wishy-washy feeling of remorse and caring and desire was rolling around in there and he was tongue-tied.

"Dina, you know this is as much as I can do right now. Why can't you just enjoy things the way they are?"

She flipped the handle and hopped out of the car, leaving the campaign paraphernalia lying across her seat. She stood in the garage with her back to him, shifting from one foot to the other like a little girl who has to go to the bathroom badly.

Luke sighed. He couldn't send her home. She was too drunk to drive. And he couldn't give her what she wanted. He unlocked the door to the house and stepped inside, ignoring her, dropping his keys on the counter and loosening his tie. He pulled a beer from the refrigerator. When he shut the door, popped off its cap, and took a drink, he turned to look for her. She was standing in the great room under the deer heads, coat and shoes off, forlorn, lost, just waiting for him.

He wandered over to her, set the beer down on the fireplace mantel, and leaned down to kiss her, unzipping her dress. Dina surprised him by kissing him back and removing his clothing and hers with a ferocity he had not seen since their first night together.

He made love to her once again, right there, on the floor of his great room, with no words—just hunger and anger and need. She fell asleep almost immediately afterward. Luke carried her to the couch, covering her with an afghan, then headed up to his own bed to sleep alone.

Dina was as transparent as glass, as soft and meltingly lovely as snow. She was not an enigma or a conquest, but what was puzzling to him was that he could not seem to just end it and walk away. He liked watching her drive away each Sunday night, knowing he would miss her soon. He liked bringing her here after several days of missing her for conversation and laughs and lovemaking. He was selfish. He did not want to give up what he liked, that much he understood about himself. What he didn't understand was why he felt something a little deeper, something that wasn't enough to keep him hanging around Dina forever but was interfering with what he knew he needed to do.

CHAPTER 12

CELIA

Celia spent all morning putting together odds and ends of household furnishings she no longer wanted for Dina's apartment. Then she watched as her sister carried one lamp to the car and returned to collapse on the couch, her breathing a little ragged, her voice hoarse. It had been a month since Dina suffered from walking pneumonia, something she'd endured two years in a row and was having more and more trouble getting over each time. Celia thought she should be back to normal by now, but instead Dina was sound asleep on her couch.

Celia looked down at her sister, curled halfway to a fetal position, her skin pale and translucent. She draped a quilt across her, gently pulling it up over Dina's shoulders.

Celia shook her sister gently, "Dina, wake up, I want to talk to you."

Dina's eyelashes fluttered and she opened her eyes, focused briefly on Celia, and then closed them again.

"Dina, sit up, wake up." Celia shook her again, perching on the end of the couch near Dina's feet. Dina's eyes were tiny slits, with barely a glimmer of a pupil but they were open. With a slight cough, she pushed down with her hands and slid into an upright position, faced Celia and yawned. "What?" she asked, sleepy, a little irritated.

"Dina, something is wrong. I want you to see a doctor and find out why you've been sick so often."

"I'm just a little slow getting over the walking pneumonia."

"That was a month ago; you should be well enough to haul some things out to your car without getting winded," Celia argued. "Admit it. You know you're getting worse. Please make an appointment for some follow-up X-rays."

"Okay, okay, I'll do it on Monday." Dina closed her eyes, tipping her head back, arms still crossed.

"No, now." Celia handed her the phone. "I'll read Dr. Austin's phone number to you. Tell the answering service you need the tests by Monday."

Celia knew Dina was too tired to fight back. She watched her sister yawn and sigh, then read the numbers off as Dina dialed them. She prayed silently while Dina explained what was wrong, waiting as the answering service gave her the nurse on call.

"Done," Dina said as she hung up the phone. "I have X-rays on Monday at noon and a follow-up with the doc on Thursday at four. I'd tell you I want to go by myself, but I suppose you are going to insist on coming with me."

Celia smiled, more out of relief than over Dina's humorous crack at her overprotective stance. She curled up next to Dina, pulling the quilt over both of them and slipping her arm around her sister while Dina rested her head on Celia's shoulder.

"Do you miss Granny?"

"Yeah, Dina, I do...every day."

"I'm surprised. I figured I miss her so much because I need her to fix things for me. I'm such a screw up. But you...you have Dave. He's your family now."

"Dina, you're my family and you'll always be part of what I build with Dave."

Celia still believed something had happened in Ireland that changed her sister forever, but Dina would not talk about her final year there or about the boyfriend, Liam, who she'd professed to be madly in love with and then dumped without any explanation. Celia poked and prodded after the break-up, but Dina refused to talk about Liam and, with an ocean between them, Celia couldn't do much to change that. Once Dina came back, rather than risk the type of deeply painful argument they'd had over Dina returning to Ireland after Maeve's funeral, she'd just let it go.

Celia's insides felt so soft and comfortable now. The painful memories were just that—memories. Dina was snuggling next to her as they'd done with Maeve so long ago when they would listen to their grandmother read a book or share her wild, Irish tales until they fell asleep dreaming of adventures and heroes and fairies with mystical powers. She knew she should wait for Dave, tell him her news first, but in this moment she could not. "Dina, are you awake?"

"Uh-huh."

"I'm going to have a baby...you're going to be an aunt."

Dina's eyes flew open and she sat up straight, a wide, childlike grin breaking out on her face.

"Oh, CeCe, that's wonderful. An aunt...Aunt Dina..."

"I don't know. Dave doesn't know yet and I probably should have told him first, but I had to tell you."

Celia and Dina held hands under the quilt, their heads leaning back against the couch, facing one another and smiling. They were one again, as they had been during their childhood. Dina let go of Celia's hand and lay her palm on her sister's flat stomach. Celia closed her eyes and felt their connection reach out to her baby as well.

"Do you think it's a girl? Will you name it Justine?"

Celia's eyes flew open in horror. "NO! No, I don't think it is a girl, and no, I won't name it Justine."

They sat in silence for a few minutes.

"Just get well, Dina. I need you to be well. What do I know about taking care of a baby? I'll need you and Dave to help me raise this little one!"

A shoe scraped against the hardwood floors behind the couch. Celia and Dina turned in unison just as Dave said, "What baby?"

Celia jumped up, crashing back from nostalgic memories and sisterly bonding to reality, panicked at Dave's dark look of anger and pain. The look he gave Dina was even worse. He had never looked at her sister as though she were unwelcome. Celia saw Dina's eyes well up, then she watched Dave's back as he stormed through the kitchen beyond and out the back door. Celia told him once never to make her choose, and she hoped he would not now.

"I'll fix it, Dina," Celia assured her. "Let's get your stuff in the car and get you home. Then I'll see you Monday at noon for your X-rays."

Celia could see Dave seated out on the picnic table, waiting for her, as she loaded up Dina's car. She hoped he understood. It was foolish, what she had done in an errant moment of reminiscence when she felt so close to her sister, as worried for her as she had always been. Celia fought the push from within herself of a deep, troubling realization that it was possible she might truly need no one but Dina. She loved Dave but as he walked out, she knew she could survive without him, raise a child without him. But she could not bear to move through life without knowing Dina existed in some, if not all of the places along her journey.

CHAPTER 13

DINA

*D*ina lay in Colleen's cottage on the most comfortable mattress she'd ever known, her head buried in piles of soft pillows, her body soaked in sweat, and she cried, weakly. The
windows were open and the air was cool but Dina was on fire. She
could see the unfurling, deep green leaves on an enormous tree outside
the window, their beauty at once breathtaking and terrible. The pain
had been excruciating but that last push had done it and she could hear
a baby wailing loudly enough to break her heart. She closed her eyes,
wishing sleep would come immediately, but it did not and seconds later
she opened her eyes again, only to come face to face with the round blue
eyes of a tiny infant as the midwife placed it in her arms.

"'Tis a girl," the midwife said.

Dina breathed in and out with her tiny daughter's chest. She un-
wrapped her and smelled her, touched her, checked her fingers and toes,
then wrapped her back up in her little pink blanket. A rush of feelings

washed over her as Colleen, kind Colleen who she had come to love almost as much as Kathleen, sat on the side of the bed and watched her. She could feel fear and hunger mixing with her kindness today. Dina didn't want to let go, yet she had promised, signed papers. It was what was best for the baby but she couldn't move her leaden arms toward Colleen.

"Would you like me to take her?" Colleen asked. "Would that be easier, dear?"

Dina kissed the baby on her rosy forehead then nodded to Colleen who reached softly over and under Dina's arms to remove the baby. Dina felt emptiness more awful even than what had come after Maeve's death. She watched Colleen look at the baby with love and awe.

She needed to run for a while, far away, until she could no longer hear the wailing from her grandmother's wake mixing with the wailing of the child she had just surrendered to another woman and to another life that would not include her.

Dina woke up drenched in sweat. Ever since she'd discovered Celia was pregnant she found herself dreaming of Katie. She wanted to sleep, just to see her again, but she dreaded sleep because she lived through the pain of giving her up over and over each night. Dina was exhausted from dreaming and no amount of sleep took that away. The night sweats she assumed came with these dreams of Katie were getting worse. She felt so tired all the time that she often asked her students to do group projects because it was exhausting to stand up and teach for an hour. She just wanted to sleep.

Celia thought she was sick, but Dina thought it was depression. Along with the reoccurring nightly loss of Katie, during her waking hours she relived the night of the political fundraiser, the night when she was feeling so warm and loved that she blurted her feelings out and etched a line of demarcation, a gap between she and Luke. She'd watched him close that gap and seem to need her, want her, for months, then revert to a distant, busy, absent boyfriend. It was draining and it left her despondent, desperate, wishing she was strong like Celia, needing no one.

As much as the smells and sounds of the doctor's office were something Dina feared and disliked, she was hoping for a quick diagnosis from the X-ray results and a magic pill. She sat on the wooden chair with its orange seat cover, identical to the twenty-five other chairs neatly lining the walls of the waiting room, their backs aligned and facing the middle of the room, and she waited as if a vigorous game of musical chairs was about to begin. But there was no one to play the game with her. Celia sat quietly, flipping through baby magazines, her face a little gray from morning sickness. Somehow Dina knew that even if the room were packed with people, she would feel alone.

"Dina Benet?" The nurse stood in the open doorway to a hallway of properly numbered examining rooms, her loose, blue drawstring pants and multi-colored smock looking like easy, comfortable jogging clothes. She had Dina's file and was motioning to her.

Dina and Celia stood up at the same time.

"Can my sister come with me?" Dina felt like a child asking.

The nurse smiled and shrugged agreement. They were off down the hallway, following her quick steps, stopping to weigh Dina, then on to a room with the number two hanging from a little sign near the door and a soft pastel wallpaper border running around the circumference of its walls.

"I'm going to take your blood pressure and temperature." The nurse was moving efficiently, stacking a gown, robe, and blanket on the end of the examining table. "Then I want you to take everything off but your underwear and put on this gown. When you're ready hop up on the table and wait for the doctor."

"But I thought we were just going over X-ray results," Dina said.

"He'll give you the results and an exam, then you can talk," the nurse said cheerfully as she tightened the blood pressure cuff around Dina's arm. Seconds later she popped the thermometer in Dina's mouth while she wrote down her blood pressure on the chart. It seemed as if she extracted the thermometer, wrote down the temperature, waved, and closed the door behind her in one swift move that invited no further questions.

"I'll bet she's just as perky when she tells you that you have a terminal illness," Dina groused, removing her clothing and shivering as she donned the gown then wrapped the blanket around her. "I think something is wrong."

"Dina, that's what we're here for, to figure it out," Celia said.

Dina lay back on the paper-covered examining room table, listening to it crackle and crunch under her body, the pillow cover doing the same. She gazed up at the beige ceiling tiles filled with perforated holes and, breathing slowly, tried to block out everything around her. She had not been to yoga class for a long time. There was never much money left over in her budget and yoga was expensive; still, she missed the stress relief and the oneness of mind and body. She now tried to remember how to breathe, slowly and deeply through her nose, sinking into her own body and exhaling the bad stress while inhaling a good calm. She heard the latch click and the door swing open.

"Celia, how are you?" Dr. Austin's deep voice resonated, an appropriate fit for a large, bulky man. Dina kept her eyes closed, willing extra seconds of peace and quiet.

"Great, Dr. Austin. I'm doing great," Celia said. Dina knew she was probably giving him her stiff smile that wasn't really a smile because she was terrified for her sister. Dina called it her politically correct smile.

Dina felt a shadow, a coolness, and opened one eye. Dr. Austin, bear-like and blustery, was peering down at her. Dina smiled and winked at him.

"Ahhh, so you're joking with me. For a minute, I thought you were taking a nap on our nice, comfortable beds here." His smile, usually casually and easily loping more to one side of his face than the other, was stiff. Another smile that was not a smile. Dina sighed and sat up, eyeing the envelope of X-ray film he was setting down on the counter across from her. Like soft rain, touching and cascading, rolling across her in a leisurely manner, a sense of foreboding now traveled through her senses.

"I'm going to take my Irish self outside, catch a firefly, and wish on a fairy before you speak, to ensure good luck," Dina quipped, winking at him again.

Dr. Austin didn't even smile this time. He put his cold stethoscope on her neck and then on her back, asking her to breathe deeply. He felt her neck and shoulders, looked in her ears, then, turning, clipped her chest X-ray onto a board on the wall and flipped a switch. A skeletal picture of what she assumed was her torso lit up.

"See this here, and again here," Dr. Austin said, pointing above her left rib cage and again somewhere around where she suspected her sternum lay. Dina hopped off the table, blanket wrapped around her waist, and shuffled forward to peer closely at the X-ray. It looked like two gray smudges, or perhaps they were shadows. She was confused, unsure what it was supposed to look like.

"Is something wrong?"

Dr. Austin snapped off the light and the X-ray disappeared as quickly as it had appeared.

"Yes, Dina, something is wrong."

"Is it the smudges or shadows or whatever you pointed to?" Dina was sober now, no joking around. She glanced at Celia who looked near tears.

"Yes. Those are lymph nodes above your lung and around your trachea and diaphragm," he replied. "I'm hoping they are just infected from your nasty bout with walking pneumonia, but we are going to schedule a biopsy to make sure."

"And if they're not just infected? What are the other possibilities?" Dina's voice was high-pitched and quavering slightly with fear. Dr. Austin did not reply immediately. He opened the office door and called for a nurse, then put the films back into an envelope. Seconds later, a nurse arrived and he asked her to set up a biopsy, preferably within a few days. "So soon?" Dina said after the nurse left. "I have to work. I can't."

"Dina, there are several possibilities and I hope the lymph nodes are just inflamed or infected, but if it turns out to be the worst-case scenario and you have lymphoma, which is cancer in your lymph nodes, then I need to get you treatment quickly."

He had sucked all the air out of the room, Dina was sure of it. She clutched the sides of the exam table, breathing slowly, willing the area around her not to begin spinning. Celia was white as a sheet.

"I need you to lie down and I'm going to examine you," Dr. Austin said.

Dina sat on the table, woodenly, then slowly slid onto her back, looking up at the ceiling rather than at Dr. Austin. She could feel tears sliding down her cheeks yet she couldn't make a sound. She was afraid to speak for fear she would begin screaming and never stop.

Finally, she said, "Dr. Austin?"

"Yes, Dina?" The stethoscope was cold against her chest.

"Could you have a nurse see to Celia? She's pregnant."

Dr. Austin stopped his examination and looked over at Celia. Her head was between her knees. He opened the door and barked out an order in a harsh voice Dina had never heard him use. The nurse returned and he asked her to take Celia to the room next door and have her lie down. Then he spoke softly in the nurse's ear, patting her shoulder, and she nodded, leading an uncharacteristically compliant Celia away.

"Okay, doc, so what time is the biopsy and what am I in for?" Something was rising up in Dina. Something she did not know she possessed. She wanted to live to see Celia's baby.

As Dr. Austin continued to examine her, slowly explaining the biopsy and potential treatments depending on what it showed, Dina worked to convince herself it was just an infection. Something simple antibiotics would cure. But she felt dark and cursed and sure it was more. Something no wishing on fireflies would turn from a harsh reality into an easy solution. No one was going to rush in and fix this one for little Dina Benet, especially not Celia, who was pregnant and fragile herself. Dina was on her own, free-falling without a net.

CHAPTER 14

LUKE

Luke swung his car into the hospital parking garage entrance, shivering as the electric window lowered to let him reach out, push the big orange button, and grab the white parking ticket that automatically popped out. The arm to the security gate rose at about the same pace his window closed and he drove forward slowly, glancing at the uniformed person in the ticket booth, a young girl with a pierced eyebrow and a mouth full of bubble gum who gave him a bored look, blew a big pink bubble then bent over what looked like a celebrity magazine of some sort.

Over the last few weeks, he'd been out of town at depositions for a difficult litigation he was sure would go to trial and hadn't called Dina much. He normally stuck with real estate, estate planning, and a few divorces, but work was lean and this had come his way. He was trying to wean himself from Dina a little, knowing by spring he would end the relationship in as humane a manner as he could. He'd kept his distance from

Amber, too. She kept calling but it smelled like trouble to him right now and he still felt at odds with himself over what he'd done in the dark corner of another parking garage much like this one. Which wrapped up his dilemma in a nutshell, Luke thought, as he found a spot two levels up, exited the car, and locked it with one quick press of the button on his keychain.

He was having trouble weaning himself from Dina. The feelings were there, the desire was still there, but whatever was wrong that prevented him from taking that final step of commitment was there too. Amber was a Band-Aid, an interlude that solved nothing and, if he toyed with her while he was still with Dina, it would present endless issues he didn't need—especially now when he needed to focus on work, not on his personal life.

After he'd called Dina's apartment from Pittsburgh to see if she would pick him up later that day at the Erie airport and her bitch of a sister answered, curtly telling him Dina was undergoing some serious tests at the hospital, all those conflicting feelings and desires went off in him like tiny little explosions through the entire ride home.

"She's having tests at Hamot Hospital and has to be there a couple days," Celia said, her voice unfriendly as usual. "I'm just here getting her pajamas and a few of her books."

"What kind of tests?" Luke demanded, the panic and worry seeping into his voice. "Why didn't she tell me?"

"Maybe if you'd called a little more often she would have," Celia snapped back.

"I noticed she was sick a lot and tired, and I asked her about it...told her to go see a doctor." He knew what Celia thought of him and, regardless of whether some of it was well-deserved or not, he didn't like her. "She didn't listen. She said she was fine. I couldn't force her to go."

"Well, I forced her to go and it's not good, so if you care about her at all I suggest you make some effort here," Celia said.

"I'm on my way home," Luke had snapped, hanging up on her before she could say another word.

Twenty minutes later he was airborne and ordering a drink. He needed it to deal with this. He hated worrying about someone this much when he was steering his life in another direction. It would be better if Dina would treat him the way her sister had, then he could just wash his hands of this without guilt, without looking back. If she had been that way all along they might actually have worked out a little better. Thinking of fragile, needy, kind Dina lying there in a hospital bed, he felt deep concern. He'd been trapped this way with his ex-wife as she'd repeatedly thrown Josh into the mix when he suggested a separation. He'd finally left her, but in many ways had never really left her. One situation like that was enough. Two was over the limit.

Thirty minutes after he picked up his car in long-term parking at the airport, he was here shutting off his cell phone and leaning back against the cold steel of the hospital elevator walls as he rode up to the fourth floor where the sterile, white world of needles and tubes mingled with the smells of cafeteria food and medicine and the human body in distress. He hated hospitals second only to funeral homes.

Luke sighed and shoved his hands in the pockets of his black leather jacket. He didn't have flowers or a card. Hell, he didn't even know what Dina was in here for. He checked the signs and followed the arrows to Room 4340. Knocking tentatively, he opened the door slowly. Celia sat in a chair across from the bed, her skin a pasty color, and glared at him. Her husband, Dave, standing next to her, smiled and nodded at Luke.

"Hey, man," Luke said to Dave, ignoring Celia. Dave was a quiet guy who basically didn't get involved.

Luke turned toward the bed and stopped cold. Dina's eyes were closed, tubes were in her nose, and an I.V. ran a thin plastic trail from somewhere under the blanket up to a large bag filled with liquid hanging from a steel pole. He moved toward the bed slowly, then, leaning over, he touched her cheek lightly. He could see tiny blue veins on her temples and she was so pale the freckles were even more pronounced than usual. The corner of what seemed to be a large, white gauze bandage stuck out where the blue-patterned, hospital-issue gown had slumped down across her shoulder.

"Hey." Dina opened her eyes, blinking and trying to smile. "You're back."

"Yeah," Luke said, perching slightly on the bed, silently wishing Celia would leave. "What's going on here? Were you going to tell me about this?"

"Not much to tell yet. They did a biopsy. It might be nothing, just an infection. So sleepy, sorry," she mumbled, her eyes closing again.

Luke kissed her forehead and stood up. She looked delicate to the point of breakable. He felt the tide of his usual selfishness receding, replaced with something different, something unusual for him.

"A biopsy for what?" he said, facing Dave, his words pointedly directed away from Celia.

"If you had called every day you would know," Celia said.

"Look, I don't care what you think of me but lay off the bitch routine for right now and answer the question or I'll go find a nurse and get some answers."

To Luke's shock, Celia burst into tears and fled the room. Dave seemed frozen, immobile. He didn't immediately chase after her and Luke, a veteran of his own marital wars, wondered what was really going on there.

"Luke, she's pregnant and worried about Dina. Don't talk to her like that," Dave said. "She's not really herself. You know how close she and Dina are."

"Okay, but can you tell me what is wrong with Dina? What's going on here?" Luke asked, thinking Celia was being herself, pregnant or not. "And congratulations on the baby, by the way."

Dave folded his arms over his chest, looking angry but trying to hold his emotions in check. "Dina went in for a checkup because she's been sick a lot and tired all the time. Celia had been after her to see the doctor. He said she has an enlarged lymph node over her lung and a few more down her trachea and into her diaphragm. It could be a number of things but they had to do a biopsy. She had the procedure this morning, about eight thirty."

Luke stared down at Dina's sleeping face for several minutes.

"I need to find Celia and make sure she's alright."

"Yeah, yeah." Luke nodded at Dave, pulling up a chair next to Dina's bed. "Before you go, can you tell me what the possibilities are for what might be wrong with her?"

Dave was halfway to the door. He turned and looked at Luke for what felt like a very long moment before answering. "I can't remember all of them, but one was an infected lymph node. And the one that has Celia so upset is the possibility of cancer in her lymph nodes. You know, you should decide, man."

"Decide what?"

"Whether to step up to the plate for once," Dave said. "Either step up to the plate, Luke, or hit the road."

Then he was gone.

Cancer. Luke felt his hands shaking as he unzipped his jacket and hung it across the back of the chair. His grandmother had died of cancer when he was seven years old. He barely remembered her, but he recalled the smells and sounds of death. It was what he hated most about hospitals and funeral homes. The smells and the sobbing and wailing that accompanied human misery. Yet his grandmother had been old, gray, sad, and ready to meet Jesus, or so his mother told him then. Dina was so young and fresh. He couldn't imagine the universe handing her over to those smells and sounds, to the end of life.

Luke bent his head and put his hands together as the nuns had taught him all those years ago. He was rusty at this process. His thoughts did not naturally focus on God. He hadn't prayed much in years, usually bowing his head when he did show up at Mass, but going over his list of things to do or his plans for later in the evening while others prayed around him.

"Dear God," he started, then stopped. Maybe he should throw the Blessed Virgin or Jesus in too. Never mind, he wasn't good at this. "Dear God, please don't let Dina die," Luke said softly, out loud. "And give me the strength to do the right thing here."

He didn't know what the right thing was. His better instincts told him she'd be better off without him. Luke knew nothing about cancer or treatments or what would be expected of him. He should break it off now. But what if he did and she gave up, got so depressed or stressed that she didn't fight hard enough? Luke leaned back into the armchair and closed his eyes. Unbidden, the memory of his ninth grade English class and the priest who had insisted they each memorize a poem, rolled up in his mind. He hated poetry. The Dylan Thomas poem he'd picked was short and he liked the title. In those days, he'd thought he would move away from Erie and lead an amazing, exciting life somewhere else. But in the end he'd come home to what he knew, where he could march to his own tune without much interference, where he could be somewhat of a big fish in this small pond. Feeling all of fifteen years old again, Luke tried to recite it, softly, to the sleeping woman before him who he wanted to stay

with and he wanted to leave, but despite his best efforts, all he could resurrect was the first line.

"I have longed to move away," he thought again and again. The rest
of the lines were missing in his memory. Just then Dina opened her eyes
and smiled at him. He felt a sense of desire to save her, wrapped in the
noble rush of hope and mad belief that he could be her hero. But as she
fell asleep again, before he could say anything, Luke knew he would not
be able to hold up to that desire and he should leave.

Celia walked back into Dina's room at that moment. Luke didn't
think she'd heard anything he'd said, yet she seemed to have softened
toward him.

"Please don't leave her right now. The doctor said attitude is everything in getting well and, no matter what I think of you, Dina loves you
and she needs you to hang around."

Luke nodded, trying not to make eye contact with her. He felt like he
was going to be sick and he didn't want Celia to see that on his face. He
watched Dave come back into the room and stand behind her. He looked
away, unable to make eye contact with either of them.

"I'm not thinking about leaving her," Luke lied, staring down at Dina
as he spoke. He didn't want Dina to die but he knew himself and doing
his best might not be enough. Deep down, he knew that illness, with all
its accompanying smells and sounds, disgusted him. He knew with every
fiber of his being that he was just weak enough to run. He longed to run,
to move away, but he was afraid of what would happen to Dina and, selfishly, of what people in his little fishpond of a city would think of him.

"I have to get going," Luke said. "I came straight from the airport, but I do have to pick up my son soon. I'll be back tomorrow."

He nodded to Dave and walked out of the room. But something made him pause, just outside the door. It was still open and, although he wasn't in the habit of eavesdropping, he waited, listening.

"What do you think?" he heard Celia ask Dave.

"I think he'll give it a shot, but I wouldn't expect the sun and the moon, honey," Dave answered. "He's not in love with Dina. I told you that a long time ago."

"I know, but I just want her to get well and I don't think she can withstand a break-up and do that. I want her to live. To meet our baby."

Luke waited, but they were silent. Finally, he walked away. He knew what Dave was thinking. It was the same thing Luke would be thinking if his sister was sick and dating a guy like him. He'd think it would be better for her if the guy left rather than have him stick around and hurt her anyway in the end. But there was no way Dave was going to say that to his pregnant wife.

CHAPTER 15

CELIA

C elia sat on the edge of the examining table in Dr. Austin's office, trying to lighten the mood. She watched as Dina fidgeted, fearful.

"Let's swing our feet and wiggle our butts at the same time to get the paper on the table to make that crinkly sound like we did as kids," Celia said.

That got a smile out of Dina, but Celia could see her sister wince when she tried to twist. She was obviously still struggling against residual pain from a biopsy that required them to pry open her rib cage to get at the lymph node.

"Sorry, I can't. It hurts."

Celia hesitated. She wanted to ask what was going on with Luke, but she knew she needed to seem supportive. Dina knew her so well. If it came across as fake they would end up arguing and it was not the time for that sort of thing.

"So how's Luke?" Celia put on the new bright and shiny face she used now when she talked about Luke.

"I'll see him tonight," Dina answered. "He has a new client and is working long hours, but he calls me every day and he's sent flowers twice. He knows I'm getting results today, and he's waiting to hear."

Waiting to see if he has to stick around or whether he can go. But she hugged Dina, careful not to touch the biopsy incision.

"Let's think positive," Celia said. "It's probably just an infection. We'll get some antibiotics and go home."

"I hope so," Dina said. "But if it's something more serious I have to talk to Luke and I think I'll need to let him go. I don't think he's up to this."

Celia held her breath, trying to mask her elation. She prayed Dina was serious. That would be the best thing for her, Celia was sure. Then she could come to stay with Celia and Dave, to get well with people who loved her.

"It's okay to get excited, CeCe," Dina said with a small laugh and a grimace. "I've known for a while that this relationship isn't doing well but I love him and I can't just shut that off. But I can't expect him to stay if this is really serious, especially if he's not up for it. I'll give him a choice."

And he'll be gone faster than I can say jackrabbit. "You make the decision, honey," Celia said. "I'm here for you. Dave and I are both here for you."

"Yeah, I know." Dina's eyes teared up as they did so often lately. "I appreciate that, but you both have a new baby to think about. You don't need to deal with me."

"My baby is going to know its Aunt Dina, and I will do whatever it takes to make that happen," Celia said. "End of subject."

Just then, as if on cue, Dr. Austin walked in. One look at him and Celia's heart sank. He was definitely not smiling. Dina kept her eyes fixed on his face as he leaned his back against the counter across from the examining table, stretching his white coat further as he crossed his meaty arms over his chest, a file in one hand.

"Just give it to me straight, Dr. Austin," Dina blurted out. Celia was surprised. She would have expected Dina to avoid any unpleasant facts.

"It's not good, Dina. You have lymphoma."

Celia burst into tears. Her hormones were all over the place as it was these days and this pronouncement following all the tension that had been building over Dina's health was too much. Celia put one arm around Dina's shoulder and wiped her eyes with her free hand. Dina didn't respond. She sat, back straight, still as a stone, her eyes fixed on Dr. Austin.

"What does that mean for me?" Dina asked.

She has to be in shock, Celia thought. *She can't absorb this.*

"It is Hodgkin's disease, which, if you have to get cancer, is the easiest to cure," Dr. Austin answered. "But yours is stage three, and we think it's almost down into your spleen so we've got to begin chemo immediately."

Celia could feel Dina start shaking a little, and her sister's eyes begin to water.

"You're in for a fight. Are you up for it?"

Dina was silent for a moment, her gaze locked on the doctor's soft, brown eyes. His words were harsh, but his eyes were gentle. It all seemed so surreal to Celia; she couldn't imagine what was going on inside Dina.

"How long will it take to beat this?" Dina sounded cockier than Celia believed she felt.

"I don't know the answer to that," the doctor responded. "We made an appointment for you tomorrow morning with Dr. Gates at the cancer center. He can give you more specific answers."

"Listen, Dina." Dr. Austin leaned forward, putting his hand on her shoulder. "You should stay with Celia for a while. You need a support system around you. You don't know how you will handle the treatment, and your attitude will make all the difference in beating this thing."

"I can't impose on Celia and Dave…"

"Oh, no," Celia interrupted "I'm having Dave move you out of that apartment and you're going on medical leave from your job. Beating cancer is the most important thing right now. Don't even think about going it alone; you're coming to live with us."

Dina was, gripping the edge of the examination table so hard her knuckles were white. When she let go, she slumped, her small frame caving inward before her whole body buckled forward. As her forehead touched her thighs, Celia rubbed her back. She listened as deep, retching sobs erupted from somewhere in her sister's core, echoing off the examining room walls.

"I want to be strong, to handle this on my own," Dina gasped, sitting up slowly, her tear-streaked face nearly touching Celia's.

"You will be strong and when you can't, I'll be strong for you," Celia said. "You are coming to stay with us. I'll take care of everything."

Celia took Dina's hand and helped her off the table. The doctor handed Dina's appointment schedule to Celia without another question, then patted Dina's shoulder and told her lots of people survive cancer. Celia walked Dina out of the office, helping her into the car, and buckling the seat belt. All the while, Dina shook and shook like a small leaf broken from the sustenance of the branch, tossing and rocking in the wind as it tumbled and rolled over and over again.

"I'm here and I'll make it alright," Celia said, reaching across from the driver's seat to pull Dina's head onto her shoulder, hugging her across the hard, inflexible stick shift.

When they were children that statement would have been all Dina needed. Today, Celia said the words but wondered if they sounded hollow. She knew this was one fight that was out of her hands.

"I wish you could, CeCe," Dina said, crying again, softly now. "I wish you could fix this for me, but I'm on my own this time."

"You are never on your own, Dina," Celia said fiercely. "Never!"

CHAPTER 16

LUKE

Dina had been quiet and distant throughout dinner and the movie. Now that they were back at his house, curled up on the couch and drinking beer, Luke wondered whether he should ask her what was on her mind.

"Dina." Luke sighed before he started wading into what he was sure would be another conversation about where their relationship was going. It had been a week since she heard the results of her biopsy, and she hadn't mentioned anything, so he assumed the test came back clean. Clutching the neck of the beer bottle, Dina covered the short length of the room in one long step to sit on the fireplace hearth facing him. She had an odd, determined look on her face, her eyebrows furrowed, her beautiful mouth set in a hard line.

"I can't sit next to you while I talk about this," Dina said, her face seeming to soften slightly. "I need a little space and I need to face you."

"Is this about us again?" Luke felt mildly exasperated.

"Yes...and no," Dina said. "Let's says it is about me and about what will become of us. Were you going to ask me about the biopsy results, Luke?" Her voice was tight, angry.

"I thought about it, but I thought you would tell me if anything was wrong and, since you didn't say anything, I thought they came back negative," he answered, defensive but worried. "Why? What happened?"

Dina took a long, slow drink and looked away, focused on the backyard where the trees were barren, stripped of all color, their capes of gold, bronze and green just a distant memory.

"The trees are bare," she said. "Just like I'll soon be. I'll be bald...in the middle of chemotherapy. The biopsy showed I have Hodgkin's lymphoma. My first chemo starts in three days."

Luke experienced the same feeling he'd felt sitting by her hospital bed. Even as she displayed a new, tough exterior to him, he could feel her vulnerability, could sense it rolling off of her and surging across the room to touch him. He didn't want her to die. At this moment, he wanted to do something heroic and right and decent for her.

"I'm here, baby," he said, getting to his feet and starting toward her. "I'm not going anywhere. I'll be here for you through this."

Dina put up her hand to stop him, shaking her head. "Sit down, Luke." He heard the pleading in her voice. "I can't tackle this with you sitting next to me." As Luke sat back down, Dina took a deep breath, setting her beer bottle on the hearth and clasping her hands together. "We've had our problems and things haven't been good for a while." Dina looked down at her hands, then up at Luke again. "I know they are just fine for you when I'm accommodating and go along with just hanging out and having fun. But they're not fine for me because I want more. We've had that conversation a million times and it always ends in us drifting farther apart.

"This disease, this battle I've got to fight...it would be hard on the best—the strongest—of relationships," Dina continued. "Once I'm in the middle of fighting for my life, I can't worry about us, solve our problems, or feel sad. I've got to have a good attitude and good support. I'm not blaming you, Luke, I just don't know that we have what it takes to weather this storm."

They sat in silence for several moments. Luke watched Dina, her body taut with fear and anxiety, her hands twined into one another, knuckles white. He wanted to be insulted but the raw truth of her words hung between them. He hadn't thought dreamy Dina, lover of poetry who always waited for the fairy tale to come true, saw them—saw him—with such clarity. He had obviously underestimated her.

"I'm giving you a Get Out of Jail Free pass, Luke," Dina said quietly. "We can break it off, no hard feelings, and you can go on with your life. Or you can stay, but then you have to be in it for the long haul and stand by me. I can't deal with a break-up or relationship issues in the middle of chemo."

Luke put his head down, covering his face with his hands so she couldn't see the angry scowl that twisted his face. Taking a deep breath, he pulled himself together, positioning his expression to something bland, although his tone said enough that she probably suspected he was really ticked off.

"Nice...could you try to sound like you have some confidence in me? And of you course you're putting the whole decision on me, Dina...on my head!" Luke's mind was racing. Every fiber of his being was screaming at him to take the deal and get out. Call her and send her cards now and then but move on with his career and his life. He'd known for months he should and probably would eventually break off this relationship. And she was giving him a free pass out.

"I'll be taking a leave of absence from work and staying with Celia and Dave...probably let my apartment go too. The lease is up soon."

He had a fleeting moment of worry at what his friends, clients, and the people of this small city would think of him if he left her now. She'd be staying with Celia, who would watch like a hawk to see how he behaved. If he wasn't the model boyfriend, that bitch would tell everyone. But Dina had just told him it was alright to go. So why wasn't he flushing what little grit and fortitude he had down the toilet and going? Celia or no Celia, he knew he wasn't in love with Dina. It might be duty or guilt holding him back, but it didn't feel that way. It felt like fear. Fear of what his friends, his family, his peers in the community would think of him if he left her, high and dry, to battle this disease on her own. And somewhere, mixed into all that self-need was, surprisingly, fear that she would die, that he would lose her permanently. The thought of her death pained him. Outside of worry over what his divorce from Marianne would do to Josh, he'd rarely had a war of emotions between his head and his heart.

He functioned with his head and decisions were born out of self-need. Luke was not an introspective man. He had no desire to explore why this sudden feeling had rolled up inside of him. He wanted to believe that his feelings for Dina were tagged, labeled, and under control.

Luke could feel himself rising and walking toward her as if he were standing outside his body watching. He leaned down and pulled Dina to a standing position, wrapping her in his arms. She was warm and shaking as she leaned her head against his chest.

"I guess this is good-bye." He saw her shoulders shrug in a false nonchalance that did nothing to override the quiver in her voice.

"No, I'm staying," Luke said. "If you will let me, I'll stay. I'll be there when you're bald and sick and I'll be there when you survive this."

Dina melted against him and she began crying quietly, softly. He leaned down to kiss her salty tears as her mouth said, "Thank you." He didn't respond. His brain was still loudly admonishing him to leave as he picked her up and carried her up the stairs to his bedroom. He'd made his decision for better or worse.

CHAPTER 17

DINA

January reigned with terrible beauty, Dina thought, pulling the thick, crocheted afghan closer. The pristine white of frozen snowflake patterns on the windowpanes and the warmth of the roaring fire in the fireplace before her created a magnificent contrast that she could enjoy as long as she was lying on the couch, rather than outside in subzero temperatures that cut to the bone. A sharp Canadian wind blew across Lake Erie, picking up every last drop of moisture and dumping lake-effect snow everywhere. It decorated the lush, green pine trees that towered skyward in Luke's front yard with glittering icicles and soft, sloping white drifts that settled then fell from branch to branch. It stripped the oaks and maples of their leaves, buds, and any trace of green life.

She heard Luke banging around in the kitchen and smelled the dark, savory aroma of a roast coming from the oven. Her sense of smell was intact, but she doubted she would savor much of it. Yesterday's chemo drugs left a strange taste in her mouth that was part dry and drug-laden and part metallic. It continued to linger today as did her lack of appetite. But he was trying hard to take care of her and Dina knew better than anyone how he was stretching internally to do it. She sat up slowly to watch the snow blowing around outside like the lifting, waving veils of a million miniscule Arabian dancers, only to drift up against the window and rest there.

Dina glanced down at the pillow where her head had just been. It was covered with hair, her hair, in strands and clumps. She looked out the opposite windows into the backyard at the maple tree that had, a few short months ago, showered her with a thousand fall leaves. It now stood stark and shorn, much like Dina. Touching her head, she could feel where the tufts had dropped away to reveal open bald patches almost connected in a circle. She sighed, wishing for a crown of leaves to cover it. She was beginning to look strange and she knew it wouldn't be much longer before no hair was left. She'd tried a wig, but it made her head itch so, instead, she wrapped scarves as artfully as possible around her head. They gave the illusion of femininity, but not much more. She hurried to clean the hair off the pillow and locate the scarf that had fallen from her head before Luke came back.

"Hey, you're awake! How are you feeling?"

Dina's head was nearly down to her ankles as she retrieved her scarf from under the coffee table. She raised her head slowly, one hand clutching her hair, the other holding the scarf, and peered up at him. She had no idea what she looked like at that moment but she had a pretty good idea, by the look on his face, that it wasn't good.

"I'm okay, just lost my scarf." She laughed, dropping the hair in her lap and hurrying to twist the scarf around her head. She saw worry and concern mix with something else resting deeper in his eyes, a straining exertion of some sort. "Sorry, I guess it was inevitable that I'd lose my hair but it's still a shock, isn't it?" Dina grabbed the hair from her lap and stood. "Maybe I should just shave my head and get it over with, huh?" She laughed and he seemed to relax, laughing a little too.

"Ready to eat? It smells great, and I'm starving!"

"Me too," she lied, smiling and following him into the kitchen. "It smells awesome. Thank you so much, honey!"

While he put on his oven mitts and took the roast out, she quietly dropped her hair in the trash can. Glancing in the mirror, she could see the dark circles under her eyes. Her eyebrows and lashes were totally gone now, her face puffy from the prednisone she took daily after each treatment.

"Can I help?" Dina asked.

She wanted, more than anything, to create an oasis of normalcy. She felt such guilt for bringing this into their relationship, even though she knew it was not her fault. Luke was so changed since her biopsy, so much more attentive and worried about her, making her hope the disease would deepen their connection. Yet, as she felt the great level of energy he put forward to keep his promise to her, she did not feel a profound bond evolving between them. Dina loved him; she wanted to live and love and wake up one day completely healthy with a link between them that would not break.

"No, I've got it under control." Luke smiled at her, wrapping her in a big hug, and kissed her soundly on the lips. "Penny for your thoughts."

"Just thinking how lucky I am to have you and how much I love you for doing this for me." Dina tipped her head to look up at him, but he wrapped her back into a silent hug.

"Come on, let's eat." He pulled away and, taking her hand, walked her to the table.

Dina had no idea how she would get that big slice of roast beef down. The mashed potatoes looked like an easier option. But she was determined he would not know that his efforts were in vain. Like the beauty outside the window that would only offer a death-like chill when touched, so the dinner smelled like heaven and tasted like cardboard to her.

"It's wonderful, Luke," she said, chewing slowly. "It's just what I needed, really...it's perfect."

He nodded and smiled like the old Luke, happy and self-congratulatory. She knew he was happy with himself for doing the right thing. Dina wished it came more naturally to him. She smiled back, chewing and swallowing while the wind howled and the veils of snow blew to and fro frantically. If she stopped thinking about anything but this moment, then she was safe and loved and she knew she would live to see tomorrow.

CHAPTER 18

CELIA

Celia wished she could have a little share of Dina's anti-nausea medication as she watched the small bag of fluid draining into her sister's veins. She was about seven months pregnant now and the baby was no longer giving her long bouts of morning sickness, but the smells of the cancer center brought that familiar queasiness back with a vengeance. She'd insisted on being with Dina for every chemotherapy session, despite her sister's protest that Luke would go with her and Dave's offer to take a turn or two as well. Fiercely, silently, she would will her sister to survive this disease, even if she had to call on every saint she could think of and barter with God in a way Father John had told her was not appropriate.

"So we have a deal?" Dina looked so comfortable in the overstuffed recliner it was hard to imagine she wasn't waiting for her favorite television show to come on instead of the four bags of toxins the nurse was carrying toward them from across the room.

"Sure," Celia answered, bile rising in her throat again. "I have to run to the restroom. I'll be right back."

Maybe it was the baby. Or the poisons they were about to put in her sister to kill the poison growing inside her. Or the deal that Celia would go home to rest after chemo and let Luke come after work to sit with Dina. Celia didn't believe for a minute he could hold out and hold up for Dina through all of this. She didn't want that bastard in her house or in Dina's life, but Dave had cautioned her to let it go. A stress-free, happy Dina was going to have better odds fighting this disease.

"And what happens when he drops out in the middle of it? When he hits the road and runs?" Celia had asked.

"We'll deal with that when and if it happens." Dave had hugged her. "Just focus on what is best for Dina. I'll focus on you. Forget about Luke. We'll deal with that as problems arise, if they do."

Dave told her he thought Luke just might grow and mature during the experience, that it would bring he and Dina closer and maybe solidify their relationship. She knew he didn't really believe that. He was just saying it to ease her fears. Celia's childhood had hardened her. She knew something awful had happened to Dina in Ireland, something that made her cry out in her sleep at night. Celia sensed it while Dina was living abroad, but she'd been powerless to help or to stop whatever was burdening her little sister. Now that same feeling was screaming inside her again, only this time it had a name: Luke.

And his name was pounding in Celia's temples as she lifted the white, antiseptically clean toilet seat and dropped to her knees. Dina was so reckless with her trust, her feelings, and her life. Celia could control only so much, but that rash, careless streak in her sister never seemed to go away and she could not cage or destroy it. She stood up, flushing the toilet, then rinsed out her mouth and patted her face with a cold, wet paper towel. When Celia returned, the little med port in Dina's chest was hooked up to a bag of medicine and she seemed to be resting comfortably. Dina's veins had been too small to handle the treatment intravenously. The med port was easier and less painful.

"CeCe," Dina said softly, her face relaxed. "My test results are coming back good. I might finish treatments before you have the baby."

Celia sat down, smiled, and wrapped a blanket that was lying across the arm of the chair around her torso. She leaned back and closed her eyes. Maybe Dave was right and it would all work out for the best in the end. She felt exhausted and Dina still had two hours of treatment to go.

"That's good," she heard Dina say. "Take a nap. Remember, I'm going to get well so I can meet that baby you're carrying. You need to stay well too."

Celia opened her eyes to see Dina smiling, hand reaching out. The chair was so close to the recliner she could hold Dina's hand without moving. They sat that way as the fluid dripped slowly into her sister's body until Celia fell asleep. She awoke to a nurse gently shaking her shoulder.

"She's done and she handled everything really well," the nurse said. "Are you ready to take her home?"

Celia nodded, standing up and searching for her purse. She was ravenously hungry. It came on her like that, as if when the baby wanted to eat, the world had to stop to accommodate its appetite. Once she got Dina home and in bed, she would raid the kitchen.

"Come on, honey." The nurse was helping Dina out of the recliner.

Celia put her arm around Dina's waist and tucked the remaining wisps of her hair under the baseball cap she'd decided to wear today. Dina seemed steady but she always had this tired, spacey look after chemo. She would sleep for hours, Celia knew, then wake to reach for the phone and call Luke.

"I'm steady. I can walk," Dina said. She looped her arm through Celia's and they maneuvered around the chairs in the waiting room, out through the lobby, and into the parking lot. It was freezing cold and icy. They were used to it. Winter on the Great Lakes was not for the weak or the faint of heart.

"Three more treatments." Dina snapped the seat belt in place and tipped the seat back. Celia was sliding behind the wheel. "My test results are good. Wish I could skip those treatments. I think it's already gone, CeCe."

"Hey, you take every treatment...to the last one," Celia said. "Then we'll be sure that it's all gone."

"I just want my hair and my life back." Dina closed her eyes as they pulled out onto 38th Street and headed east. "I sleep so much I barely spend time with anyone. I miss Luke...and Josh."

Celia felt anger mix with her worry. As Dina's hair fell out and the cancer drugs caused her moods to twist in odd ways, she saw less and less of Luke. He called nearly every night, but his earlier promises to see her often had lasted about two months before the excuses—as Celia saw them—began. It was work or his son or his parents. But she bit her tongue as she was doing now. *Keep your eye on the goal,* Dave kept telling her. *The goal is for Dina to get well.*

"Luke is so special and different from any guy I've ever known," Dina mumbled sleepily. "He only sees the best in me."

"Uh-huh." Celia kept her eye on the road.

She could hear Dave as they left the hospital after the biopsy telling her there were a million guys like Luke and he'd known tons of them—well-meaning but weak and selfish—but Dina was one in a million. He wished she could see that and get her act together. Celia glanced at Dina sitting next to her and falling asleep. Celia had always seen her sister as loving but weak and foolish. Dave disagreed. He said Dina was a lot stronger than Celia gave her credit for and would show her that one day. Celia wondered when that day would come.

"Hey, Dina? We're home." Celia shook her sister gently. Dina moved slightly but did not wake. This was becoming a problem as her energy waned after each treatment and Celia's stomach grew. She couldn't get her out of the car and into the house if Dina didn't get up and walk on her own.

Celia opened the car door and stepped out onto the driveway, her boots crunching across the salt chips mixed with snow and ice as she walked around to Dina's side, opened her door, and unhooked the seat belt. Celia talked to her the entire time, but Dina remained sound asleep. Celia stood up, looking around the neighborhood for someone who might help, but the street was deserted. She looked down at Dina again then shut the door, leaving her in the car. She needed the keys to open the house and get to the phone, but she couldn't leave Dina out in the freezing cold for long without running the engine again for heat. Unable to run, Celia moved as quickly as she was able, her bulky torso shuffling along the sidewalk to the front door and then the phone as hastily as was possible.

"Luke, it's Celia, can you do me a favor?"

She thought he hesitated but maybe it was her imagination. "Sure, what is it?"

"I can't get Dina out of the car. She's sound asleep and won't wake up. Can you come over?"

The silence hung there for seconds that seemed like minutes before he answered.

"Don't you think something might be wrong if she won't wake up after chemo? Maybe you should call the paramedics or her doctor?"

"She does this every time." Celia was exasperated. If he was as involved as he'd said he would be, he would know that each time it was Dave or a neighbor who helped her wake up Dina and get her in the house. "Usually I have someone around to help, but I don't today. I'm seven months pregnant. And with this weather..."

"Well, I've got a closing in an hour..." Luke's voice trailed.

Celia hung up on him without even a good-bye. She didn't care what Dave said, she was done with Luke. It took about fifteen minutes to get from his downtown office to her house. He could do it and be back for his meeting in forty-five minutes. She planted her hands on the kitchen counter and leaned forward as much as her belly would allow, breathing slowly to control her anger. The whir of a small motor came from across the neighborhood backyards. Craning her neck, Celia looked out the kitchen window to the right, but she saw nothing.

She went back outside and got into the car, starting the engine and turning up the heat. Dina was still asleep. Celia touched Dina's cheek and was relieved that her skin was still warm and dry. Celia heard the motor again and looked up. Three houses down, Louie Palermo methodically moved a snow blower up and down his driveway. With his head covered in a knitted ski mask, his bulky body in a black jacket, and black leather gloves covering his hands, he looked more like a helpful burglar than the solid, salt-of-the-earth father and husband Celia knew.

She sighed with relief and got out of the car, leaving it running. She headed for Louie, her arms waving to catch his attention over the whining and rasping of the snow blower. Fifteen minutes later, Dina was sound asleep in her bed, wrapped in a quilt, while Celia offered Louie a cup of coffee and broke out a package of cookies.

"Oh, Louie, you can't imagine how happy I was to see you were home." Celia kicked off her shoes, set down a mug of coffee in front of him and a cup of tea for her, then grabbed a cookie.

"Yeah, I'm usually at work but I took off a couple a days to get some stuff done around the house," he said with a grin. "Angie's been on me to do some work at home. Weather was so bad this morning I wanted to make sure she could get back in the driveway later."

"It's getting tougher and tougher as Dina gets weaker and sleepier," Celia said. "If I can't wake her up then I'm not physically able to drag her in the house."

"So how's she doing? I mean with the cancer and all." Louie crossed his muscular arms on the table, the T-shirt revealing half a tattoo of a bald eagle and an American flag on his right bicep, the gold Italian horn around his neck shifting and swinging with the movement of his arms. He'd peeled off his jacket and sweatshirt in two quick moves and sat down as if he'd been coming to her kitchen table all his life.

"She thinks it's gone because they've told her she's doing better, but the doctor told me it is not all gone yet. She has three more treatments, then, if she passes her tests and it's gone, she's done. I want to tell her, in a way, but attitude is everything right now. She's trying to handle a lot. I don't want her feeling depressed if a couple more treatments will make the belief the truth."

But it will be touch and go the first year to keep her in remission and get her immune system stronger. If she doesn't pass, then more chemo and we talk about clinical trials." Celia sighed.

"Tough on you, Celia," Louie said. "And you got your own little guy coming, huh?"

"Did I say it was a little guy?" Celia laughed.

"And what about Dina's job?" he asked. "Did she have to quit or is she taking a leave?"

"Fortunately, she was teaching full-time for about a year before she got sick so she has health insurance," Celia said. "They aren't thrilled about her being out in the middle of the semester, but the insurance is paying for the treatments and, on the weeks when she feels well enough, she grades papers for her substitute teacher and sometimes for other teachers.

"But the disability paycheck isn't enough for her to live on her own, so she's here," Celia added.

"So if the chemo's working, why does she seem so weak?"

Celia smiled at Louie, thinking what a good guy he was, his eyebrows furrowed with worry over a total stranger, sipping coffee with her in the middle of the day and trying to give her support and comfort in his simple way.

"It eats all her rapidly dividing cells—cancer cells, white cells, hair follicles." Celia's fingers played with the crumbs on the table as she spoke. "She's got to survive the chemo along with the cancer it's trying to kill. Her type of cancer moves pretty quickly so she's got a very strong chemo."

"Whew! I didn't know all of that," Louie said. "Listen, give me the dates of her next treatments and the times you'll be coming home. I work for the parks department and we're always running around the city checking on things here and there. Me and the guys will swing by and help you get Dina in the house."

"Oh, Louie, I could hug you!" Celia could feel her eyes watering. She tried not to cry.

"Well, well, now, don't cry. I guess you could hug me. But don't be tellin' Angie I was down here hugging you and eating cookies when I'm supposed to be working through my chores list up at the house." Louie stood up, laughing, and Celia felt her own laughter bubble up amidst the tears. She gave Louie a big hug. He left with a list of Dina's treatment dates and, ten minutes later, she could hear the snow blower humming again.

CHAPTER 19

DINA

I arnród Eireann's run from Sligo to Dublin would give her three hours through the beauty of the Irish countryside to adjust, mourn, and begin to recover. She wasn't sure what to feel and so she was feeling everything in spurts and painful jumbles of guilt and sadness. Numbness would be good right now, but it refused to come and save her. Just a week earlier she'd taken the same train in the opposite direction, her hands resting comfortably on her large stomach, filled to capacity, full of her baby kicking beneath her heart. Now she was as empty as the rolling fields the train was passing at a good clip.

Low stone walls that looked as though a Celtic king might walk out of the mist and step over them to greet her zipped by outside the window, followed by sudden modernity in the form of brand new houses clustered together across the street from older, whitewashed cottages. Each home, in each village, new and old, sported a small wall enclosing either the house itself or a cluster of homes. On the way to Sligo she'd imagined simply getting off at a stop and joining the village life, raising her baby in a small cottage behind their own little wall, flowers in baskets hanging from the porch and growing everywhere in the yard. Now she looked at the same homes with hollow longing. All that had seemed full and lush and green rolled by outside her window and spilled over her as she crouched in her seat, barren, futile. Nothing was growing within her and all that was growing here was out of her reach, a fleeting glimpse as the train hurtled from stop to stop, taking her farther and farther away from a central heartbeat she needed.

She felt unbalanced, almost carsick, and she wanted to flag down the train's ticket man and ask him to stop immediately, put the train in reverse and go back. Instead, she changed her seat so she was facing Dublin rather than Sligo, creating a feeling of moving forward rather than backwards. Forward into a black hole that was of her own making, despite the sunshine spiking through the train's windows. She had done the right thing. She had nothing to offer her daughter. Her life hurtled forward as empty as her womb now and no baby should shoulder that burden with her. And yet, she felt that if she never left the train, if she just didn't get off, and it went on and on, over the months and years of her days, eventually Katie would climb aboard and they would change the course of what she had put in place this week.

She curled her body into the seat, knees up, head on the window, and prayed for a release from the ache. "Next stop, Dublin!" was the only answer she received. And so she stepped out onto the platform and stood, blinking. Then she turned around and around, choosing no direction, her senses distorted and dizzy...

Dina blinked as she awoke, adjusting her eyes to the dark room. For a split second it felt as though the bed was spinning, but she knew it was only a residual effect of her dream. She'd had this dream many times before. Sometimes Katie was riding with her, always at a different age, but most times she was alone, sad and confused. The dream never resolved itself. She just became too dizzy to remain asleep and her subconscious pushed her awake. Only the streetlight, trickling through a crack where the curtains met, and the neon green glow of the digital clock lent any light to the room tonight. She licked her lips and swallowed hard, trying to remove the metallic aftertaste of chemo from her mouth. Flicking on the bedside light, she reached for her cell phone on the nightstand.

There were no voicemail messages. Dina sat up slowly, holding onto the cell phone. It was about ten thirty. She figured she had slept eight or nine hours. The house was silent. Celia and Dave must've been asleep. Dina needed to go to the bathroom and get some water, maybe something to eat too. But she sat there, staring at the phone. It was probably too late to call, but she dialed Luke's number anyway, listening to it ring and ring until the answering machine picked up. She hung up without leaving a message. Then she tried his cell phone. It rang into voicemail, but this time she left a short message. "Hey, baby, where are you? Give me a call."

Something felt very wrong to Dina and, even as she tried to shake the feeling off as an aftereffect of either the chemo or her recurrent dream, she couldn't help but feel her sixth sense was screaming for her attention. She padded off to the bathroom, flushing the toilet before she realized she might wake Celia up. Then she headed out to the kitchen, wide awake and hungry.

Dina was halfway through making a sandwich, sipping a tall, cold glass of milk in between slathering extra peanut butter on the thick Italian bread to wash the chemo taste out of her mouth, when Dave appeared in the kitchen doorway.

"Hey, sorry if I woke you," Dina said as she plopped a dollop of jelly on the sandwich and began spreading it around.

"No problem, I wasn't really sleeping, just lying there to make sure your sister fell asleep," he said.

"Yeah, I'm worried about her, Dave. I think being pregnant and trying to help me is too much for her. I wish she would let someone else come to chemo with me."

"You know better than to try to get her to change her mind, Dina. You mean everything to her." He was standing at the sink with a glass of water, wearing a t-shirt and pajama bottoms, his hair a mess and his face more resigned than resentful.

"Dave, she loves you and she loves that baby...you know that," Dina said. "She's just felt responsible for me since we were so little, it's hard for her to imagine not being in control of me or not having me in her life somehow."

Dina took a bite then handed him the knife and pushed the bread toward him. Dave started making his own sandwich, cutting the silence between them with the clink of the knife against the jar.

"I know I've given her a really hard time trying to break that control, and I know the choices I make cause her to worry all the time," Dina said. "I don't do it on purpose any more than she purposely tries to rule my life."

Dave laughed, pouring a glass of milk for himself.

"Okay, maybe she does consciously try to rule my life." Dina laughed too.

"She's worried about this thing with Luke, Dina."

"Yeah? Are you worried too, Dave?"

Dave didn't answer immediately. For several minutes they ate standing up at the island in the middle of the kitchen in companionable silence. "Yeah, I'm worried. I don't think he's the guy you think he is." Dave seemed uncomfortable.

"I'm not exactly a prize, Dave. Mid-thirties with no stable job, no money, pipe dreams of becoming a writer that never came true. A closet full of skeletons you know nothing about." Dina shrugged her shoulders and smiled.

"Dina, you're talented and capable of doing so much more. The only person who doesn't know it is you," he said. "There are a million Lukes. He's a run-of-the-mill, average guy who can't totally commit and enjoys being selfish." Dave looked startled, surprised at his own candor. "Sorry. I shouldn't have said all of that. But Dina, I could never run off to Ireland or understand poetry or write a story about something I'd just made up. I could never do one of the things that come so naturally to you and nei-ther could Luke."

Dina suddenly felt tired. She walked into the den and sat down in the recliner, leaning back a little.

"Hey, are you alright? Did I upset you too much?" Dave was standing in the doorway.

"No, I guess I'm still a little weak from the chemo. I needed to sit down." Dina motioned Dave to come in and he sat on the couch across from her.

"Celia ever tell you about our mother?" Dina asked.

"Not much," he answered. "She won't talk about her."

"She needs to let go of all that anger she has for poor Justine." Dina sighed. "That was our mother, Justine O'Malley Benet. The first person in a long line of people that Celia tried to protect me from. Justine and Pierre, our incompetent parents, are the reason CeCe is obsessive about orderliness, cleanliness, and security."

It was a slow, malevolent kind of pain for Dina to think of the days before she and Celia came to live with their Granny Maeve. Dina had been very young. The memories were dim and had to be fleshed out with what Maeve told her later, when she was older. But what memories she did have were lodged like a tiny piece of hurt in her middle that she'd just as soon not experience too often. Dina looked at Dave and knew he and Celia didn't stand a chance at a good marriage if he didn't understand her sister the way she did, and Celia certainly wasn't going to tell him if she hadn't already. Dina decided that if she died, it would be something she could leave behind, the knowledge that he would understand and help Celia with the demons inside that drove her mad with worry and anger.

"She's been protecting me longer than Granny, longer than my own memories can carry me back to, longer than anyone on this earth," Dina began. "From the day I was born and Celia was only two years old herself, she began protecting me primarily from our mother, Justine, and, at times, from our father, Pierre."

She told him the bits and pieces Maeve had shared with her and Celia, combined with things she'd heard here and there as she grew up from people who knew her mother. How, in 1961, Justine fell madly in love with a college boy who had been drafted in the Vietnam War. He didn't want to go and Justine didn't want him to go, so they did the only thing they could think of. They ran right over the border to Niagara Falls and into Canada, then just kept on going. At some point they reached Montreal where the boyfriend tired of Justine and left her alone in a boarding house, penniless. She was forced to wait tables at a local restaurant to earn enough money to live and, during that time, Justine met Pierre Benet.

"I overheard things, here and there, when I was older...and I do remember my parents. I think they were more obsessed than in love and a lot of the relationship was based on sex and drugs." Although physically tired, Dina was wide awake and in a story-telling mode, time-traveling with Dave in tow. "Justine and Pierre moved from one low-rent apartment to another, barely making ends meet. Granny knew Justine was alive because every so often she received a letter with a little bit of news and a request for money. Granny sent the money every time, first taking it to St. Patrick's where she sprinkled it with holy water then lit a candle and prayed for Justine to come home." Dave laughed along with Dina at the thought of Maeve praying over the money.

Eventually, Dina told him, Justine and Pierre returned to Erie with Celia in tow. She was about a year old, very sick and hungry. Justine brought her to St. Vincent Hospital's emergency room where the nurse on duty called Maeve, then a night-duty server in the cafeteria. Maeve let them live with her for about a month, but when they refused to get jobs and drank too much, Maeve got them an apartment two blocks away and jobs at the hospital, in an effort to force both Justine and Pierre to straightened up and get their lives on track. They didn't hold those jobs or any others they managed to get for very long, and they definitely didn't change. A year and a half later, Dina was born and, by that time, the family was on public welfare assistance. Justine and Pierre began supplementing their meager income by selling drugs, and then eventually began selling only what they didn't consume themselves. Celia made sure Dina had something to eat and every week they went to Maeve's for a few days where they had baths, hot food, hugs, and a clean bed to sleep in.

"It would have been better for us to just live with Granny. At first, I think Justine really loved us when she wasn't high, and our father, when sober, was a pretty nice guy," Dina said. "Granny said Justine barely drank at all while she was pregnant with me. But by the time I was three or four, Celia and I were just vehicles to help them get welfare support. They got less if we weren't there, so Justine wouldn't let us go.

"I can't tell you everything we saw by the time CeCe was twelve and I was nine, but it was very bad." Dina shivered and crossed her arms over her chest. "There was very little food, strangers in and out at all hours. We slept on a mattress on the floor. The mornings we woke up to the sweet smell of marijuana, we knew there would be food laying around because they got hungry smoking it. Other mornings there were harsher smells or no smells, our parents passed out or maybe not there at all and we were on our own. My memories are cloudy, but Celia's are raw and sharp, as if it were yesterday."

Dina continued to remember out loud in a rambling way, forgetting Dave was there at times. She told him her clearest memory was when old Mr. Petrone caught Celia stealing food from his corner store then hiding it in Dina's backpack, and he called the police. They hadn't had a bath for several days or clean clothes in a week. Celia, at ten years old, was blunt with the police officer and the store ownerstoreowner.

"We're hungry," Celia had said, as Dina began to cry.

"Where is your mother?" the policeman asked.

Celia shrugged, long, tangled reddish curls falling forward as she looked down at her shoes and picked nervously at the front of her stained shirt.

"Well, little girl, I have to call someone about this, or I'll have to take you down to the police station," he said.

"Do they have food there?" Celia had asked him, ever the opportunist.

"Yes, we have food, and we can call the social workers to help you find a place to stay," he answered.

Celia looked worried. Dina remembered she'd begun shaking and sobbing but Celia remained stoic.

"Call Granny," Celia told him. "Maeve O'Malley. That's our granny. Call her."

"Even at ten she was ordering bigger people around," Dina told Dave with a laugh. "Mr. Petrone looked relieved. He nodded his head in the direction of the counter and pulled the police officer away. I've turned that day over in my mind like a badly bent, blackened penny for years, looking at it from every angle, hoping for the impossible, hoping to make it shiny and new again. But I can still only see my sister frantic and hungry, while I sobbed, helpless, unable to do anything."

"The mother is no good. A drug addict," Dina heard Petrone tell the police officer. "The children are probably very hungry and desperate. The grandmother is a good person. She lives a block away. I'll call her."

The only time Dina laughed at this memory was with Celia, who always imitated Mr. Petrone in a horrible stage whisper. In her memories, Dina could still hear herself whimpering as the police officer sighed. "I really should call social services and have them put in a foster home," he said.

"Just let me get the grandmother here and we will work this out." Petrone hurried to the phone behind the counter to dial Granny's number.

Dina remembered Maeve standing like a statue with her straight back and solid, laced, white orthopedic work shoes, hands folded in front of her calmly. She talked to the policeman on the sidewalk outside the store for a long time while Mr. Petrone fed Dina and Celia ham sandwiches, milk, and Ritz crackers at the little table in the back room.

"Ever see Celia really stressed and make that same little meal for herself?" Dina asked Dave.

He nodded. His eyes were wide with recognition coupled with shock and disbelief that his strong, meticulous wife had had such a childhood. "Years later Celia went to Mr. Petrone's funeral even though she never had another interaction with him after that day. It was her way of thanking him for the simple compassion of food and the complex intercession that saved us from going into the foster care system. Granny took us home that day and gave us hot baths, clean pajamas, and an ice cream treat, tucking us into bed with old Irish poetry, songs, and kisses.

"Even today, just the sound of someone reciting Yeats or singing old Celtic tunes brings back the powdery smell of Granny and the illusion of comfort, safety, and love." Dina smiled, her eyes filled with tears she and Celia could never shed for their parents. "So, for the next year and a half, CeCe and I were shuffled back and forth between Granny's home and our parents' filthy apartment. Justine cleaned the apartment and picked us up from Granny's when it was time for the welfare caseworker to come by. She'd keep us for a week or so until she got high and forgot about us again. Then CeCe would pack a few things in her backpack and hold my hand tightly while we walked two blocks and crossed busy Cherry Street to go to Granny's house. We had each other and Granny and then you came along and Celia had Granny and me and you. Even though Granny is gone, Celia will soon have a baby. Then maybe she won't be so distraught about me."

They sat in companionable silence or a few minutes. Dina waited, thinking Dave would have questions, but he said nothing. "You see now, huh, Dave? I was her first baby, her first responsibility, and I'm the only person who carries the same pain inside that she does. I just handle it differently. I forgive Justine and Pierre, where Celia cannot."

Dina curled partially into a fetal position on the recliner and turned toward Dave. Then she continued, describing the apartment she and Celia shared with Justine and Pierre. It was littered with pipes, needles, and drug paraphernalia of every kind. At times Justine's eyes were on the girls. Like two deer caught in the headlights they would freeze and wait, exhaling only if the moment passed and they were, once more, invisible. Sometimes Justine stared at her daughters then moved on, floating over to Pierre, to a needle, to a drink, to her next fix—Celia and Dina completely forgotten in a second. At other times, high and disoriented, she would yank them from their coloring books, demanding to know if they were telling Maeve about what went on at the apartment. Dina remembered how they would shake their heads and mumble "No," holding hands and waiting for the moment to pass. Going to school was their reprieve, their salvation. Even when the other children called them stinky or they had very little in their lunch bag, it was better than hanging around with Justine.

Their father didn't care too much about what Maeve or anyone thought. He would get high and pull out his guitar, patting them on the heads and letting them sit together, curled up into a big floor pillow, while he played and sang to them. He skated in and out of remembering their names, but he was kind to them and they wanted to love him. But they did not want to love their mother. Her inner pain and torture were Celia and Dina's constant nightmare, while their warm, albeit sporadic, relationship with their father irritated Justine. Dina remembered how, once, Celia had bravely ventured forth and asked Pierre about Justine.

"Papa, what is wrong with her?"

"She has no father," he replied. "She knows him not and her soul is in pain from needing and searching for his love."

"Oh." Celia scratched her head, puzzled.

"You are lucky, *mon petit chou*," Pierre said with a grin. "You have me."

A week later, their strangely elusive father was gone. They never saw him again.

"It was the last unbearable loss of a man for Justine. Like a small ship, adrift on ever more powerful waves, her last anchor was lost and she capsized," Dina said. "Celia and I came home from school to discover Justine lying on the floor. She had been dead from an overdose for several hours. I was so scared. Celia called 911 then took me to Granny's. But we ended up coming back to the apartment with Granny and then all hell broke loose. Granny went nuts, screaming and wailing. The police and the paramedics showed up and took us outside."

Dina and Dave sat in silence with just the tick of the clock on the mantel disrupting the hush. Only Dina knew how much CeCe needed Dave, even if she acted as though she could handle anything and when she was obstinate and stubborn and seemingly obsessed with Dina. She needed Dave to give her a stable home and love.

"Now you know why she hates Luke," Dina said. "In a way he reminds her of Pierre and me. Pierre's selfishness, willing to leave without thought for us. My inability or unwillingness to adhere to CeCe's idea of what is right, secure, and stable. I scare her in the way Justine or the memory of Justine has scared her every day of her life."

"Keep this between us and just get her to relax during this pregnancy. Whatever will happen to me will happen—good or bad...we'll know the outcome of all this treatment soon."

Dave stood up, yawning himself, and picked up their glasses and plates, strolling off to the kitchen to put them in the dishwasher. Dina waved good-night to him as she curled deeper into the recliner and fell asleep, still holding on to her cell phone, willing it to ring.

CHAPTER 20

LUKE

The sound of running water penetrated Luke's conscious mind slowly, splashing rhythmically with the pounding in his head. He opened his eyes carefully. Early morning sunlight filtered in through the slats of vertical blinds across cheap, red satin sheets and he felt disoriented for a moment, trying to move beyond the ache in his head and neck to situate himself in this space, in this room. He wasn't sure where he was or how had he gotten to this place.

Luke moved and the bed moved with him. A waterbed. The kind he'd had in college because it seemed fun and kinky, but now it just made his back hurt. He lay sideways, sliding his legs over the bed's bumper pad sides, the movement causing a near tidal wave of sloshing. He sat up and eyed the clock. It was nine a.m. and he was late. His cell phone sat in front of the alarm clock, turned off. He reached for it and gazed around the room while he waited for it to turn on. He was naked, his clothes strewn everywhere on the floor. A child's bulletin board hung crookedly on the wall near the chipped dresser, covered with pictures of Amber.

Luke sighed as it all came back to him. His phone was beeping. He had four missed calls and a couple messages. Clicking through he saw there were three from Dina and one from Josh. He laid the phone back down. He didn't want to deal with any responsibility now. That fucking bitch Celia had called him as he was about to leave for a loan closing for Benton, his primary client, claiming she couldn't get Dina from the car to the house. He could hear the disapproval in her voice when he explained he couldn't make it to her house and back in time. Luke had no idea what Celia thought he did all day, but he had a business to run. If Dina was suddenly that bad, a medical professional should be helping out, not him.

A mix of anger and shame had surged through him as he jumped in his car and headed out to the bank for the closing. Even now, anger at Celia, anger at the blame that spun around him not only from her but from his own self-reproach, welled up in him and he felt trapped, rebellious. Amber had been at the courthouse, working on some title searches for another attorney, when he raced in to file the closing documents before the prothonotary's office closed. She'd invited him for drinks at a slouchy little tavern across the street from her apartment.

"Hey, how are you feeling?" He looked up to see Amber standing in the doorway, wet and wrapped in a towel.

"Not great; got any aspirin?" Luke asked.

She turned and left. He could hear her rummaging around in the bathroom then the water began running. He dialed his office on the phone.

"Hey, I won't be in today," he told the receptionist. "Can you cancel anything I've got and reschedule? I'm not feeling great." Luke listened intently for a moment. "Yeah, I turned my cell phone off to get some sleep. I see messages from them so I'll call back."

He hung up as Amber reappeared with a glass of water and what looked like two ibuprofen. He popped them in his mouth and chased them down with a big gulp, then, putting his finger to his lips to indicate she should keep quiet, he dialed Marianne's number and asked to speak to Josh. Fifteen minutes later, after promising to sign Josh up for soccer that weekend and help him with his homework, he hung up. Amber sat on the edge of the bed, sliding next to him.

"Want to play hooky from work today?" Luke asked her with a grin. The headache was receding, but the fury and agitation were not.

She smiled and nodded. Luke could feel the heat of her large, comfortable body as it radiated soap and talcum and sex in equal measure. She wasn't much to look at but she had beautiful hair that cascaded in curls down her back and over her fleshy shoulders. He liked the ease of her, the lack of complication. She needed so little, nothing almost. No complex conversations or piercing desires, no requirement that he analyze himself and try to be something he might not want to be today. He turned his phone off again.

"So guess what I want to do first on our day off?" He unhooked her towel and ran his hand over her breasts, watching her giggle.

They slid back onto the waterbed and he closed his eyes. *Fuck Celia,* he thought. *I've done everything right and I deserve just this one day to let loose.* Later tonight or tomorrow he knew he would deal with Dina, make it up to her. She would forgive him. He was sure of it. She always did.

CHAPTER 21

CELIA

"It's been a week, Dave." Celia felt the heat of wrath rise upward from her neck to her cheeks. "She had what might have been one of her last chemotherapy treatments and no word from him. He's a rat and I'm going to tell her to break up with him."

"No, you're not." Dave was uncharacteristically firm. "She's sick, Celia. Her immune system is depleted, she's tired, but she's beating this thing. A big break-up with someone she loves and sees as supporting her through this would set her back."

Celia crossed her arms over her chest and squeezed, hugging herself hard, then released the pressure and exhaled. It was a habit from childhood. She didn't know how to slow down her anger right now.

"Look, I agree with you." Dave wrapped his arms around her, her protruding tummy in between them. "He's not cutting it and who knows what he is up to, but you have to think of Dina and keep your eye on the prize. She has to get well. Then she will deal with this."

"Ha," Celia snapped. "Dina, deal with this? She's too weak." She'd never said it out loud before, what she believed about her little sister. Celia was struggling against taking control and just breaking up with Luke herself, on Dina's behalf.

"You're wrong. Dina is much stronger than you give her credit for," Dave said. "She always has been and you need to let go and let her handle this, Celia. For your sake, for the baby's sake, and for Dina's."

Celia was silent. She could hear Dina's voice upstairs. Probably on the phone. *Hopefully,* Celia thought, *not with* him. Dave was rubbing her back now with one hand, and trying to unclench her fists with the other. He was wrong, wrong, wrong. She, Celia, was the strong one. She always had been. Dina was unable to make the hard decisions life required of her. When Dina came downstairs and told her that she still had not heard from Luke, Celia was going to tell her to get rid of that guy.

The sound of socks shuffling along the hardwood floor in the hallway made Celia turn her head toward the kitchen doorway. Dina stood there smiling, bald head wrapped in a soft blue silk scarf and wearing a Hard Rock sweatshirt over old jeans, her big, rag-wool socks hanging off the front of her tiny feet. Celia could feel Dave hold her shoulders to keep her steady.

"Hey, Dina, sleep well?" Dave asked.

"Yeah, I'm taking so many naps now but I feel great." Dina yawned, smiling.

The three of them stood there in silence as Dina looked dreamily out the kitchen window, seemingly at nothing.

"It's a winter wonderland out there, CeCe," Dina said. "Just like me. Everything is pale and bare. But it'll be spring soon. I'll be sprouting hair again."

"Did you hear from the doctor?" Celia watched Dina grin ear to ear.

"Yes, I did," she said slyly.

"Dina, tell me now," Celia demanded. "Don't play games."

"Oh, CeCe, you're so impatient...and that temper." Dina laughed. "He said he thinks the cancer is gone but one more chemo just to be sure. I'm almost there...cancer-free and healthy!" Dina danced a little shuffle across the floor in her floppy socks, heading toward her sister.

"Whoo-hoo!" Dave yelled. "Group hug!"

Celia felt Dave wrap she and Dina in a big hug, her baby belly in the middle, and tears of gratitude began streaming down her face. "Dina, let's got to St. Patrick's and light a candle." Celia was grabbing her car keys.

"Whoa, wait, CeCe," Dina said. "How about tomorrow? Luke is picking me up in a couple hours and taking me out to celebrate."

Celia had to turn away so Dina couldn't see her face. Dave's hand was on her shoulder as if holding her at bay. She stared out the window at her barren magnolia tree, still awaiting the buds that would be the beginnings of small leaves, and she knew he was right. Just a little longer, until Dina was out of the woods and stronger.

"Sounds good." Celia turned, smiling, to hug her sister. "Tomorrow we'll go to St. Patrick's and say a prayer for you and for Granny."

"And for your baby," Dina said. "Maybe you can finally relax now and take care of yourself."

"Amen," Dave said. "Let's keep her in line, Dina, and make her do that!"

Dina smiled and waved as she left the room, walking upstairs to get ready for Luke.

"Celia?"

She felt Dave close behind her but she did not turn as he spoke.

"You did great. You did the right thing," he said.

"For now, Dave. For now. But when she is better, he goes, once and for all," Celia answered.

"Celia, did you ever consider something else might break up their relationship eventually?" Dave asked.

"No, that guy will hang around and use her for as long as he can," Celia retorted.

"Well, you can get as mad as you want, honey," Dave said. "He's the one who's weak. And I think as much as he wants to pull this off, he will screw it up on his own and then you'll see how strong Dina can be."

Well, Celia thought, *let him see Luke any way he wants to*. As long as she would see him leave Dina's life soon—and for good.

CHAPTER 22

LUKE

Sweat ran in rivulets down the side of his face, partially drying in the cool spring breeze as he heaved the old, rotting railroad tie up out of the ground and onto the patio where Henry had just laid another one. Worms wiggled in the dark earth sticking to the bottom of the wood, extricating themselves and flopping on the tiled patio to begin making their way to a safer spot in the yard. It was the last day in March and, although it was still cool enough outside to require sweatshirts, it had rained all week, softening the hard winter ground and making soil texture that was perfect for digging.

"Two more and we'll have all six out," Henry said, wiping his burly forearm across his brow. "You sure you want to put a fence in?"

"Yeah, I don't want to have to pull another set of these up ten years from now," Luke grinned. "You up for sticking around to put a fence in?"

Henry slapped together the work gloves on his big hands and nodded. "I don't think we'll get it all done today, though," he said. "I'll probably have to come back tomorrow...finish off the fence and the beer!"

They laughed together, moving their shovels to leverage the last two ties, then dipping, grasping, pulling, and using the shovels again in some sort of dance that was at once harmonious and primitive. By noon, they had all the railroad ties out and stacked by the house. Luke began smoothing the earth around the patio, preparing it for the solid oak fencing he'd purchased, complete with a tiny gated entry point, while Henry went inside to grab some sandwiches, chips, and beer for their lunch. Luke could hear him whistling and see him moving around in the kitchen.

What a good guy he is, Luke thought, one part envy and one part solid comfort. He began rinsing the dirt off his hands, arms, and face, spraying them with the garden hose, then wiped himself off with a clean towel hanging near the door in the garage. Luke slipped out of his dirty running shoes and stepped inside the screened-in porch. Sitting on the picnic table were two beers, the condensation sliding down from the bottlenecks, two thick ham and cheese sandwiches, and a couple bags of chips, even napkins, although they were now lifting on the breeze and flying across the porch. Luke heard the sound of running water upstairs. Henry preferred a bathroom with soap and water to a hose for cleaning up.

"Hey, look what I found." Henry slapped a pack of Marlboros on the picnic table.

Luke took a bite of his sandwich and stared at Henry without speaking.

"Now, I'd say I thought you quit, but it seems there was one other time you jumped off the wagon and started smoking again." Henry flipped a potato chip into his mouth, crunching away while he rolled the beer bottle back and forth in his hands. It left a watery glaze on his fingertips.

"Yeah? When was that?" Luke asked, grabbing a few chips himself. "I don't remember. Just picked those up to take the edge off at work this week."

"Hmm...Okay," Henry said. "Good thing that's all it is, because last time it was to take the edge off when you were cheating on Marianne and your marriage was, you know, kind of flushing down the toilet." Henry took a bite of his sandwich and they ate in silence. Luke offered nothing. He felt flushed but his earlier sweat had dried and he knew the heat came from somewhere else. He hoped Henry would let it go. "So how's Dina?"

"Fine." Luke took another big bite. Henry wasn't giving up.

Henry fished out a cigarette and twirled it around in his fingers, then rolled it on the picnic table, back and forth, back and forth, until Luke finally snatched it from him and threw it across the porch.

"Hey, don't take it out on the little cancer stick," Henry said. "Never was interested myself. Guess I can't see much use for them except to roll them around on a picnic table. Can you?"

"Just eat, Henry."

Henry picked up his sandwich again and they continued eating in silence. It lay between them in a weighty, disturbed sort of way, like a pause in a warped record, the needle unable to jump to the end until the wrinkle is somehow smoothed out. Luke watched Henry. He was calm.

He was waiting for an answer. He knew Luke better than anyone and there would be no point in lying. Luke sighed, wiping his mouth and picking up the beer bottle.

"You know I've never been in love with Dina," he said.

"You made a promise," Henry shot back.

"And I'm keeping it," Luke said. "I'm supporting her through this cancer. I'm helping her to get better. I'm trying to be there for her as much as possible."

"And you're getting some on the side."

"One time."

"Uh-huh," Henry said. "So it ends there and Dina never finds out. She gets better and you two go on as you have been."

"Oh, I don't know." Luke felt tired. "I haven't thought that far. I was thinking this relationship should end before she got sick."

"Then you shouldn't have agreed to stand by her," Henry said. "You weren't honest. You know she thinks this means you have deep feelings for her and the relationship is going to get better."

"I do have feelings for her," Luke snapped. "That's the problem. I've got enough feelings not to want to leave but not enough to take things further."

"Well, what does a woman need to have for you to go further and commit?" Henry asked. "I mean, I thought the stuff that happened with Marianne was you getting married too young...and she was a pain in the ass. I figured you were staying for Josh. But now...you've been through tons of women. What are you looking for?"

"Maybe I'm looking for a no-commitment commitment." Luke laughed, but Henry did not. "I just want to have fun. I don't want to be tied down. I didn't expect to feel anything for Dina but whatever I feel, it's not enough."

Henry stood up and starting cleaning up the table. Luke tried to look him in the eye, and then he looked away. He felt guilt, anger, and disappointment all rolled into a small knot in his chest.

"Man, you should have told her all of that and then walked away when you found out she was sick," Henry said. "You set expectations that are going to come back and haunt you."

"Quit fucking judging me." Luke's voice rose. "I'm not you. I can't live up to your family-man standards. Hey, maybe some people are just meant to be single."

Henry was through the doorway between the porch and the house. He turned around and looked back at Luke for a long minute.

"You're selfish, Luke," he said. "If being honest means I set a standard you can't reach, then I feel sorry for you, because that sets the bar pretty low."

Luke sauntered out onto the patio, slamming the door behind him. He put his shoes and gloves back on, grabbed a shovel, and began digging holes for the fence posts. He heard a toilet flush upstairs and a car door slam simultaneously. He stood up and leaned the shovel against the house, wiping his forehead with his sleeve. Today wasn't his scheduled day with Josh, so it must be his father, bored and coming to see how the fence installation was going.

Amber appeared around the side of the house in a pair of too-tight jeans and a tank top just as Henry walked out onto the patio. Henry's anger set his face in a stone-like expression. His back was ramrod straight, his barrel chest pushed out, arms across it. When he finally turned toward Luke, the anger was gone, replaced by disgust.

"This time," Henry said, peeling off his work gloves, "I'm not going to be able to help you with the fallout, buddy. You're really blowing it."

Luke covered his embarrassment with a look of defiance, daring Henry to say more. But Henry obviously had no intention of speaking to Luke or staying here with him and Amber. He turned and walked away, his head ducking slightly as his broad back passed through the small man-door and into the garage. Luke closed his eyes and listened to Henry's truck start up, then back slowly out of the driveway.

"What did he mean, Luke?" Amber asked.

"Nothing, just guy talk. We've been friends a long time, but sometimes he thinks he knows everything," Luke said. "Why don't you go sit in the house and watch TV until I'm done out here?"

Luke watched Amber open the door to the porch and walk inside. He heard her open the refrigerator, followed by the clink of a bottle just before he slammed his foot onto the shovel, driving it into the soil below. He was going to have to talk to Amber about just showing up that way. But what would he say to her? That he'd made a commitment and he couldn't see her unless it was very private? He knew he should just tell her it was a one-night thing and it couldn't happen again. That was what Henry would do. Henry was probably expecting Luke to handle it that way and had given him the space to have a talk with Amber. Luke stopped digging and wiped his brow. The holes were larger than they needed to be. He'd been taking his anger out with the shovel a little more than he should have.

"I'm not Henry," Luke said out loud, to the sky, to the trees, to no one in particular. He waited in the silence following his words, but nothing had changed. He still felt trapped and angry. He still needed to go inside that house and do the right thing, send Amber home and stick to his commitment to stay with Dina through this illness.

He found Amber slouched across the couch in the great room, feet half up, head resting on her arm which was slung across the pillow at one end. She was watching the comedy channel and laughing. Easy, carefree. As if she lived here.

"Hey, done with your yard work?" Amber smiled at him.

"Yeah, done for today," he said.

She started to get up.

"No, stay there, let me get a beer, then I have to talk to you," Luke said.

He padded out to the kitchen in his bare feet and grabbed another beer out of the refrigerator, popping the top and taking a long swallow before walking back into the living room to sit on the rocker across from her.

"Did I do something wrong?" Amber asked.

"Yes, you did, but you couldn't have known, not really." Luke sighed. He rolled the beer bottle between his hands for a few seconds like Henry had done before confronting him at lunch. He leaned back in the chair to face her. "Amber, the other night..." Luke hesitated. "It was just one night. You can't just show up here like...like..."

"Like a girlfriend," she said.

He nodded, silent.

"Because Dina is your girlfriend?" Amber asked. "I haven't seen you with her in a long time. You look like a free agent to me."

Luke wanted to be a free agent. He wanted to give in to every selfish feeling running through him right now. He tried to put Henry's face in front of his own. Then he thought of Dina.

"Dina has cancer," Luke said. "She's very sick. That's why you haven't seen her. I promised to stand by her through this. I shouldn't have done what I did the other night. I just...well...it's been tough."

"Wow! That's intense," Amber said.

Luke watched her, so young and immature, yet not at all moved by what he'd just said. Not horrified by what they had done, just curious about this discovery. He knew then that she was missing the same piece he was, the internal piece that prevented him time and time again from putting other people's needs before his own. He was aware of it and it filled him with remorse at times, at others he was resigned to this as part of his character. But at her age, he'd been just as unaware. She was going to satisfy herself and that was it, no remorse. He realized, with surprise, that in an odd, perverted way, he admired her for that. He waited for revulsion, but none came, only nostalgia for his youth when he had yet to see the aftermath of the headlong pursuit of his own desires.

"So, standing by her must be tough and you probably need to blow off some steam once in a while." Amber shrugged. Her look said this issue was resolved.

"It's a little more complicated than that," Luke said. "I have a business to run. Other people will really think I'm a monster to cheat on a woman who's that sick."

"I might be young but even I know you are not the commitment type, Luke," Amber said. "Are you just trying to help her out and support her? I mean, that's okay with me. I don't want her to die."

"Right now, my best friend, who knows I have trouble with commitment, is disgusted with me because you just showed up with no notice and he found out I was fooling around behind Dina's back." Luke was harsh. "I should kick you out and send you packing, but I'm sick of suffering and going without. I'm not sick, Dina is, and I shouldn't have to pay the full price just because I'm helping her. But if you want to hang around with me, you don't show up unannounced and no one—I mean *no one*—knows about us but you and me."

"And when she gets better?" Amber asked.

"We'll see." Luke was sure she'd leave now, sparing him the decision of which part of him—mind or body—would win the struggle. Any self-respecting woman would go.

"I can live with that," Amber said with a shrug.

He was a hardened, cynical lawyer. He'd seen all sides of people in divorce or hostile contract negotiations. But Amber's nonchalance, her immunity to it all, nearly shocked him. Her face hadn't changed much since they'd started this conversation. She was still happily slouched on the couch, not an ounce of guilt or confusion.

"So, you look pretty dirty," Amber said. "What do you say we take a shower then we'll order a pizza and hang around naked all evening?"

He wanted to go for it. But Luke could see her, even with her lacka-daisical demeanor, taking some sort of control and he would not have that.

"You have to leave, Amber," he said calmly. "I'll call you and let you know when I can see you again."

For a fleeting moment he saw anger flash across her face and he felt some satisfaction. He still saw difficult moments ahead with Henry because of her.

"Okay, I'm outta here," she said. Getting up, she approached him and he began rocking the chair slowly.

"I'll call you, Amber," he said.

She stopped in her tracks, momentarily, then turned, picking up her keys and purse, and left.

Luke was dialing Dina's number even as he heard Amber's car pulling out of the driveway. He needed to hear her voice and smooth out the feelings inside him, push the selfish needs back into a corner to be dealt with later. He would call Henry next. Amber could wait a few days, but he knew those needs couldn't be locked down for long. He would see her, but on his own terms.

CHAPTER 23

DINA

The long line of ancient cottonwood trees and red maples towered above, waving slightly in the breeze, arched over the roadway to create a lush, green cathedral. Every few minutes the electric blue of the bay and the sky above, dotted only with a few soft white clouds, exploded into view on her right. Occasionally, a stalwart man or woman, bundled in a sweatshirt and jeans or sweatpants, ears covered, whizzed by on rollerblades as Dina drove the mandated twenty-five miles per hour. It was mid-April and still a little chilly on the Great Lakes, especially here at Presque Isle State Park.

Dina opened the window, breathing in deeply until she felt too cold, and then closed it. She had borrowed Celia's car to come down here to the place she loved most in the world, where she could quiet her soul and think. She'd sold her own car months ago to help cover some of her bills. Celia had been frantic when she'd said she wanted to drive to the beach. She'd practically sanitized the whole interior for Dina and the smell of Lysol and 409 was still a little overpowering with the window closed. Three weeks ago she had what she hoped was her last chemo treatment and Dina knew her white cells weren't at their best right now. She should be at home in mini-quarantine, avoiding germs and waiting a few more days for her immune system to get back on the upswing and provide enough white and red cells to protect her.

But she couldn't seem to focus on her illness or the long-awaited remission. All she could think of was that she had not heard from Luke in over a week, not since she called with her last test results, telling him she thought her chemo treatments were over and she was finally well.

"I feel positive, Dina, that it was the last chemo," he'd said during that conversation.

"I hope so, I'm so tired...I hope it's over," she had answered.

"I've gotta go get ready for work, but I'll be thinking of you." She heard water running in the background.

"Are you calling me from the bathroom?" she asked. "I can hear the shower."

"Uh, I started running the water just before the phone rang. Just letting it run to make sure it's hot when I hop in." He sounded strange.

"Okay, you'd better get going." She heard the water shut off. "Call me later?"

"Later." He hung up before she could say another word.

She felt a shift deep within herself. A knowing that had just come upon her or perhaps had been there for a long time, delicately avoided and carefully swept into a corner. Now she felt a heavy stone in her middle, weighing upon her esophagus and making even breathing difficult, just as she had when she'd entered her apartment in Ireland to find Liam and that girl, just as she had when she'd released Katie from her arms. She felt as if she were five years old again and, if she just told Celia that something was wrong, her sister would fix things. But she couldn't tell her about Ireland or what she suspected—perhaps subconsciously, perhaps not—about Luke now. Too many secrets she'd kept from her sister. Too many mistakes that turned into secrets that turned into lies.

She turned left then right onto Mill Road and drove past the beaches on the lakeside, heading toward Sunset Point. The road curved before her in a wide S-shape, flanked by pine trees—red pine, jack pine, pitch pine. She'd learned them all on high school field trips that now seemed like a soft, dim dream from another life altogether. She had a blanket and an extra sweatshirt, and she'd wanted to just sit on a piece of driftwood for a while and write, but Celia screamed so loudly about germs and bugs that she'd agreed to take the sanitized beach chair Celia handed her. Thankfully, cell phone reception wasn't so good out here, preventing her sister from calling every thirty minutes to see how she was doing.

Dina pulled into a small area off the left berm of the road that was more sand than concrete. A few die-hard kite enthusiasts were out creating a beautiful splash of primary colors against that blue of sky and water. Locals often called it the "kite beach" with fond amusement. After parking, she plopped her purse in the trunk and removed the blanket and chair and a canvas tote.

The breeze was blowing from the west and much cooler out here. After setting up the chair, she pulled the blanket up to her chest, its bottom resting in the sand, and closed her eyes, listening to the waves, the gulls, and the rustling beach grass mingling with flapping kites. About five people dotted the small beach, sitting in chairs or on blankets. Each, like Dina, was alone, a tiny island of humanity seeking the private solitude only available this time of year. In a couple months the shoreline would be packed with sunbathers, screaming children, lifeguards blowing whistles, and the occasional dog barking. But for now, it was chilly, calm, serene.

Dina was thinking about Katie again and about Celia's baby not yet born. She had a notebook and pen in the canvas tote, but she wasn't sure she could write. She felt so drained that she doubted even the least little bit of prose would roll up from inside of her. She needed to slowly refill from the utter physical and emotional exhaustion of the past six months. She'd also brought her Granny Maeve's journal with her, well-worn with age and well-thumbed by Dina who had read it often since Maeve's death. She pulled it out then and sat it on her lap as she looked at the endless blue of water and sky and wondered if they were in heaven together, Justine and Maeve. She wondered if mothers and daughters, no matter what pain they suffered together during their earthly life, were reunited in peace in heaven. Dina opened the journal and flipped to the passage about her mother's birth. She'd read it many times while waiting for the birth of her own little one. Katie, her beautiful little secret.

July 1944

I heard a gentle voice saying "there, there," and turned my head to see but my vision was blurred. I knew I was in my own bedroom, but the man and woman at the end of the bed looked fuzzy and their voices were unfamiliar. "Mick?" I called. My voice was hoarse. But it was Dr. Jones. I heard his deep bass voice and closed my eyes, soothed by its sound. I heard him say they had to get the baby out. I'm eighteen years old and strong as a horse, but something was wrong. I heard it in his voice, felt it in my bones. I want my mother with her strong hands, familiar voice, and scent of lavender, but she's an ocean away from me. A firm arm settled across my back, pushing me partially upright. I could see a nun's habit. She told me to take a deep breath and push. The final pain was terrible, beyond any I'd ever known, and then there was silence, followed by a weak cry. I heard it as if I was at the end of a long tunnel and then I must have blacked out.

When I came round and had my wits about me, I heard birds chattering outside the window and felt a breeze, unusual for July, moving its heat across my face. I didn't know, at that moment, how long I'd been asleep. I called for Mick but there was only silence. Then I heard a chair scrape on the hardwood floor in the outer room and slow steps came towards me. I couldn't move or sit up. A dark form knelt by my bed and a kind face peeked out at me from beneath a black and white wimple. She was holding something. She moved the bundle from her arms to mine and Justine looked up at me for the first time. Oh, how I loved my baby in an instant. The nun came around to the other the side of the bed and moved me to a sitting position, propping pillows behind me. I asked her name and she said Sister Mary Jude. She looked no older than I, this Sister Mary Jude, but with a practiced hand she helped me begin to breastfeed Justine. As I watched her sucking hungrily on my body I knew we were one, my tiny daughter and I.

I asked Sister Mary Jude where my husband had gone off to. When she looked uncomfortable, I knew something was wrong. I looked around my bedroom and saw that Mick's watch and the picture of his father were missing from our chest of drawers. It was a nicked and paint-spattered piece of furniture we'd found on the sidewalk after neighbors set it out as garbage and it's peculiar to remember now how, at that moment, all I thought about was painting the chest of drawers green to cover its scars.

Mick and I fought often over how poor we were and how we couldn't afford a baby. Mick wanted to become rich in America. He wanted to wait a long time for children. I couldn't defy the Church and try to prevent pregnancy. It is a mortal sin. Besides, I have no idea how to keep from getting pregnant and no one to ask. When I realized I was pregnant, I knew something terrible was going to happen. I felt it in my bones. A premonition, my mother said, always settles in your bones and you feel the weight of what is to come.

Dr. Jones said Justine was a beautiful, healthy baby, but I could have no more after her. He said I couldn't survive giving birth again, that I'd had too hard a time of it. Perhaps he was right, or maybe I just didn't know any better, but I believed him. My mother birthed five children, four of whom lived, and I wish, desperately, that she was here to help me. I yelled at Dr. Jones, asking how I was supposed to keep from having more children. He had no solutions but to leave my marital bed and cease sexual relations with Mick. Then I asked Dr. Jones if he'd told this news to Mick. When he admitted he had, I knew for sure that Mick was gone.

I looked down at Justine, now sleeping in my arms, and began to cry. I had no idea what I would do or how I would care for my baby. Dr. Jones asked me if I would return to Ireland. I remembered my mother warning me not to leave for America with Mick. But, oh, how I'd loved him then. I wanted to take Justine and go home to my family but pride and shame stood in my way. Failure is never a good reason for hiding and staying away.

I told Dr. Jones I'd make a way for Justine and me in the world and hope for the best. When Dr. Jones told me Mick had seen Justine before he left, I stopped loving him in that moment and screamed a curse on his Irish head so loudly that Justine awoke and began screaming as well.

Justine needed a father, even one such as Mick, so I did my best to find him, but it was hopeless. Father John used some of the church's resources to help me. But Mick had vanished into the vast new country that was now my home and I never found him, may he rot in hell.

Dina looked up from the journal and watched as a thin, weathered man traversed the water's edge, slowly swinging a metal detector back and forth, the round obelisk seeking the lost treasures of others. He was still several yards from Dina but she could see his craggy face, the deep grooves a roadmap of a lifetime spent on an endless treasure hunt, the tangled mane of hair braided and tucked under a knotted bandana that circled his head. He looked as though he lived as he worked, out in the open, no part of him tamed or domesticated. Perhaps he had begun as a child, enamored with pirates and riches and mystery, then, unable to let go, found it had now cost him the comforts of a home, wife, and children.

Or maybe it had cost him security but brought him a freedom few could know. He was still several yards away but heading toward her like an elephant, tusk swinging with the folds on his face, legs taut, brown, and muscular.

The weight in her chest seemed to shift and push, reminding her why she was here. She wished she could just drink a bottle of wine and go to sleep, waking up to find that her hair had grown back and her boyfriend loved her and her world was as solid as Celia's. Celia would tell her she needed to take control and create her own solid world rather than close her eyes and wait for it to come. Celia thought she was so weak and foolish, a woman in need of constant care.

Dina sighed. She was neither weak nor foolish, just an avoider of pain. She had seen little signs, small things in Luke's behavior as her treatments continued, that left her with concern. But she blamed herself in many ways for bringing this disease into their fragile relationship and putting added pressure where it was not needed. In a logical, clinical way she knew it was not her fault and yet she felt the current state of things to be her responsibility. Everyone had weaknesses and strengths. It was best, in Dina's opinion, to be honest about the weakness and work to develop the strength. She knew what Luke's weaknesses were and she'd watched him struggle with her changing looks, with her prednisone-puffy face, with his feelings for her and his desire to have no feelings for her. But she had continued to believe that he loved her in his own tortured, maladjusted way.

Now, a tear or two rolling down her face in rhythm with the tide before her, she was not so sure. Perhaps Celia, in her dark cynicism, was right. *Luke might be more than just weak and a little vain. He might be twisted and nefarious at the core. He might not be struggling to be strong and to save this relationship.* As these thoughts rolled through her brain, she wondered if perhaps his ego had taken to the noble idea of helping save her life, but then the ugly realities of her runny noses, hair loss, bloating, and dizziness had mingled with a sense of entitlement in him so large it was a defect rather than an immaturity not yet outgrown. Celia would be surprised at Dina's thoughts. "Dina of the rose-tinted glasses" she called her. Dina laughed out loud, even as she wiped the tear away, realizing as she did so that the old treasure hunter was nearly upon her.

"Am I in your way?" she asked. He was very close to her chair and she could smell a mixture of cigarettes, sweat, and cocoa butter.

He looked startled, as if he hadn't realized she was in his path, so intent was he on his quest. The arm of the metal detector seemed merely an extension of his gnarled hand, the yellowed nails on his bare toes mere inches away from the detector's disk. Wisps of yellowish-white hair sprouted like alfalfa from his soft brown braid. A brown hat that looked more suitable for the Australian Outback hung off the back of his neck and had, perhaps at one time, been a definable suede or leather of some sort. Dina wondered whether his bare feet were freezing in the cold or if he'd become such a part of nature, of the landscape and the seasons, that he'd adapted in ways others could not imagine doing.

"Are you talking to God today?" he asked.

His voice sounded unused, out of practice, billowing up from the depths of a remembrance of conversation. He seemed to have heard her voice but not her question. Dina wondered if she should move.

"I'm working my way up to that," she said. "I'm thinking through which troubles to present to him first, I guess."

He shut off the metal detector but it stayed attached to him, a part of his body. He stared out across the lake for several minutes. Dina knew she should feel vulnerable and uncomfortable with this odd creature, but she did not. She felt safe and still.

"Are you going to ask him if you will live?" he said.

"No, I'm going ask him to help me live a little better," Dina said.

She realized he had recognized her bandana scarf held in place on her head by a baseball cap for what it was and for what it was hiding. And she knew, in the moment of their exchange, that somehow she would live.

"Do something you have a passion for, live with a freedom in your heart, and you will live just fine," he said. "Don't take the weight of others with you."

"Do you talk to God out here?" Dina asked.

"Every day," the old man said. "He helps me find my treasures."

He turned his metal detector back on and, as abruptly as he had spoken to her, he left without so much as a good-bye. God might want to work on his social skills a little, Dina thought. Yet, as he disappeared around the curve of the beach, she realized the pain in her chest had lessened, lifted perhaps by his metal detector and spirited away, washed clean by the water, drifting up to the sky on the wings of a kite. She was sure it would return. She could hear Maeve's voice, lost to her over the years, quoting some mythical Irish poet:

I am the wind of the sea, I am the wave of the ocean, I am a powerful bull, I am an eagle on the rock.

Dina could remember no more of it, although she'd recited it with her grandmother often as a child. She opened her notebook and wrote one line, then laid it on her lap, reading the line several times.

"God, let me find the treasures in my life that will help me live," she read the line aloud to herself. It had seemed an almost profound prayer when she wrote it down. Now it felt powerless and small as the wind lifted her words and carried them away across the expanse of Lake Erie then up into the sky. She shut the notebook and got up, carrying the blanket and chair to the car. Celia would be waiting. Dina needed to rest before dealing with Luke.

CHAPTER 24

CELIA

"I hope last week was her last chemo," Dave said. "Then maybe you'll concentrate on your pregnancy and our baby."

Celia watched as he slammed the dresser drawer shut and headed to the bathroom carrying his clothes. She hoped Dina had had her last chemo too, on so many levels. They were all in a holding pattern, waiting for her test results, waiting to see if Dina could enter remission and they could all find their way to some type of normalcy. Dave was angry because the doctor had told them this morning that Celia was having such a stressful pregnancy he was worried about her blood pressure and saw some signs that the baby might come too early. He wanted her to take it easy. Dave hadn't spoken to her all the way home then he exploded when they pulled into their driveway.

"I told you over and over that you need to worry about this baby, our baby, but all you do is stress out over Dina and Dina's illness and Dina's boyfriend!" Dave's voice thundered in the closed car. "Now you have a high-risk pregnancy. You know what that means, Celia? You put our baby at risk."

"Are you blaming Dina?" Celia thought her voiced sounded small. "She's waiting on her test results, if that makes you feel better."

"Dina? No, I bet Dina would like to be treated like an adult, and I've heard her tell you to take it easy for the baby's sake," Dave said. "But you are just obsessed with being Dina's mother. She's a lot stronger than you think, Celia. She doesn't need a mother. Our baby does."

Celia sat there shaking, unable to cry, as he opened his door, slammed it shut, and marched into the house. She lay back in her seat and felt the baby kick. His kicks were much harder than they had been. They knew it was a boy now. He had a name and he would be here in another six to eight weeks. She sat quietly for another five minutes before she followed Dave inside. When she walked through the front door she could hear him on the phone telling someone she would not be in to work for a while, possibly until the baby was born.

"So you called my boss?" she asked. "You couldn't let me handle my own job?"

Celia felt bone-weary. Dropping her purse onto the kitchen table, she laid her jacket across the back of the small, oak chair then turned to face her husband. His face and neck were red and he was looking at her in a way she had never seen before. Or maybe she had been so wrapped up in saving Dina she had not really looked at him in a long time. But there it was, a dark anger, seething and twisting from his brown eyes, traveling across the grim set of his mouth and cascading from the furrows in his brow. It was Dave and yet not her Dave and she wondered if he loved her anymore.

"You have put our child at risk, you have put our marriage at risk, and now I'm going to make you follow the doctor's orders for bed rest and no stress, if I have to work from home to do it," Dave said. "This is not Dina's fault, this is not my fault, this is not anyone's fault but yours, Celia. You and your stubborn, obsessive ownership of your sister."

Celia put her hand on the back of the chair to steady herself. All the years she had dated Dave, lived with Dave, been married to Dave, she had never seen this side of him and it scared her. She wanted to cry and ask him to forgive her, but a hard knot in her throat and even harder places deep in her heart and mind would not allow her. She knew it was pride, but she could not stop herself from stepping into the fall.

"So are we over? Is that what you're saying? You don't love me anymore?" Celia wanted to take control but her voice trickled out and fell between them soft as a feather.

"I don't know what we are, but we are both going to do what it takes to bring a healthy child into the world," Dave answered. He seemed to soften for a moment then his face set in a stone mask again. "Let me help you upstairs."

Celia wanted to protest that she could do this—like everything else—on her own, but she felt a terrible weariness that settled in her shoulders and her back with a weighty pressure that made her too heavy to make it alone. So Dave helped her up the stairs and into bed. She wished he would lay there with her until all the anger between them faded away, but he simply began banging dresser drawers and grabbing clothing.

She could see him in the hallway now, tying his running shoes, then the door below shut and he was gone. She hoped he would run off his rage and come back able to talk to her. Celia put her hand on her enormous belly. He was quiet now, her little John David. He wasn't moving around as he had been earlier. She closed her eyes and sleep washed over her in light, foamy waves, pulling her out to sea and into a deep, dreamless slumber.

When Celia woke it was dark outside. The streetlight, a beacon slashing across the bedspread, illuminated Dina's bald head and the outlines of her face as she lay next to her. Celia watched her sister breathing softly, her eyelids devoid of lashes, fluttering now and then. At the same moment that relief washed over her, she wondered where Dave was. The breeze blowing in the window was cold. She glanced at the digital clock. It was midnight. Trying to slide quietly out of bed was going to be nearly impossible at her current size. She moved slowly, sitting upright on the edge of the bed first. Dina did not wake up. Celia stood, shut the window, and headed downstairs to find Dave. She was very hungry but first she needed to know he was safely home.

She saw his feet hanging over the side of the couch before she even entered the family room. It looked like he'd grabbed a pillow and a couple of blankets and was deep in sleep, his light snores floating through the doorway where she stood. Celia's slippers shuffled lightly across the kitchen floor as she headed for the refrigerator. She pulled out lunch meat, cheese, lettuce, tomatoes—everything for a monster sandwich. She was leaning over the deep-bottomed bread drawer when she felt a funny pang and stood up quickly, gasping and clutching the counter. After a very long minute or two, it passed and Celia relaxed.

"Looks good, CeCe," she heard Dina say a few minutes later.

Celia turned around to see Dina eyeing her beautiful sandwich, which now sat on a pink plastic plate with chips around it. She put her finger to her lips and pointed toward the doorway to the family room. Dina paused, listening to the snores, and then smiled. They sat down at the little kitchen table.

"Want half of this?" Celia asked.

"No way, you need to eat that," Dina said. "I'll just make some peanut butter toast."

"Good, because I'm starving." Celia smiled. She ate comfortably, listening to her husband's snores, watching her sister move through the kitchen collecting milk, bread, and peanut butter to put her snack together. Celia felt a gentle peace fall over her. Things would be fine. Dina would live, the baby would be born, and she and Dave would work things out. It had been a tough winter, but the leaves were back on the trees and the dogwood buds were ripe and ready to bloom. Life was about to begin again and it was filled with promise.

"CeCe, are you okay?" Dina asked.

"Why?" Celia took a big bite of her sandwich.

Dina sat down, a filmy milk moustache across her upper lip, two big slices of toast with melting peanut butter stacked on a paper plate. She laid down two napkins. Dina always had two napkins—one for her lap, one to wipe her fingers on. She probably didn't even notice this unusual habit that Celia found so amusing.

"Dave was back from running when I came home," Dina said. "He was pretty upset and angry. He told me what the doctor said."

Celia continued to chew, washing her food down with milk before speaking. "He shouldn't have taken it out on you, it's not your fault," Celia said.

"He never blamed me, CeCe, but you have to take better care of yourself. And I blame myself for being so wrapped up in my illness and my own problems that I didn't insist you take it easy and quit running around taking care of me, your job, the house, Dave, the baby, and everything else."

"You couldn't have stopped me, Dina. I wouldn't have listened."

They both laughed at the frank truth of her statement.

"Do you think he still loves me?" Celia asked. She could see Dina's astonished look.

"Yes, Celia, he loves you, he's just so worried that he's angry. I'm angry too. You have to start respecting other people enough to listen to them. And you have to forgive yourself."

"Forgive myself for what?"

"Forgive yourself for how I turned out. You did the best job you could, trying to mother me when you were too young for the responsibility. I made all my mistakes on my own, as an adult, and I'm big enough to take the fallout from that and handle it." Dina paused. "You have to let go and just be my sister. You're someone else's mother now."

Celia watched her sister's smooth, hairless head bend over her plate. She could not change Dina or make her find a happy life. Celia knew that now and she hoped she hadn't learned too late for her baby or her marriage. "Dave says you're a lot stronger than I give you credit for."

"I'm not our mother, CeCe," Dina answered. "I'm a bit of a dreamer and I don't always make the best decisions, but I want the same things you do. I just make more mistakes trying to get there."

"So what are you going to do next?" Celia asked.

"Well, while I wait for my test results, I'm staying here to take care of you for a while."

"And Luke?"

"I haven't heard from him in three days. Once I know whether I'm in remission, I'll go see Luke and have it out. I don't feel physically strong enough now."

Celia stood up and took her plate and glass to the sink. There was that pain again. She felt Dina at her side, her arm slipping around Celia's waist.

"What's wrong? Are you okay?"

"It's just a pain, probably false labor, nothing more," Celia said. "He's not due for another five weeks."

"Let me help you back upstairs." Dina was rubbing her back.

Celia straightened up and put her arms around Dina, this woman she had mothered and sistered and who she loved so much. Dina hugged her back. "Does it feel odd to let someone else help you out?"

Dina was giggling softly at the irony and Celia began laughing with her. They were hugging and laughing when she felt the puddle of liquid spill between them. She let go of Dina, doubling over in pain at the same time. She could hear Dina yelling for Dave and then he was there, holding her up while Dina got her suitcase and they headed for the car.

"Oh, my God," Celia sobbed, "it's too early…it's too early…"

"It will be okay, CeCe!" Dina called to her as she ran out the door to the garage.

Celia couldn't look at Dave, couldn't face what she was sure was anger. Then she felt his arms around her, saw his concerned face, heard him say he loved her as the next wave of pain hit and she was at once vulnerable, scared, and determined to save her baby.

CHAPTER 25

LUKE

Luke could see her standing midway down the sterile white hall, intently focused on whatever lay beyond the big window her forehead rested upon, the back of her head hidden by a scarf secured with a baseball cap as usual. A wallpaper border of teddy bears amidst colorful balloons pleasantly disrupted the otherwise monochrome décor. Josh was holding a blue teddy bear in one hand, Luke's palm in the other. He was excited, so excited that Luke had been unable to talk him out of coming to see what a new, fairly premature baby looked like. Josh had been premature and the young boy's curiosity had the best of him now. Luke hoped the child's enthusiasm would cut through the tension he'd felt between he and Dina when he called her earlier that day.

Dina looked up at the sound of Josh's sneakers slapping on the linoleum floor as he ran toward her. Luke met her eyes and saw no anger. She looked tired and frail, dark circles floating below her lash-less eyes. Her shoulders felt thin and bony as he put his arm around them and looked through the window with her. Below was a row of fat, healthy babies, sleeping, crying, or simply looking back at them through the glass.

"Which one is he, Dina?" Josh asked.

Luke knew the answer. He could see, in a covered, oxygenated crib behind the other babies, one lone infant with a blue knit cap and tubes entering his arm and his nose. It was like looking at Josh all over again. He felt Dina shrug off his arm and squat down until her head was level with Josh's.

"See that bed in the back, behind the others?" she said.

Josh stood on his toes and nodded vigorously. "Is that him?" he whispered.

"Yes, it is. He's smaller than all the others because he arrived too early."

"Can I give him this teddy bear?" Josh fiddled with the bear's arm.

"Not yet," Dina said. "He's in the special bed because his lungs and his immune system and lots of other things aren't quite big enough. He has to stay away from any germs."

Josh looked disappointed. Dina hugged him softly. "Josh, would it be okay if I kept the bear until he's bigger and stronger and then gave it to him? I'll make sure to tell him it's from you."

Josh smiled, his small face relaxing, and thrust the bear at Dina.

"So what's his name?" Luke asked casually.

"John David," Dina answered. "J.D. for short."

She wasn't looking at him yet, but she leaned against him, her arm around Josh, and they watched little J.D. breathing in and out, his tiny hands balled in fists, flailing now and again against the world.

It was always this way with them, Luke thought. He and Dina would feel so close, then a deep, hopeless canyon would open up between them, and then later something would pull them together again. He knew it couldn't work. He even knew they were through, technically. Yet he wanted to touch Dina, pull her and Josh close to him, and inhale. She smelled like new leaves and dogwood blossoms. Or maybe he was just willing the hospital smells away.

"Would you like to see Celia and Dave?" Dina asked.

Luke stiffened, pulling away. "No, we just stopped by to see how the little guy was doing and to bring a present."

"And say congratulations you're an aunt." Josh laughed.

"Yes, I am, aren't I?" Dina smiled.

"I'll call you later," Luke said.

He couldn't quite meet her eyes. He didn't know if he would call or not. He owed her an explanation, something, after all she had been through, but that trapped feeling was rolling in now, a thin, filmy miasma pushing him backward and away.

"Luke?"

He had turned to go when he heard her.

"Yeah?"

"Luke, I passed my tests," she said. "They called a few hours ago. I'm cancer-free."

He couldn't move. He was free. He wasn't responsible anymore. Turning to face her, he found her watching him, searching for something in his face. Luke moved back to her in two strides and wrapped her in a big hug.

"Dina, that's wonderful," he said. "That's so great! This calls for champagne."

"Later?" she said.

"Um, I have Josh for a while," he said. "Call me tomorrow morning?"

"Sure." She smiled again, waved, and turned to go, holding the blue teddy bear to her chest and heading down the hallway away from him.

***

The next morning, Luke paced nervously in his kitchen. He hadn't slept well. He knew what he had to do and he was going to do it the coward's way, at least that was the description Henry used when he'd stopped by to pick up Josh and take him home. After finishing a bowl of cereal, Josh had grabbed his backpack and climbed into Henry's truck.

"Have you told Josh?" Henry stood in the garage, out of earshot from Josh.

"Not yet," Luke said.

"Are you going to tell him something?" Henry was looking out at the driveway rather than at Luke.

"I'll tell him the same thing I'm telling her."

"Hmmph." The noise rolled up from Henry's throat.

Luke watched as Josh waved from Henry's truck. Henry just nodded quickly and drove away. Since then he'd left Dina two messages and was waiting for her to call. Unlike Henry, who thought this was all about Luke thinking of himself and trying to slither—"like a snake" he'd said—under a rock to avoid the backlash that would come, Luke thought he was offering up what would be the easiest way for both he and Dina. Just as the phone began ringing, he saw Amber's car pull in.

Shit, what is she doing showing up so early?

"Hello?" Luke answered the phone, watching Amber pull her backpack out of the car and lock the door.

"Luke, hey, it's Dina." Her voice was soft and confident.

"Dina, give me one second. I see my neighbor outside and I need to return an extra shovel he loaned me." Luke put the phone down before she could respond. He stopped Amber in the garage, grabbing her little overnight bag and steering her out onto the patio. "Listen, sweetie, I need you to sit out here for a while until I come get you. I have an important business call and it's confidential. You can't come in until it's over."

Amber smiled, acquiescent, and wandered over to one of the two folding chairs he'd placed there that morning when he and Henry went outside to talk where Josh couldn't hear them.

"No problem." She giggled. "Don't be too long."

Luke was back inside in two long strides and picked up the phone.

"Dina, hey, I'm sorry," he said.

"That's okay. Are you busy tonight? I think we need to talk." She paused. "I think you know why."

"I know I haven't been around for a few days," he said.

"Try a week or more," she shot back.

Luke was surprised. So she was angry and sure of herself. He'd thought she would slide into this pretty easily. Maybe he was wrong.

"I needed to think about us," he blurted out. "Dina, I think we should take a break."

"Take a break?" she said. "What the hell does that mean? Take a break? Isn't that what you've been doing for a couple weeks by not calling?"

"I just think we've been through a really hard, intense time in our relationship and we need a little space from one another to think about where we go from here. I need a break to think a little." Luke tried to sound reassuring.

The silence seemed to go on and on, even though he knew it was only a few minutes. He should have just said he was breaking up with her. Henry was right, he was a coward. He shouldn't be doing any of this over the phone, regardless of how he handled it. He watched Amber wiggling in her chair outside, talking on her cell phone. She was unpredictable and it would be just like her to come waltzing into the kitchen, loudly looking for water or the bathroom. He liked that about her. That and her laissez-faire, easy come-and-go attitude. No serious talks of love or commitment. She was happy with raw, uninhibited sex and a kiss good-bye. No guilt, no struggles with Amber.

"Are you seeing someone else?" Dina asked.

"No, of course not." Even to Luke his voice sounded small and fake.

"This doesn't make any sense to me." Her voice was a little less assured. "How long are we on this break for?"

"Just a few weeks, maybe a month." Luke fidgeted, tapping the counter, looking at the clock.

"You're seeing someone else. I know you, Luke. You're not the kind to go without for a month, or even a week."

"Dina, there's no one else. Things have just been so serious with us and we've been through this huge experience. I need some time to think." He felt no guilt. He didn't consider what he was doing with Amber as actual dating, like he had with Dina. She was just a sunny, easy plateau where he could go and do whatever he pleased, feel as young as he wanted, without repercussions. He didn't feel trapped or guilty or conflicted with her, he just felt simple, crude pleasure and, after that, he felt nothing. Luke needed her like a wanderer needed a bridge to get from the complexities of the forest across to the simple, lush green of a manicured lawn. She was his way out and he was cutting this last piece of twine to follow her back to his old life. But Dina didn't know any of that, and he didn't want her to know. Three more weeks with Amber and he'd be thoroughly sick of her, letting her go to move on into the real dating world again, with Dina none the wiser.

"This isn't what I want, Luke," Dina said. "Why is everything about what you want? I think my illness should have made us closer and we should work through whatever is bothering you, together."

He couldn't believe she was giving him a hard time. He had expected her usual desperation and need to please. Perhaps he'd been spending too much time with Amber and Dina had grown too much spine in his absence.

"I'm sorry, Dina, but I'm taking a break. I need some space," he said. "I have to go. I have a meeting with a new client in an hour then I'm stopping by to see my parents. I'll call you in a few weeks and we'll talk. I promise. But for now, if people ask, we're just taking a break." Luke was pretty sure he mumbled good-bye when he hung up, but the phone began ringing again as he let Amber in. The caller ID showed it was Dina. Luke shut off the ringer and handed Amber a beer.

"Don't you want to answer that?" she asked.

"No, I'm all about shutting off the world right now," Luke said, smiling. "And you're going to help me."

CHAPTER 26

DINA

A sense of long, suppressed knowing was emerging, clashing with raw pain and disbelief as Dina clutched the steering wheel. She wanted to turn the car around and drive to Luke's house, but to do what, she asked herself. At the same time she wanted to drive a hundred miles an hour and get away from him for good. Instead, she was following the speed limit and all the traffic signals on autopilot, wrestling with herself, aiming her car toward the only place she could go to think clearly.

At a red light, she glanced over to see the man in the car to her left staring at her oddly and, in that moment with a stranger, she felt the stark clarity of her hair loss, her missing eyebrows, her puffy prednisone-inflated face, and she finally began to cry. Putting her head down on the steering wheel she sobbed until someone honked their horn and she raised her head to realize the light was green and the curious stranger was long gone.

Dina's car was the only one parked in the lot at the kite beach, its lonely, windswept area devoid of all but the scavenger gulls. Even the old treasure hunter with his metal detector was nowhere to be seen. She needed the solitude, the open blue expanse of sky and water, the quiet lapping of the waves. Her body and mind were working so efficiently, while her gut and her heart were in such chaos that it felt as though simple movements had become difficult.

The sand was cold to the touch as she sat down in the beach chair and pulled the old quilt around her. The sun was hazy despite the huge white clouds that dotted the clear sky. The water looked so beautiful but she knew it was like ice. What would it be like to strip down to nothing but her hairless, scarred, cancer-softened skin and just walk into those waters, disappearing?

Dina began crying again, not for Luke, who she knew was gone despite his reassuring words, but for the sheer enormity of her mistake this time. She had known, deep in her soul and all along, that he could not go the distance with her. She had loved him in spite of his weak center. Dina wanted to believe he loved her in his own, troubled, distorted way—and that was the sorrow of it. He had just proved he did not love her in any way that was worth having and she still refused to accept any other truth. She couldn't let go and yet she knew she had to flee from Luke quickly.

"Oh, God, what is wrong with me?" Dina called to the sky, to the water, to the wind. "Why didn't I tell him to get lost?" She listened and waited, but nothing spoke back. Dina closed her eyes. She knew this stress was bad for her condition. She might be in remission but she was at risk.

"I'm weak, God...please don't leave me alone without someone to love," Dina called to the sky again, an old childhood habit of believing

God lived in the firmament above her rather than in the circumference around her. A distant, bearded sage on a cloud rather than the spirit within the aura of her being that had come to fill in the spaces left after Katie's birth. Her nose was running profusely. She pulled a tissue out of her pocket and wiped her nostrils, then burrowed down into the quilt, pulling her hat over her eyes. The deepest part of her muscles and her bones were fatigued and she did not think she could get up and move toward the car if she wanted to. She was back on the beach in Sligo one moment, then staring out across Lake Erie in another. She rocked her body slowly, letting out first a weak cry to the heavens, then a stronger shriek and a yell. Alone with the wind and the sky, she howled and keened like Maeve, until her anguish diminished to gentle sobbing and she fell asleep.

***

The wind was icy when she awoke and the sun was close to the horizon. She had no idea how long she'd been sleeping in the beach chair. Her arms and legs were stiff and cold. She wanted to close her eyes again, but something had awakened her. A voice in her dream, perhaps, a thought more than a voice, or maybe just the rush of the wind playing games with her mind. She could feel it, hear it, yet she was still alone out here, only the wind and the waves reverberating around her.

Yet, Dina could have sworn someone just told her to go to Luke's house to see the truth. She laughed, standing up slowly, and folded the

chair. Her mind had played funny tricks on her all through chemotherapy, jerking her feelings in every direction, giving her bizarre dreams or
deep, dreamless sleeps. With so many toxins and drugs pumped into her
in such a short amount of time, she was probably just losing what little
was left of her sanity over the demise of what was left of she and Luke.
She crawled into her car and turned on the ignition, cranking up the heat
until she felt warm.

"Well, it will nag at me until I go talk to him," Dina said out loud to
the endless blue water stretching before her. The only sounds that returned were the lapping waves and the screeching gulls.

She backed the car out onto the road and headed for Luke's house.
Something felt unfinished, just as it had with Liam, just as it always
would with Katie. She needed to see him and resolve their phone conversation. Dina wondered if she was too sleepy to drive, let alone deal with
creating closure with Luke, so she pulled into a convenience store on
West 12th Street and bought a small cup of coffee. It warmed and stirred
her all at once. Still the feeling, the persistent, voice-like thought from
her dream did not leave her.

It was dusky, grayish, with the street's lights just about an hour away
from coming on when Dina turned into Luke's driveway. There was a car
she didn't recognize parked there. She backed into the street and continued driving as if by instinct, wondering why she hadn't just continued to
pull into his driveway anyway. It was probably some friend or business
associate, most of whom she knew. Dina shook her head and took a long
drink of the partially cooled coffee. She was just spooked by her odd
beach delusions.

She parked on the street above Luke's, walking down through the neighbor's backyard to reach his. She stopped under a huge oak tree, her shoes crunching the few dead, brown leaves left scattered across its foundation, new green buds unfurling above her head. It would be months before they colored and fell again, before she could make a crown of leaves and smell the autumn as she and Luke and Josh raked in harmony.

She could see movement in the great room under the shadows of the deer heads. She froze.

It was Luke...with a woman. They were standing, naked, moving slowly. *No. No, this can't possibly be happening again.* She could almost hear Liam's laughter, raining down through time to surround her. Rage surged through Dina, her hands balled in small fists.

Seconds later, she was pure anger as she slammed the porch door open and burst into the great room, the shock on Luke's face registering only moments before Dina pulled back and punched the strange woman in the face.

"Hey! Dina! Are you insane?" Luke was trying to pull his pants on with one hand and push her away with the other.

Dina glared at him, pulling her arm back for another swing when suddenly she faltered, dizziness sweeping over her. "You lying, cheating bastard!" She tried to yell but it seeped out in a hiss and a sigh, like a cheesy line from a bad soap opera. She looked at the plump, young girl lying naked on the floor, rubbing her jaw as she stared boldly up at Dina. "I'm battling cancer and you're sleeping with my boyfriend?"

The girl shrugged her indifference.

In that moment, Dina remembered her. She remembered the long-ago political fundraiser, the young woman stuffed in a tight dress following Luke around, and how he had disappeared only to come back flushed and sweaty. She felt sick.

"The entire time, even before I knew I was sick," Dina said to Luke. "I remember her. You've been doing this the entire time! How could you?" Dina could feel the bile rising in her mouth and she tried to control herself. She could not throw up right now, or fall or collapse.

"Dina, I tried, I really did, but you knew all along that we didn't have a commitment, that I wasn't the kind to, you know, settle down."

"You should have left when I got sick! You promised."

"And I kept my promise, Dina. I stuck with you the entire time. You're cured now. I need my space. I need to take a break. I told you that, but you just wouldn't listen, would you? You just couldn't walk away and give me just a teeny, tiny break from you."

Dina thought he seemed to be hissing at her, a human snake of sorts, and she realized she was getting dizzy again. *The hissing of the spent lie.* In that odd moment she could hear Luke reciting Dylan Thomas to her in the hospital. She clutched the back of a chair. The room was spinning a little, disorienting her. "I can't believe it's happening again."

She could feel Luke hand her some water. "What do you mean 'again'? Here, sit down, Dina." She drank the water, watching the girl grab her clothing and head up the stairs. She thought Luke had ordered her to get dressed but she couldn't be sure. Then she sat in the chair and set the water glass on the floor beside it.

"Are you okay?" Luke's hands were on her shoulders. She couldn't stand the feel of his touch.

"I just felt really dizzy. Give me a minute, the water is helping." Dina handed the empty glass back to him and stood, clutching the side of the chair until she was sure she was steady. Then she looked Luke squarely in the eye, her mind clear. "I knew we had problems, but I thought you loved me in your own way. You lied."

"I didn't lie, I'm just not who you want me to be," Luke replied. "I'm not made of that stuff."

Dina laughed sarcastically and began walking toward the porch.

"I don't think you're okay to drive," he said.

"I don't think that's your call." She walked through the porch, head held high, willing herself not to collapse. Dina alternately heard Luke's voice, then Liam's lilting brogue in her head, which let her know she was on the verge of losing it altogether. She hadn't seen or thought of Liam in years. Her body felt sick and exhausted. She needed to get out of here. Get as far away as possible.

"Dina, please, let's talk tomorrow," Luke said. "Get some rest and then let's sort this out, you and I."

"Why don't you ask her to leave and we'll talk now?"

He was silent, crossing his arms over his chest, his face stubborn and angry. Luke would have it his way or no way, of course, and she knew he wanted it all. He sat down in the Adirondack rocker on the porch and began rocking, eyeing Dina as she paused with her hand on the door handle, hesitant. If he was trying to make her feel guilty, she hoped she wasn't tired enough to give in.

Then, as she had done for all of this day that had started out with celebrating yesterday's joyful news and deteriorated into the nightmare she found herself confronting now, she began speaking without forethought. Dina spoke the words Luke had said to her not so long ago, expelling them from her mind and somehow deciding what the way of this thing between them would be.

"I have longed to move away, from the hissing of the spent lie, and the old terrors' continual cry, growing more terrible as the day, goes over the hill into the deep sea."

Luke's body tensed and he stopped rocking. Their eyes locked together, neither giving in nor taking anything away.

"Good-bye, Luke," Dina said with what felt like her last surge of available energy.

She couldn't tell if he'd heard her. She felt like the words were screaming in her head and she was blowing them out on a whisper. Luke had the oddest look on his face as he began rocking back and forth again.

Dina pushed the door open and, unable to run, moved as quickly through the yard and into the darkness as she could, inhaling the nighttime air and the smell of grass embedded in dark soil below, half hoping he would beg her to stop and half relieved when he did not. An alarm bell was sounding within her as she slid into the driver's side seat of her car and shut the door, rolled sideways, and curled into a fetal position. Her body was giving her a warning that she was far beyond the limits of exhaustion and stress than was safe for her, but her heart would not listen, thumping hard against her pain which stretched across the miles and decades of her life.

It had happened again. Dina closed her eyes to shut out the image of Luke and Amber, only to resurrect Ireland and Liam.

She needed to drive away but her body wasn't moving or responding easily. Eyes open, she saw Luke's light on in the distance. Eyes closed, she was back in Ireland, dropping her duffel bag and backpack on the floor outside her room. She'd just returned from burying Maeve to find two notices on her door from her landlord, saying that her rent was past due. The door was three quarters shut but not latched. Dina pocketed the notices at the same time she pushed it open. She could see Liam's curly head on the pillow and she walked across the tiny room in two steps to shake him awake.

"Liam, why didn't you pay the rent?" Dina asked.

Liam raised his head, rubbing his eyes, and the covers to his left moved. Then a head of sandy, spikey hair appeared, and a young girl with a pixyish face and large green eyes, her eyeliner like highway skid marks, popped up to a sitting position and smiled.

"Hello, luv." She smiled. "I'm Deidre; who are you?"

"This is what you do while I'm gone burying my granny in America?" Dina's voice had cracked before it hit the high notes.

"Your granny died, luv? I'm really sorry," Deidre continued, unaware.

"You should be sorry, you little slut." Dina moved toward Deidre. "This is my room, that's my boyfriend, and you've been having the time of your life on my rent while I'm left with these."

Dina waved the rent notices with one hand while grabbing Deidre by her spiky locks with the other and yanking. Deidre began screaming and thrashing, while a naked Liam jumped up and moved between them, protecting Deidre.

"Get out!" Dina said. "Get out before I call the police and have you arrested for trespassing."

She didn't have to tell Deidre twice. She was nearly shoving herself into her clothing and running out the door. Liam dressed more slowly, then walked toward Dina.

"Dina, darlin', you can't own me," he said. "I'm a free spirit."

"I don't care what kind of spirit you are, leave what's left of the rent money on the dresser and go. I don't want to see you again, *ever*." Dina remembered her voice shaking, but she had been so much stronger then. Her feelings had nearly shut off for him at that instant and she'd felt like a prizefighter twitching to take him down.

Liam fished around in his pants pockets, turning them inside out to indicate there was no money. He was grinning. Dina shoved him against the door and grabbed his jacket from the chair. She found fifty dollars in the pocket and the key to her room. Throwing the empty jacket at him, she stood clutching the money and key as if they were hard-fought winnings. Liam began to protest, moving toward her again.

"Come near me one more time and I'll kill you," Dina threatened. "This is half of what you took, but it'll keep a roof over my head until I work something out. Now get out, Liam, I mean it. And don't come back."

He shrugged, unconcerned, and walked out. No words, no poetry, no care for her soul which had just wrestled throughout the long transatlantic flight with despair over the loss of Maeve and the feeling that Celia had betrayed her. Dina ran to the bathroom down the hallway, still clutching the money, as she heard the door to the sidewalk below her open and close, then threw up in the toilet. She sat on her knees, bent forward over the commode for a long time before she felt a hand on her shoulder and saw Kathleen standing next to her. Dina opened her mouth but couldn't speak.

"It's okay, Dina. I'm wise to what's been going on here while you were gone." Kathleen had gently pulled Dina to her feet. "Now, rinse out your mouth and come back to your room. You need to lie down."

Dina splashed water on her face over and over then cupped it in her hands to rinse the vomit and stale taste from her mouth before she walked to her room and collapsed in a chair.

"How did you know I was home?"

"John and Connor called me from the airport saying they were picking you up and bringing you here. They might have suspected what Liam

Janet Roberts

was doing, but I knew for sure. Deidre's in one of my classes. So I came looking for you. I wish I'd gotten here a little sooner. I would have liked to give that Liam a good punch."

"I won't touch those sheets until they've been washed," Dina said softly. "I found them here, Kathleen. He spent my rent money on her and this is all I got back." Dina released the pound notes from her hand, watching them float down onto the floor and blow around in the slight breeze. Kathleen picked them up and laid them on the dresser, using a brush to hold them in place. Then she stripped the bed as Dina sat motionless in the chair, watching her. When she finished, Kathleen helped Dina lie down. Curled in a fetal position, Dina began sobbing, silently at first, then loudly, as Kathleen curled up behind her and wrapped her arms around Dina's back.

"You're a good friend, Kathleen."

"You deserve a good friend, girl. Now I'm going to give you something to help you sleep, then I'll talk with your landlord and get things straightened out. I'll be back to check on you later. And don't be chasing after Liam when you wake up."

"He's gone, Kathleen, and I can't say I care as much as I should."

"Well, and that's as it should be. It's for the best, luv. So what are you crying for?" Kathleen handed her a glass of water and a sleeping pill.

Dina shook her head. "I can't take those pills," she whispered. "I'm crying because I think I'm pregnant."

It was the first time she'd said it out loud, admitted to herself what her body had been telling her for several months. She'd planned to talk to Liam about it today, but that was out of the question now.

She could see Kathleen's shocked face as she leaned over to hug Dina closer. "We'll take these things one at a time then," Kathleen had whispered.

And now, alone in her car, bald, sad, and exhausted, just yards from Luke's home, Dina began to sob. For Kathleen, for Maeve, for her baby, Katie, for all she'd lost and all she needed. If only she could shut off the feelings for Luke as easily as she had for Liam. If only there was someone to help her handle things one at a time once again.

"God...why did you save my life, only to put me through this pain?" Dina wailed to the heavens beyond the roof of her car.

Sitting up slowly, she strapped herself in and turned the key in the ignition. She did not want to stay here a minute longer, to face the shame of Luke or his neighbors finding her. Dina knew exhaustion would overtake her soon and she needed to sleep, but not here, not in this car, not in this place. She could and she would make it home to Celia.

CHAPTER 27

The roll and creak of the barrels was comforting to Dina as she lay on her side under an afghan on the well-worn couch listening to music on the radio and ignoring the ring of her cell phone. Morning sun filtered through the skylights above, while birds sang and squawked outside, flying here and there in search of breakfast. She was safe to heal and think here.

Luke had called a number of times, each voicemail increasingly frantic, but Dina didn't answer. She felt sheltered here, someplace where virtually no one could find her. She was cleaning them all out of her head and out of her system—Liam, Luke, even her father, Pierre, who she hadn't thought of in years, and, of course, her mother. All those voices mixed with the petulant wail of Katie as she left Dina's arms and the insolent shrug of a naked girl—whether she was in Liam's bed or in Luke's house—and finally Luke's cold denial of the bond between them. They felt like failures she needed to let go of. She only wanted to hear her granny's singsong voice giving her sage advice. Or perhaps she just wanted to see the fairies of her childhood dreams mixed with the voice of God. Most of all, she wanted peace and the feeling that she was not losing her sanity.

Dina's first instinct as she drove away from Luke's house that night, the image of that naked girl in her mind, was to leave town immediately. Dave had come home to find her packing her things, her cap off, her face flushed and tired. When she'd broken down and told him what happened, she was grateful beyond imagining that he didn't yell and scream as Celia would have done. He hugged her and let her cry until she was too spent to do more than sit there and listen to him.

"Dina, you can't go anywhere," he said. "You're not well yet. At least rest, grow some hair, heal."

"He'll come looking for me, Dave, when that woman is gone," Dina sobbed. "I'm not strong enough yet to walk away, to say no. I still want to forgive him."

"Celia will go nuts if you leave before she gets home with the baby," Dave answered. "But you're right, you need to hide and heal." He seemed to think for a moment. "Stay right here, Dina. Don't move and don't leave yet." He walked out of the room.

Dina couldn't have moved much if she'd wanted to. She felt unwell in a deep, resonating way that rolled through her in waves and wrapped around her with the soft lightness of a baby's blanket and, yet, was still stifling. She lay slumped sideways on the bed, her feet dangling over the edge, her face lying just inches from the open suitcase and duffel bag. Dave was on the phone in the next room, his voice rising and falling in an even pattern.

"Dina, I have a solution." He stood in the bedroom doorway looking at her but she couldn't sit up and answer him. "Listen. My buddy Chuck has a houseboat out on Horseshoe Pond at the peninsula. He and his family only use it sporadically in the summer. He said you could stay there a while, no questions asked. You'd just be on the other side of town, but well hidden."

Dina pushed herself slowly to a sitting position and stared at Dave.

"No one will know you're there, least of all Luke...unless you tell him. And even if he did, he'd need a boat to get to you from the dock."

Dina lowered her head to her chest, arms crossed over her stomach. *A hideout, a place to think and heal.* Dave and Celia could visit sometimes, but she would primarily be alone to read and write and forget.

"I think that's a good idea, Dave." When she finally spoke it was with a wan, appreciative smile. "I'm too tired to run away tonight anyway."

Dave laughed and she grinned weakly along with him.

"Okay, get some sleep, then first thing in the morning we'll finish packing you up and head down there," Dave said. "We'll stop to get groceries, and Chuck will meet us at the dock."

"And Celia?"

"I'll talk to Celia."

"Dave? I can't promise I won't eventually run away."

"I know, Dina. And hell, maybe you should. But not now. You're not ready."

Dina nodded as he moved the suitcases to the floor and lifted her legs up on the bed, covering her with a blanket.

"Sleep, Dina," Dave said. "You finally beat the cancer. That's all that matters. Don't let this knock you out of remission. I'll take care of everything."

"Dave, you're so good," Dina mumbled. "Celia is so damn lucky." Then everything went black and she was asleep.

When Dina awoke, Dave had packed her suitcases, her laptop, and several books, and even added pictures of him, Celia, and the baby.

"I'm not going to live out there forever," Dina said.

"It's good for you to have pictures of your family. Celia and I will come out, but you won't feel alone."

"How will you visit me?"

"Chuck has two small motorboats, one moored to the houseboat and one to the dock," Dave said. "We can grab the one at the dock any time and come see you. You can run to the dock using the one at the houseboat. From there, you can call a cab or one of us to pick you up."

They bought enough groceries to last a few weeks, then drove out to the North Pier. Standing on the dock as Dave pointed to the closest houseboat, only five or six feet away, Dina sighed with pleasure and relief.

Rocking gently on the water was a pristine white haven, beckoning her. Its long, sloping roof peppered with skylights came down far enough to create an overhang. The roof and the white railing encircling the houseboat created a lovely shaded deck on every side. The clean lines of the modern siding were broken only by a sliding glass door leading out to the deck on one side and regular doors opening to the deck from the opposite side. A motorboat was moored at its side.

Chuck had been waiting for them. He hopped out of his blue Ford truck and loaded the groceries and Dina's bags into another motorboat tied to the dock. Then they all climbed in the boat, Chuck pulled the throttle on the engine, and they headed out to the houseboat. Chuck and Dave puttered around for about thirty minutes, giving her a few instructions on using the motorboat, helping to put the groceries away, showing her where the flashlights and First Aid kit were stored. Finally, they seemed to run out of things to say and, once she assured them she'd be fine alone, they left.

Dina let Celia leave a few messages on her cell phone before she called her back, and they talked for a long time. Then she'd slept for nearly twelve hours straight, emotional and physical exhaustion overtaking her at last.

In the three weeks since then, she'd only moved from the couch during the day to eat, shower, use the bathroom, and go outside. She never wanted to leave. In the early morning and at night, she sat out on the small deck that ran around the perimeter of the houseboat and drank a cup of coffee or a beer, occasionally smoking a cigarette from a pack of Marlboro Lights that Chuck must have forgotten he'd left there, tucked in the back of the silverware drawer. She knew the last thing a cancer survivor should do is smoke a cigarette, but it felt so good to gaze up at the stars and feel the houseboat rock with the slight movement of the water, inhaling and exhaling all the toxins of her life in a most unhealthy but relaxing way. She often lit a few tiki torches on the deck, enjoying the dark quiet of the night broken only by fireflies and the soft glow of the tiki torches.

If only Luke would quit calling. Dina never answered, but she listened to his voicemails over and over again despite the pain they caused. Celia urged her to start writing, and each night before she fell asleep, Dina promised herself that tomorrow would be the day she would pull out the laptop and begin. But each time she looked at the keyboard, she worried she wouldn't know what to say or would be unable to spill out her thoughts in a way that would rid her of all this pain and despair. She needed to move on, and to figure out a location to physically move on to.

Erie was too small and Celia was busy telling everyone from fellow employees at Erie Insurance to the parishioners at St. Patrick's to her neighbors on Sunset Drive what Luke had done. These houseboats were the last bastion of privacy where one could hide in Erie, but, with the tourist season beginning in a month or so, Dina knew her solitude wouldn't last. Chuck and his family would want their houseboat back and Dina would either face the community and Luke, or move on.

Dave was coming out tomorrow to take her to the doctor for a few tests and a checkup. Celia had already called ahead to petition for a written excuse that would keep Dina on long-term disability from work. Not that her employer cared. A substitute teacher had handled the classes this far and the semester would soon be over. But she had to decide, within a month, whether to go back or quit. The checks would not continue showing up forever.

Dina stood up from the comfy couch and stretched, eyeing the coffee pot in the kitchen area to her left. The light was still on and it looked like there was enough left over from the pot she'd made an hour ago to give her one more cup. Chuck was obviously a Pirates fan, she thought as she poured the last of the coffee into a black, ceramic mug that said "Go Bucs!" on the side in gold lettering, shut off the machine, then headed out to the little deck. It was midday and balmy, but the breeze was still a little cool. It wouldn't really warm up around here until late May or June.

There were twenty-four houseboats, including Chuck's, all forty by sixty feet, and all connected to underwater lines that provided power and water. She laughed, wondering if she would have lasted this long out here without the amenity of a hot shower. Dina began walking around the house, touching the smooth white surface of the outer wall. The white railing seemed sturdy, but she didn't want to risk leaning on it and falling into the water. Still, curiosity made her lean over it to take a look at the barrels the house was erected on. She'd been fascinated with these houses since grade school, when Maeve took her and Celia to Beach 11 and veered off the main path and down the side road to Horseshoe Pond to show them how people could live on the water. Once back in school, Dina had peppered her teacher with so many questions that they'd had a "houseboat day" where they all learned about the houseboats that had been there since the early 1900's.

Dina looked out across the softly rocking rooftops of the other homes to the entrance of Horseshoe Pond, remembering that once the houseboats had been scattered in the western end of the bay. Until the State of Pennsylvania mandated they be moved to Misery Bay and then, in 1964, established Horseshoe Pond as the only site for the location of these floating homes. No more than twenty-four were allowed in the pond now and, although many of the houseboats had been updated and modernized, others still showed signs of age and decay. Fortunately, Chuck rebuilt this houseboat, once owned by his great-grandfather, two years ago.

She could see white birch trees on the shore, lush and green and filled with flocks of finches singing and chirping. She leaned into a corner spot against the wall, drinking in the smell of coffee and fresh air and the decaying fish floating just left of the houseboat.

Suddenly, she heard a sudden rustle of feathers and the scratch of clawed feet and froze, her body still, as a great blue heron landed on the corner of the deck opposite her. He was about twenty-five feet away but she could see him clearly, standing proud and indifferent, as though she was an interloper on his property but he would politely allow her to share his space for a time. One of his bright eyes, sitting just at the end of his large harpoon bill, watched Dina cautiously. He was beautiful, with the sun glinting off his blue-tinged feathers, and a second, soft black tuft to crown his head, sloping like pieces of hair toward his neck.

Suddenly, Dina felt filled with energy. The wind and the sun moved over her with quick electricity and she knew what she wanted to do. She wanted to run back inside, but she moved cautiously around the perimeter so as not to startle the beautiful bird until she was back in the houseboat, then she headed to the bathroom for a steamy shower. She was ready to write and she was living in the perfect setting for the poem—and perhaps a story—bubbling up inside of her.

Janet Roberts

Three hours later, when Celia and Dave arrived with little J.D., a pizza, and a bag of groceries, the blue heron was long gone, but Dina was happily typing away on the laptop.

"Dina...you're writing!" Celia's face lit up.

"CeCe, I'm ready." Dina reached for J.D. "I have one poem and the beginnings of a short story."

"Great!" Dave put the pizza down on the small kitchen table along with napkins, a couple paper plates, and some Pepsis. "Let's eat and you can tell us about it."

J.D. began crying in Dina's arms when Celia tried to wrap both of them in a hug. They laughed and Dina handed him back to his mother, running her hand through the little head of strawberry curls so much like Celia's.

Dina told them how she'd been inspired by her haughty, feathered morning visitor, by the houseboats and their history, as well as the seclusion and healing she felt here, and the mystery of hiding out.

"How long will you stay out here?" Celia asked.

"Celia, don't push her," Dave said.

Dina shifted in her seat, crumbling her napkin into a ball and putting it on the paper plate littered with pieces of crust and sauce smears, without looking at Celia. An idea had emerged during her writing but she wasn't going to tell her sister. She was sure Celia wouldn't like it.

"I've only been out here a couple of weeks," Dina said. "Luke keeps calling, although I never answer, and he seems to be giving up a little. I'm just not ready to face him or anyone else. I need at least a month here. But I think I can call a cab and start running into town for my own groceries soon."

"He hasn't had the nerve to call us." Celia's mouth was set in a hard line, but motherhood had changed some things, Dina thought. Before J.D., Celia would have been vocal and insistent about Luke by now. But she kept her voice soft and quiet and refrained from going in a direction that would make her angry enough to lose her temper and yell. Dina smiled, watching her tough, controlling sister as her face and body softened when she looked at J.D. He was adorable. Dina wished she could stick around to watch him grow up.

"Celia, I know you don't want to hear this but I'm the one who's been hurt and betrayed and I've had a little time to think here. I do believe he cares about me in some stunted way that would never have rolled into a good relationship...and he is somewhat remorseful in his own way for what happened." Celia's face went red and she opened her mouth to protest, but Dina put up her hand and motioned her into silence. "Don't get me wrong, he doesn't care about me the way Dave does about you. I don't think Luke can care about anyone more than he cares about himself and satisfying his own needs. That's his weakness. Which is why he'll never truly think what he did to me was wrong...because he was satisfying his own wants and needs.

"But on some level, he wanted to be noble and good," Dina continued. "He thought that in standing by me he could expand beyond a self-centered coward who can't exert the control he needs to or summon the depth of character others have on hand or commit whole-heartedly to another person, to put another's needs first."

"He has no integrity," Dave said.

"No, he doesn't." Dina sighed. "And, sadly, he knows it but is missing some level within himself where integrity and other traits you see in people you respect for their sheer sense of being...of humanness toward others...grows and unfolds."

"So you're saying he's trying desperately to be something he's not?" Dave looked skeptical.

They were all quiet for a few minutes. Celia had undone her shirt and bra and was breastfeeding J.D., fixing her eyes on him and trying to steer clear of the discussion for once.

"No, he's not trying," Dina said. "Not in the real sense of the concept. He's saying all the right words and he's trying to imitate others, but in the end he only exerts energy for things that satisfy his needs...primarily his ego needs and his physical needs, I suppose."

Celia looked disgusted. "So you're going to leave this houseboat one day, forgive him for his uncontrollable weakness, which you seem to think is not his fault somehow, and take him back, aren't you?"

"Celia!" Dave said.

Celia kept her eyes fixed on Dina, patting J.D. softly, soothing him. Dave's voice had startled him and a small wail began to rise up from his tiny mouth, but even at this age Celia could control him with a touch.

"I never want to see him again and I'm never going to if I can help it, CeCe," Dina said. "I'm going to leave Erie for good without seeing him or saying good-bye. I decided this morning."

Dina felt the heaviness of her words and of her own sadness as she watched the sorrow and disappointment grow in her sister's eyes. Celia thought she was so weak, almost worse than Luke. For Celia, all problems were solved by rushing in and doing battle. This was the way of true strength and the way to win. But Dina was learning there were many ways to be strong and many ways, some soft and patient, to become a winner. Dave, she knew, understood this just as Celia never would.

"Where will you go?" Celia asked. "And when?"

"I don't know where yet," Dina said. "I'm thinking about it. I'll go when I have a little hair, look a little more normal, and after I get my last paycheck next month."

Celia sighed, rocking J.D. with her body as the houseboat softly rocked all of them. Dina breathed in the sight of her sister, her heart and soul, and the tiny baby in her arms, waiting for a sense of peace to settle between them. Then Celia reached one hand over to clasp Dina's fingers, and she smiled, reluctantly but with a new level of acceptance in her eyes.

After they left, Dina slipped open the laptop and began writing again. She had lied to Celia. She knew exactly where she was going. But she had not lied about Luke. She never wanted to see him again. She would make one phone call before she left town and it would not be to Luke, but it would be her way of letting him know that he'd passed the point where he could talk his way out of it. He would find out that she was not as easy, weak, and pliable as he thought she was.

CHAPTER 28

LUKE

L uke set his beer on the small, scarred wooden table and sat down across from Henry. They met at the Docksider on a Saturday afternoon now and then. It had moved several blocks south on State Street from its original location near the public dock and had gone through a renovation, but it was still dark, cool, woody, and smelled of beer, cleaning solution, and a few undefinable smells from the Friday night college crowd.

It was mid-June and the weather outside was beautiful, but the Docksider had no deck or courtyard where they could hang out and drink. Henry seemed absorbed in a baseball game on several of the televisions perched high above the bar. The Pittsburgh Pirates were playing and Henry loved the Pirates, even though winning seemed more a part of their history than their future these days.

"The fence looks good and it's holding up well," Luke said.

"Good." Henry nodded in Luke's direction then back to the television. "Maybe you can come over one day and help me with mine."

Luke wondered if Henry would follow up with that. Recently, things had been a little tense between them and Luke thought Henry often avoided him. This was the first time they'd gotten together in about a month, although they talked on the phone off and on, so Luke had been surprised when Henry called and suggested they have a few beers at the Docksider. Henry had been uncharacteristically quiet as Luke complained that he couldn't find Dina and she wasn't returning his calls.

Henry stood up, stretching his large frame a little, and walked over to the bar. A couple of minutes later he returned with two beers and two bags of pretzels, tossing one to Luke and opening one for himself. They watched the game for a while in a comfortable silence broken only by the crunching of pretzels and the noises behind the bar as the bartender cleaned, replaced kegs, and set up for the evening. Luke had missed the silent bond of brothers that had always existed between them and he relaxed back into it easily, putting his feet up on an empty chair and soaking it in. His cell phone rang, a raucous, irritating invader into the peace and calm between them. He looked at the caller ID then pushed a button, sending it to voicemail, and put the phone's volume on silent.

"Sorry." Luke grinned.

"Amber, I'll bet," Henry said, his unsmiling face fixed on the television.

"She's starting to get on my nerves," Luke admitted.

"Not so much fun when you're not sneaking around, is it?"

"Hey," Luke's voice rose. "If you want to be an asshole, I can leave."

"Yep, you can leave," Henry said, "but not before I tell you about the call I got yesterday." He turned his attention from the television to Luke, his steady, serious gaze making Luke uncomfortable. "Dina called me."

Luke had just lifted the beer bottle to his lips when Henry spoke. Anger ran through him like wildfire and he slammed the bottle back on the table. "She fucking called you and she hasn't returned my calls in two months? Where is she?"

The bartender walked to the end of the L-shaped bar closest to their table. "Everything okay?"

Henry raised his hand and nodded that everything was fine. The bartender shrugged and returned to what he was doing.

"Give me one good reason why she should return your calls, Luke."

"Human decency. Respect for me and for our former relationship. To give me the chance to apologize."

Henry laughed and tipped his head back to take a swig of his beer. It wasn't the nice, hearty Henry-laugh Luke knew, but something hard and sarcastic that unnerved him. "Stop thinking about yourself and what you want for a minute, Luke, and ask yourself if you showed her any human decency by taking up with that little slut while she was fighting for her life. Why should she respect you? Why should she even think what you had was a relationship?"

Luke thought he was going to explode from the sheer energy of his resentment. He didn't know who it was aimed at now, Dina or Henry, he just wanted to punch something or tip the table over. He should leave.

But Henry suddenly looked smug to him, although his expression hadn't changed much since he first sat down. Luke was sure that Henry, simple and honest to the core, was not capable of hiding much—and he knew something.

"Did you really want to apologize?" Henry asked. "Are you sorry? You really hurt her."

"Of course I want to apologize," Luke said, "and explain. I'm very sorry I hurt her."

"But you would do it again, wouldn't you?"

"Hey, she wasn't my wife. I did my best to stand by her but I didn't love her and that's what she wanted, love and commitment. Eventually, it would have come to some sort of break-up. I'm just sorry it happened this way."

"I think you're mainly sorry people found out that you cheated on a nice girl while she had cancer, and it's ruining that public image your ego is in love with." Henry stood and Luke stood with him, pulling back his arms, one hand in a fist. Henry looked at him and laughed.

Right then, Luke knew they would never be the same again. Henry, his brother buddy, his friend for life, had lost respect for him. The sound of his laugh punched Luke in the gut and made his arm go limp worse than any fist would have done.

Henry picked up his car keys. "I apologized to her," he said. "Not necessarily on your behalf."

"I didn't love her," Luke said. "At least I wasn't *in love* with her."

"She's gone, Luke. She left town and she's not coming back. She went to New York City. Good luck finding her among eight or nine million people, not that I think you'll bother to try." Henry had the door to the bar half open, sunlight filtering in through the dingy darkness, fingering the scratches on the hardwood floors.

"Henry," Luke called, walking toward him as Henry turned. "Don't let her come between us. We've been friends for too long."

"She didn't come between us, Luke. You did. As we grew up, you became one thing and I became another. I just didn't want to see it. Good luck, buddy." Henry waved and he was gone, the door closing behind him with a soft thud.

Luke turned to face the empty bar. Even the bartender had gone back into the kitchen. Luke wanted to put his head down on the table and cry tears of sorrow and anger, but he wouldn't give in to it.

Damn that woman. No one had ever cost him so much. He hoped she rotted in hell. And yet, deep down, he wanted her to come back. To come back and forgive him, change him. She could convince Henry he could change, that it wasn't too late.

But she was gone and she would never come back. She would never forgive him.

CHAPTER 29

DINA

Dina sat on a bench in Central Park and smiled, inhaling the clean, crisp smell of the trees into each cell of her damaged but healing body. The stately American elm trees had unfurled leaves bright green with promise.

A slight, gentle breeze rustled the newspaper on her lap, which was open to the classified ads. She held it down a little more firmly with her left hand while her right skimmed lightly over the inch of short, spiky hair that covered her scalp. It felt so good to know it was back that she reached up again and again to touch it. Like the trees that towered over her, she was sprouting fresh buds, renewed. In Erie, she'd looked strange among girls who often still gravitated toward big, 1980's hair, so she'd worn a baseball cap much of the time. But here it seemed hip and trendy to be shorn, and she wondered if she would decide to keep her hair this way or actually let it grow out.

She'd paid homage to Lennon at Strawberry Fields and then found a bench on Literary Walk, which felt fitting to her somehow. She could sit here and meditate for hours, but the realities of life dictated she do otherwise. Dina rummaged in her purse, pulling out a red pen, and began perusing the ads for apartments in earnest. Dave and Celia had insisted on paying for a week at the Day's Inn Hotel on Broadway. That, a job interview tomorrow, one big suitcase, and $5,000 were all she had. She'd sent a poem and three short stories she'd written to a number of magazines while she was living on the houseboat. *Redbook* took a short story and *Savvy*, the new hip magazine for young working women, had taken a poem. Celine, the editor of *Savvy*, had called her personally.

"We're still small and personable here at Savvy." Celine's voice was a smile with a distinct Brooklyn accent. "I'd like to say hello and ask you a few questions about yourself. We'll publish a little bio about you under the poem."

"Wow! That's great!" Dina had answered.

They'd chatted up a storm, as if they'd known each other a lifetime, and when the conversation ended Dina had the names of three editors at different publishing houses, a list of affordable neighborhoods in Brooklyn, and a promise from Celine to call ahead and help grease the skids toward getting job interviews when Dina moved to New York.

"Call me when you get here and we'll do lunch," Celine said. "Maybe you can do a little freelance work for me. You know, to pick up some extra cash. It's expensive here, honey; you'll need it."

Dina called each editor two days later and, true to her word, Celine had called ahead to put in a good word. They all asked for a resume so Dina grabbed the laptop, gingerly slid into the little motorboat moored by the houseboat, and motored to shore where she had a cab pick her up and drive her to the nearest Kinko's. The next week, she had an interview lined up and two weeks to box up her stuff at Celia's, pack a suitcase, get a plane ticket, and go. She would have just gone, feeling fearless and invincible since she'd beaten death, but Celia was beside herself with worry. So she'd agreed to let them book the hotel for her, promising to let Celia know if she ran out of money before she had a job. She'd also made sure the Regional Cancer Center faxed her records to Sloane-Kettering in New York. She was still required to get a checkup every month and that wouldn't change until she hit a year in remission.

Celine told her to check out Park Slope or Carroll Gardens in Brooklyn but they were looking a little pricey for her wallet. One month there and her money would be gone. The well-worn ex-cop she'd sat next to on the plane told her Red Hook was the place to go. A little gritty, but up and coming in a slow, artsy, methodical way. She'd have to take the bus to the subway, he said, but that made the rents lower.

She dropped her head and skimmed the listings for Red Hook. A big drop in price, almost half the amount of the more convenient areas Celine recommended. The cop, Louie, said he'd put in forty years with the NYPD but now he just bought old properties, fixed them up, and sold them. He'd given her his card and wrote on the back the name of a friend who he said had an apartment for rent.

"It's nicer on the inside than it looks outside," Louie said. "And the bus stops in front of the building across the street. No grocery store close by and a couple blocks up, the neighborhood is still a little rough, but new stuff is coming. Give it a couple years and it'll get better."

Millions of apartment ads were swimming in front of her eyes now, the streets running together as she tried to match them with her still clean, well-folded tourist's map of Manhattan and the five boroughs. She reached into her jacket pocket and pulled out Louie's card, then her cell phone. The card said *Louis J. Palluzo, Real Estate Development*. She flipped it over. The name scrawled on the back looked like it said Bud Risotti, but she wasn't sure. The number, however, was clear. She dialed it.

"Yeah?" The voice on the other end was gruff.

"May I speak to Bud?"

"Speakin'."

"Uh, hmm, uh, your friend Louie Palluzo told me to call about the apartment for rent."

"The one on Van Brunt...down from Wolcott?"

"Uh, yes, I think so."

"How you know Louie? You his girlfriend or something?"

Dina could feel her face flushing with embarrassment and anger. This guy was rude. She wanted to hang up but she needed a place to live and it needed to be an affordable place.

"I met him on the plane. I just moved to New York. And I'm not his girlfriend."

"Hey, I was just kiddin' with ya! Louie's got a wife. Not that that would stop him, ya hear, but I was kiddin'. You're kinda serious. You got a job?"

"I have an interview at Crown Publishing tomorrow. And, uh, I have some freelance work lined up."

"Okay, okay, normally you need to have a job to rent from me, but I'll tell you what. You come down here today and we'll talk," Bud said. "I'll show you the apartment, and you tell me if you think you can get that job."

"So, how do I get there from Manhattan?" Dina asked nervously. "Can I meet you around two thirty?"

"Sure, that'd be a good time. The bus will let you off across the street from the building. I'll be waitin' there. I'm the good-lookin' guy with the Yankees hat."

Dina was silent.

"Man, you got no sense of humor. You'll need to learn 'bout New Yorkers."

Dina laughed nervously and apologized. He gave her directions on how to take the subway to Jay Street in Brooklyn and catch the B61 bus headed to Van Brunt Street in Red Hook. She hoped she could get there and back in one piece. Her invincible shield felt like it was melting and her hand shook as she put the card back in her pocket. She felt safe in Central Park or in a Manhattan hotel with lots of security. Now she was venturing out and a panic-driven need to run back to Horseshoe Pond and Chuck's houseboat washed over her.

She tipped her head back and stared up into the vast bows of an ancient, tree then closed her eyes. In that second, she was back in Luke's yard with Josh writhing happily in a pile of leaves as she raked up grass and dark soil with crackling, drying foliage and smiled at him. She opened her eyes and tears of nostalgia for what she'd had and yet never really owned trickled down her cheeks, mingling with fear at this big step she was taking. Several leaves gently settled on the bench beside her, a gift from the giant elm, and she picked them up. They were so green, rubbery soft and pliable, new and vibrant. Dina wanted to iron them between two pieces of wax as she and Maeve had done long ago and keep them for a snowy, cold day when she needed to feel as alive in her fear and pain as she did in the prospect of her new strength.

She stood up and stepped forward onto the pathway without looking, so intent was she on putting the leaves into her roomy purse, her first memento of this new sensory canvas she would learn to call home. Michael ran into her at that precise moment.

He was jogging, earphones in and radio strapped to his left bicep, humming to himself. Her head came up just as he slammed into her and she yelped, trying to jump out of the way without falling as he struggled not to fall back into the path of a teenage girl on rollerblades zooming by on his right.

"Oh, God, I'm so sorry," Dina said.

He was half kneeling on the pavement, his hand on his ankle, his face hidden by long, soft dreadlocks bunched together in a ponytail and hanging over his shoulder like a partially sashed curtain.

"Are you alright?" Dina asked anxiously. "I should have looked before I stepped out."

A pair of hazel eyes with a slight upward slant set in skin like cafe au lait looked over at her and he smiled broadly. When he stood he was much taller than her, slim and athletic with broad shoulders, and she had to tip her head back to look at him.

"Are you alright?" she asked again.

"Yes, I'm just fine." He laughed and she felt a sense of lightness about him that was contagious. "Hey, it's not often I get lucky enough to run into a beautiful woman...literally." He winked.

For the first time since she'd left Luke, she didn't want to run away from a man. Her stomach felt funny, a bit wobbly with excitement.

"Dina Benet." She put out her hand, laughing with him, and he shook it, leaving little beads of sweat on her palm.

"Hmm, nice, exotic...Dina Benet," he said. "I'm Michael Mann. I'm Michael. I'm a man..." He grinned. "Nothing special. I like your name."

Dina absorbed the sheer sensation of him in harmony with the distant sounds of jazz and rock bands coming from somewhere near the East Green and the murmurs and rustles of young lovers moving across the grass behind her to curl into one another's bodies. A troupe of Saturday morning actors worked out a scene under the trees a few yards away.

Shouts arose from a pick-up soccer game as the rapidly moving feet of shirtless, lean men of all ages exhaled clouds of dirt like so many Pig-Pen characters in a Charlie Brown cartoon.

"Could I interest you in lunch?" Michael asked.

"Oh, thanks, but I'm not that hungry," she said. "I was just going to go look for an apartment."

"Could'a fooled me with the way your stomach is growling."

Dina blushed. The quivers in her belly she thought were nerves were making noises and she realized maybe she should eat something. But she could hear Celia's voice warning her to be careful. Despite the instant connection she felt with him, he was a stranger to her.

"Okay, I have a couple hours before I'm meeting with a landlord in Red Hook. Where do you want to eat? I could meet you at the restaurant."

"Red Hook? Pretty brave girl. I live in the East Village and, if you don't mind coming with me so I can clean up and change, there's a little restaurant across the street from my townhouse. If I still seem scary to you when we get there, you can wait at the restaurant.

"Oh, and I'll be happy to go to Red Hook with you if you like," he added. "It might be good to have a friend with you the first time."

Dina stood rooted to the walkway in Central Park grinning, unable to move.

"What? Did I say something?" Michael asked.

"No...I mean yes...you said 'friend.' I think, Michael, that you are my first friend in New York City."

"Sounds good to me," he answered. "Now, let's hop on the subway and get going. I'm starved."

It is illogical, Dina thought as she followed him out of the park, that in a moment of need she would agree to go with this stranger. And yet, she felt at home with him in a way she had never felt before with anyone, not even Celia. It was all part of her New York adventure.

They grabbed the F train at Lexington and exited at Broadway, walking a few short blocks to a tall brownstone in the middle of a row of similar townhouses near Bleecker Street.

"See that little restaurant half a block down? You can wait there if you like, or you can come in."

Dina hesitated. She could tell it was a nice, upscale neighborhood. People were walking by and a few waved to Michael. Just then a woman emerged from the brownstone next door.

"Hello, Michael? How's your mother doing?" She smiled at Dina.

"She's great. She'll be here next weekend. This is my friend, Dina Benet, brand new to the city." Michael laughed. "Dina, my neighbor, Sue Owens."

They chatted for another minute, then Sue left. Michael looked at Dina and waited.

"I'm going inside," he finally said. "Are you coming in or heading to the restaurant?"

Dina felt shy but curious. "I'll come inside."

She followed him up the five concrete steps, hesitating slightly as he held the door open for her, then stepping inside. She felt enveloped by the cool interior of the foyer, its tiled floor meeting deep brown carpeting that stretched out to her right and up the stairway ahead, melding with the polished wooden rail to extend in one mellifluous motion upward. Dina could hear jazz music coming from far above, sifting down as if from the heavens, yet she was sure it was somewhere in the house. She stared up the stairs and into the darkness of the landing, straining to hear.

"It's my brother," Michael said, flipping his thumb toward the ceiling. "He rents the third floor from me. I own the place but it helps him and helps me...I'd get lonely around here without him."

"Oh, sure...I wondered where the music was coming from." Dina was embarrassed at her obvious curiosity.

"Have a seat in the living room or help yourself to something to drink in the kitchen," he said, taking the stairs two at a time. "I'll be back in about ten or fifteen minutes."

Dina moved slowly toward the living room to her right. She wondered what he did for a living. The brown leather couch rustled rather than squeaked as she sat down and leaned into its overstuffed back. An enormous rug that looked Persian covered most of the wall-to-wall carpeting here. A faux fireplace with gas jets behind the pretend logs looked inviting, and Dina thought how wonderful and warm this room must be in the winter.

She stood, wandering over to the fireplace mantel to look at the three pictures carefully placed on one side, balanced by candles on the opposite end. The first was obviously a family portrait, the kind she and Celia had longed for growing up, with a mother and two adult boys. One boy was obviously Michael but if the other was his brother, they looked nothing alike. The next was of him and what appeared to be a bunch of college friends, mostly guys, in some sort of pub or bar. They all sported University of Michigan T-shirts and jerseys. The last was Michael and a beautiful woman. They matched, he and this woman, complementing one another with identical skin, hair, and eyes. Their arms were gently entwined as they gazed into each other's eyes with happiness that jumped from the photo frame out to Dina, its power implicit and potent with promise. She had no idea how long she stood there, gazing at the photo, wishing that what she saw there would enter her own life, before she realized Michael was behind her. She felt him rather than heard him. When she turned and met his eyes they were sad and hooded, his mouth set in a straight line.

"She's beautiful," Dina said. She had meant to tell him his home was beautiful, but the photo overwhelmed her. The woman seemed to be there with them, and it just erupted from her mouth. She was immediately sorry when she saw his face shut down, his hands shoving into jean pockets. He looked at the floor rather than at her.

"Was," Michael said. "She was beautiful. She passed away."

"I'm so sorry." It seemed little to offer. Not enough to be sorry. The promise in the picture heightened Dina's realization of what the enormity of his loss must be. She wanted him to flash that winning smile again, but he seemed to shrink and deflate before her eyes. "I've dealt with a lot of loss in my life. I'm sorry for yours, and I'm really sorry I opened my mouth."

A silence hung between them for seconds, moments that seemed like an endless vacuum of time with no end.

"Her name was Aleta." Michael paused, a weighty sadness resting upon his face. Then he seemed to shake it off a bit, looking her in the eye. "She loved that little restaurant down the street. So what do you say we go eat, then find you an apartment?"

Dina relaxed in measured time with his change in demeanor. She nodded gratefully, following him out the door. She wondered if the ghost of Aleta trailed behind her or, if she shut the door firmly, they would once again be alone.

CHAPTER 30

S everal hours later, they exited a bus in front of a small pharmacy on Van Brunt Street in Red Hook. The neighborhood must have looked dismal to Michael, but to Dina it was much like the neighborhood at Third & Cherry in Erie, where she had grown up. The water just a few short blocks away, the houses varying from those being improved and on the upswing to those that looked like only the poorest of the poor would set foot inside and even then, only out of desperation. The homes on Maeve's block had been a little nicer, with green grass and some trees, rather than the row houses with iron bars across the doors and windows that faced her now. Still, it was a place where people either started out on their journey or gently fluttered down into oblivion. For Dina, it was the former.

A portly, balding, middle-aged man stood across the street in front of a row house with an "apartment for rent" sign, smoking a cigarette, obviously waiting. Dina crossed the street, Michael in tow.

"Bud?" she said.

"Hey, there," he answered, staring at Michael. "You Dina?"

She nodded.

"I thought you was the only one renting. Youse thinkin' a movin' in here together?"

"No, no." Dina's assurance was rushed. "This is my friend, Michael. He came with me to make sure I found my way."

"Uh-huh." Bud didn't seem convinced, but he pulled a key out of his pocket and opened the door in front of them. "It's upstairs." He started climbing up a dingy stairwell as they followed him. The walls were stained and dull, some of the drywall mildly chipped and gouged. But when they entered the apartment it was clean and freshly painted. The carpet and appliances weren't new, but they could pass for gently used and in good condition.

"Wow, this is nice," Dina said.

Michael was nodding, surprised, although Dina wondered how this could look anything but rundown and awful to him. There was one big room that served as the living room and dining area, with a galley kitchen and a nice-sized walk-in pantry. Off of the living room area was a small hallway with a tiny bathroom to the right and dead-ending at a small bedroom. A tired looking air conditioner hung out of the bedroom window and on the opposite wall was a small closet. It wasn't much, but Dina could afford it.

"There's a small antique store that opened next door, and down the block there are a couple secondhand furniture stores," Bud said. "You might be able to get a few things, unless you're shipping them from home."

"I have a few things to ship from home, but I'll pretty much be starting from scratch." They all stood there in silence, looking around the apartment then looking at one another. "So the rent is $1,000 a month plus utilities?"

"Yep, you fill out an application and pass the credit check and you can put down a deposit plus a month's rent and have it," Bud said. "Your credit comes up bad, I'll charge you first and last month's rent before I give it to you."

Dina nodded.

"So you think you can get that job?"

"Yes." Dina was not at all sure.

"Well, tell you what," Bud said. "I don't have a lot of responsible types like you looking for a place down here yet. The neighborhood is still emerging, if you know what I mean." He looked at Michael when he said this but Michael made no expression or response. "I'll give you the application and I'll hold it for a week. You go on the job interview, fill out the application and, if you get the job, send it to me. If not, call me and I'll decide whether to give it to you on a trial basis until you get employed."

Dina was silent. She wanted to tell him she could waitress to make the rent if she had to, but she was still not sure her physical strength was up to that. "Okay."

Dina felt at loose ends when they left, her mind in a million places. The bus wouldn't be there for another forty-five minutes. She wanted to apologize somehow for Bud's rudeness, for the way he looked at Michael sideways and unsure, but Michael seemed unperturbed by it all.

"Look, Dina," Michael said. "You can see the Statue of Liberty from here. This is a good place to buy property right now."

Dina gazed at the green lady with her lamp held high, the line of Manhattan skyscrapers behind her. Dina felt like part of the poor, huddled masses. Her earlier euphoria was gone and worry had set in as she thought about finding work and paying the rent. They headed down to the waterfront, leaning against two solid, wood pylons to gaze at the famous statue.

"Do you think Crown might hire me on the spot?" Dina looked over at Michael.

"What are you interviewing for?"

"Editorial assistant...with someone named Pam Posey."

"I bet you're a shoe-in, and I'll be taking you out to celebrate by the weekend."

"Why are you so sure?" Dina asked.

"Because I bet she gets a lot of young, immature kids for that type of job and she'll be so glad to see someone responsible and a little older that she'll just grab you before someone else does."

Dina nodded absent-mindedly as they walked back to the area where they would pick up the bus on Van Brunt.

"We've still got some time. Let's grab coffee."

Dina could see Michael pointing to a corner diner. Its sign said "Hope & Anchor," and its name made her smile. Inside, they chose to sit at the counter and sip coffee, in order to keep one eye trained on the front window in case the bus showed up early.

"So what do you do when you're not running into women in Central Park?"

"You mean how do I earn my keep?" Michael laughed. "I'm a business relationship manager. I actually only work a few blocks from Crown Publishing, so if you get the job, maybe we can have lunch?"

Dina laughed. "You're not a loan shark or something shady, are you?"

"No...no...I'm hoping to move to a new role next week, a promotion, but I can't talk about it because it's not a done deal."

"I'm just checking. I've known you for all of three hours now?"

"Four, I think. At least by the time we get back to the city it will be four...and all I know is you're a writer."

He was grinning at her. She could see the bus in the distance over his shoulder.

"I see the bus. We've got to go."

"Are you nervous about your interview?" Michael's comment hit a tender spot in Dina. She was terrified. She needed the job so badly. And she was tired and a little overwhelmed with the newness of everything, including this kind man beside her. Michael did his best to make conversation with her on the ride back but she was distant, lost in thought. Luke came crashing into her consciousness at times like this, when she least expected it, when she was fearful of new things and wishing she were back in the safeness and warmth of his great room. But it hadn't been safe. She had to remember that. It had been anything but safe. Dangerous to her health, to her heart, to her soul. Thirty minutes later, Dina smiled at Michael as the subway approached his stop. She would stay on for a few more minutes to reach her hotel.

"So you promise you'll call me after the job interview?" he said.

"Sure, I promise," Dina said. "Who else would I call? Besides Celine, you're my first friend here."

He stood on the platform waving, muscled arms exiting his loose T-shirt, his hair tied back away from his face in a way that was at once funky, sexy and mellow, then the train rounded the bend and he disappeared altogether.

CHAPTER 31

Pam Posey was a tiny sparrow of a woman, with smooth brown hair touched with random caramel highlights that were about two months old, judging by the inch or so of brown and gray at her part and wiry gray strands sprouting from inopportune spots here and there on her head. Her half-glasses hung from a strand of agate-colored beads and her nails were bitten to the quick. Even as she sat in silence, reviewing Dina's resume and writing samples, some part of her was moving nervously. It was the continuous dance of a tapping foot or a finger twisting a strand of hair, legs crossing and re-crossing as eyelids double blinked and lips pursed and then opened slightly.

Dina waited, trying to appear calm despite the churning fear in her stomach. This woman had the power to dismiss her and, with that, she would have to pack and return to Erie or pick up a waitressing job and pad it with freelance work. None of her other resumes had panned out into interviews. Michael had called her this morning to wish her luck and she'd silently willed his confidence and absolute assurance that she would obtain this job to come through the phone line and fill her body and conscious mind. But it had not. So here she sat like a stone statue, immobile in her effort not to join Pam Posey's nervous twitching which looked like the greatest kind of release she could engage in right now. But she refrained and she waited.

"So your references in Erie checked out, although one said you were out on medical leave for a while," Pam said. "I'm assuming you are okay to come back to work?"

"Yes, I'm just fine," Dina said.

She had promised Celia she would not divulge her illness in case it might damage her chances of employment. Dina was so proud of surviving it all—cancer, Luke, the depression that followed. But ever-cynical Celia said employers would not see it that way. She was a health risk, a possible insurance expense, and they were not allowed to ask her about it so if she didn't share then they could not penalize her.

"Celine thinks very highly of you and your writing abilities," Pam said. "You seem to have done some type of editing or another at each of these jobs as well."

"I am a very detailed-oriented person and a great editor," Dina said. "You won't be sorry if you hire me. I'll work very hard and do a wonderful job for you."

She was trying hard not to plead and beg; it was unbecoming. But she could feel the desperation rising in her voice. She didn't want to go back. She didn't want to see Luke ever again. This was a new life and she couldn't leave it before the adventure of it all had even begun.

"You know, this is an entry-level job, usually for someone much younger than you, and it doesn't pay all that well," Pam said.

"Well, I found a reasonably priced apartment in Brooklyn and as soon as I have a job I can put down the deposit and move in," Dina said. "I've lived on a lot less than the salary listed for this job. I think I'll do so well that you'll want to give me a raise soon." She smiled.

Pam smiled too. Then they both laughed. Dina had never been so forward but she had never wanted something so badly. She longed to dive into the pile of manuscripts on Pam's desk, or perhaps the stack by her feet, and see what other writers were saying, feeling, toiling away to emote on paper, hopeful their words would wend their way into print.

"How much will your rent be?" Pam asked.

"$1,000 a month plus electric. The heat is paid."

Pam pulled a calculator over and punched some numbers in. Dina held her breath.

"Okay, the salary for this job will cover your rent, utilities, subway pass, food, and there will be some left over, but not much," Pam said. "I'm okay with you freelancing to make a little extra, but I really don't want you pulling waitressing shifts to try to get ahead. I need you here mentally and physically one hundred percent and sometimes that will involve longer hours."

"Well, maybe I'll get enough freelance work to pad the paycheck and help me cover expenses," Dina said.

"You really aren't much of a negotiator, are you?" Pam laughed. "You'll have to work on that if you want to move forward here. What I'm trying to say is I'm going to offer you five thousand more than we originally discussed to make sure you can make it. Like I said, I don't care if you freelance but don't let it interfere with this job."

"Yes—I mean, thank you, thank you." Dina exhaled and smiled at the same time.

"So do we have a deal?" Pam asked.

"Yes, we have a deal," Dina answered.

"Okay, be here at eight thirty Monday morning. My assistant will take you to human resources where they'll take care of your benefits and payroll and order a phone and computer for you, and we'll get you going," Pam said. "Dress code is business casual, jeans on Friday only."

Dina wanted to jump up and hug her but instead she stood and extended her hand.

"I look forward to working for you," Dina said. "I guess I'll go get that apartment now. And my local bank in Erie doesn't have an office here. I need to set up a new checking account, transfer the funds and close my old account, buy a subway pass..."

They both laughed again at her rambling.

"See my assistant, Ruth, on the way out and get the name of the banks we have a business relationship with," Pam said. "I think they'll offer you some good deals."

Dina nodded, making a mental list as she shook Pam's hand and headed out of her office toward Ruth's desk. Her right hand pinched her left, hard, to make sure it was all real. She wished she knew where Michael worked and whether it was close by. She wanted to see him. *How odd*, Dina thought, *that I spent all day with him yesterday and I hardly know the guy.*

She walked out into the sunshine and fresh air of Madison Avenue and she felt alive in a way she should have felt when she'd gone into remission. Then, it had been as though she were wading through a pit of quicksand trying to hold her head up, to pull away, to free herself of the sheer emotional weight of it all. Today, she had done that. Luke was gone and there was only the blue sky above, millions of strangers swarming around her, and somewhere, among them, a man named Michael who made her feel good about herself and what her life could be. She pulled out her cell phone and called Celia.

"CeCe? I got a job at Crown Publishing and I found an apartment in Brooklyn."

"Dina, I want to be sad because you're not coming back ever again, are you? But you sound so happy. Something sounds very right. So I'll just miss you."

"Are you letting go, CeCe?" Dina chuckled.

"Never!" Celia laughed. "Well, I have to, don't I? You have to find happiness. And, Dina, I hope that means a guy like Dave, someone who really loves you."

"You know, Celia, I bumped into, literally bumped into, the nicest guy yesterday. His name is Michael." Dina could feel Celia tense up, but rather than back down defensively, she plunged into an animated recounting of how she met Michael. With cars honking and the noises of the city around her, Dina stood on the sidewalk and told Celia her story. When she finished, her sister's voice felt like a smile undulating through the cell phone waves.

"Well, I think you can do it now, Dina, without me. I think you'll be fine. So how about you call me with the new address and I'll ship your stuff? Then maybe, in a few months, Dave and J.D. and I will come for a visit."

"I'd love that, CeCe. As soon as I have an e-mail address at work, I'll send it to you. I think I'll have more to tell you than my little cell phone minutes will allow!"

"I'll be checking every day. We love you, Dina!"

"Hug that baby for me, CeCe! Talk to you soon!"

Dina hung up and looked right and left until she saw the sign for Chase Bank. She had a number of traveler's checks to deposit to get her account open. She dialed Bud's number as she walked toward the sign.

"Yeah?"

"Hey, Bud, it's Dina Benet. Remember, I looked at the apartment yesterday?"

"I remember you, you came by with that brown fella."

"Well, I got a job at Crown Publishing today, Bud, so I'd like to give you a deposit and a month's rent for the apartment."

"I'll be in that building this afternoon fixin' up another apartment. Come on by. I think we can work out giving you the keys without waiting on a long check-in process. You want to move in soon, don't you?"

"Yeah, I'd like to move in soon. And Bud?"

"Yeah?"

"I'll be a good tenant, but you need to be nice to the brown fella as long as I'm paying rent, you hear me?"

"Hmmph...yeah...just get down here with the money."

Dina smiled and hung up, pushing the wide revolving doors of the bank. She stepped into the hushed lobby and realized her face hurt from smiling so much. She hadn't stopped since she left Pam's office. Something new, something good was starting for her. She looked across the lobby and gasped.

Luke was here.

And then he turned around, and it was someone else. The same build, the same gray hair cut short, but it wasn't him.

Dina suddenly felt one ankle mired in the bog she'd run away from. She shook her head as if it were covered with cobwebs and moved forward to a desk where a plump woman continued typing into a computer without looking up at her.

"Could you help me? I want to open a checking account," Dina said.

"Sure, honey, just sit down." The woman kept her eyes on the screen. "I'll be with you in a minute."

It wasn't like home where people knew her name, but maybe the anonymity would help her heal. One day soon, Dina was sure she would not feel as though betrayal and loss were just around the corner. One day she would not care if the ghosts of her past were still trying to haunt her or were gone for good. She swore on Maeve's grave that she would reach that point even if it was a promise that took her many years to accomplish.

"So, what kind of checking account do you need?" The woman was facing her now.

"I have a lot of traveler's checks. I need to use half of them to open the account and then I need a cashier's check for this amount." Dina wrote down the total of the rent and deposit.

The woman began typing in her information. Dina looked around the bank's lobby. The man who looked like Luke was gone. She felt relieved and, when the woman finally smiled at her and handed her papers to sign, Dina smiled back, filled with excitement. For once she was sure she was not making a mistake.

CHAPTER 32

LUKE

It was midnight and the Docksider was smoky and loud, pulsating to the beat of the live rock band, college kids dancing and milling around and bartenders of every age running back and forth trying to keep up with the orders. Luke leaned against the wall at the far end of the bar where its scarred wooden surface curved and then stopped short. Amber was in here somewhere, half-drunk and talking with friends. He'd wanted to leave a half hour ago but she refused, poking fun at him and making remarks about his age that grated on his nerves. Now it was past midnight and he was just tired.

His eyes stung from the smoke and his head throbbed from the bad music. Amber was getting a little too confident and possessive for his taste. He was going to have to do something about her. But he'd taken such a public backlash over her after Celia told anyone who would listen that he'd cheated on Dina during her battle with cancer that he'd even faced private anger from his own family and friends. In childish rebellion, he stuck with Amber, stubbornly insistent that he could do as he pleased.

"Hello, is this seat taken?" An attractive blonde was pointing to the stool next to his.

"No, no, have a seat," Luke answered, moving his feet off the stool's lower rungs and shifting his body to let her in.

She was pretty, in an overdone, celebrity wannabe sort of way. From what he could see, she had a great body.

"You come here often?" Luke asked.

"No, not really." She laughed. "My friends dragged me here. I'm going through a divorce. They thought it was a good idea."

"Do you think it was a good idea?" Luke put her age around mid-thirties.

"Not really," she said. "I'm not too old to have some fun, but I'm too old for this place, and I'm not used to this much smoke."

They sat in silence for a few minutes drinking their beers.

"Stacy...Stacy Sinclair," she yelled over the band.

"Oh, sorry, Luke Daniels," he answered.

"So where do you work, Luke?

"I have a small law practice...I work for myself. How about you?"

"Erie Insurance."

"Really? I know a few people there, not that they like me much."

"Hey, maybe I know them," Stacy said.

"If you do, you won't hear anything good about me." Luke shifted his weight until he was partially sitting and partially standing on the bar stool. "But, okay, her name is Celia...it was Celia Benet before she married Dave. I don't remember his last name."

"Ahh, so you're the evil Luke who dated Dina." Stacy laughed. "Celia's not my favorite person. She's hard on people. But yes, I know her. We work in the same department, although not in the same area."

"So aren't you going to run out the front door now? You want to sit next to the evil Luke?"

Stacy eyed him for a few minutes in silence, drinking her beer. Luke could feel his headache receding as his eyes slid over her tight sweater and jeans. He wondered if she would go out with him. "I think it must have been hard to go through cancer with someone and deal with Celia at the same time. I'm sure you did the best you could, you just weren't in love with Dina."

"I care about Dina a lot. I wish I could talk to her, explain things my way, but she took off to New York City. I have no idea where she is or how she's doing."

"All I know is that she just got a job at Crown Publishing and she found an apartment in Brooklyn," Stacy said. "I think she met a guy too."

Luke could feel anger rising in him. The pounding in his head returned with a vengeance. He had been so sure Dina was too weak, emotionally and physically, to make it in New York. He'd been waiting for someone to tell him she was back in Erie with her tail between her legs because she didn't have the talent or the spine to make it out there on her own. Luke couldn't imagine her loving anyone but him. He knew the hold he had on her. *Let her date another guy.* As soon as she saw him again it would be over. Luke could see Amber making her way through the throng toward him.

"Hey, Stacy, it was nice meeting you," Luke said. "I have a pounding headache from this place so I'm going home. Call me if you'd like to go out some time. I'd like to see you again."

He laid his business card on the bar and slid it toward her. He wanted to get her number too, but there was no time. Amber was too close. He set out for the door, grabbing Amber by the arm and shoving her in front of him so she looked like just another college student walking out ahead of him. Luke hoped Stacy would call. He was ready for someone new and she would keep him informed about Dina, which was a bonus. Even as the thought popped into his mind he questioned why he would want to know, why he would even care. He was better off rid of her. It just irked him, like a case he hadn't closed or a fence he never finished building. He hated unfinished business and Dina owed it to him to come back and straighten out the shambles she'd left his reputation in. He'd been there for her. He'd kept his promise, he told himself. Some people in town wouldn't even do business with him once they found out he'd been seeing Amber while Dina was sick. This little city was his entire world and he needed her to convince people that he was not at fault, that he had done his best, that he never led her to believe he was in love or they would be married. He needed her to come back and prove she was in love with him so he could lay the guilt on her.

It sounded good, even to him, as it played out in his head while Amber babbled away next to him in the car. The scenario helped Luke push down the persistent, annoying twinge of desire to see Dina again, to curl up next to her in front of the fireplace and smell her hair, to feel supremely in charge in the wake of her vulnerability. As he followed Amber into her apartment his cell phone rang. He didn't recognize the number on the caller ID.

"Hello?"

"Hi, Luke, this is Stacy." He realized she must be outside the bar. He couldn't hear the sounds of the band and the crowd.

"Hey, that was fast." He laughed, mouthed to Amber it was business, and walked back into the hallway of the apartment building.

"So, how would you like to take me to dinner tomorrow night? My kids are with their father for two more days."

"I'd love to take you to dinner," Luke said. "E-mail me your address and I'll pick you up around six thirty. Okay?"

"Six thirty sounds good! See you then," she said.

He hung up, smiling, as Amber opened the door, glaring at him. "Who calls about business at one in the morning?" she demanded.

"Someone I saw in the Docksider," Luke replied. "It was too loud in there to talk, so we set up a meeting for tomorrow over dinner."

He really had to let Amber go. It had been a nice, easy thing and he thought that was understood between both of them. She was a great stress reliever, that was all. She'd made him feel young and erased Dina's illness and the guilt he felt about every aspect of that relationship. But ever since Dina left town, Amber was becoming increasingly proprietary and he was becoming progressively bored with her.

Luke walked into her tiny bathroom and opened the medicine cabinet, hunting for aspirin. When he emerged, she was standing there naked, waiting. He rubbed his temples and walked past her to the bedroom, sitting on the edge of the waterbed and removing his shoes and socks. The rocking of the bed as she entered from the other side made him slightly nauseous and he lay back, closing his eyes. He could feel her removing his clothes. Luke knew he should leave and go home. He didn't even want her anymore. He thought about Stacy in her form-fitting sweater and jeans and felt his body responding. Without a word, he moved on top of Amber and began having sex with her, all the while his eyes were closed and he was pretending she was Stacy.

Afterward, he fell asleep almost immediately, his dreams dark and painful, interspersed with Dina, Stacy, and even his ex-wife. He awoke in the wee hours of the morning, dressed silently, and left, knowing he would never return to Amber's apartment again. Getting rid of her wouldn't take much work as nearly everyone in his circle of family and friends wanted her gone. In this, unlike with Dina, he would have an abundance of help and support.

"Ah, Dina," Luke said out loud as the hot water of his shower at home flowed across his back, steaming Amber and the dull ache of a hangover out of each of his pores. "I know where you are now. So, what shall I do with that information?"

CHAPTER 33

DINA

The stack of manuscripts was endless. No matter how many hours she put in or how hard she worked she couldn't reach the bottom before a new wave arrived. Dina had never been busier or happier at any job she'd held in her life. This morning, she arrived at seven o'clock to beat the subway crowds and get a head start on her work, a bagel and a cup of coffee in her hand. It had been hot in the city last night, more Indian summer than cool fall, and her air conditioner seemed to work randomly, if at all. She'd been unable to sleep and, by five o'clock, decided to hop in the shower and leave for her nice, cool office space at the publishing house. Now, the extra time was paying off and she had been able to organize her work from the past two weeks into piles, with those she recommended Pam take a look at stacked and ready to hand over.

Dina checked her watch, wondering where Pam was. It was a quarter after nine. She was usually here by now. Dina walked into Pam's office and her eyes immediately registered what her mind could not absorb—the huge, black clouds of smoke she could see through Pam's office windows. At the same time she heard Ruth gasp from behind her.

Dina stood, frozen with shock, still holding the stack of manuscripts, mesmerized and appalled by what she could see unfolding across town. When she finally turned around, Pam was standing in the doorway, but she was covered with some sort of white film, tears streaking the powder on her face, her body shaking uncontrollably. Ruth moved her toward a chair. Dina dumped the manuscripts unceremoniously on the floor, the spell broken, and lurched toward Pam and Ruth, wanting to help.

"What happened?" Dina asked.

Ruth ignored her, frantically trying to dial for paramedics. But all medical personnel were racing to the burning building. Pam sat frozen, sobbing, the fine white substance covering her.

"Isn't there a nurse here a couple days a week? Maybe she's around," Dina said. "If not, we have to try to get her to a hospital. I think she's in shock."

Ruth managed to reach a friend, a nurse, at a nearby doctor's office. Whatever her friend was saying, it made Ruth begin to cry. All Dina could hear was Ruth's "Oh, my God!" again and again. For what seemed like an endless amount of time after she hung up the phone, Ruth just stood as still and somber as a statue, staring out the window, wiping her eyes, lost in thought.

"Ruth?" Dina called softly to her. "I think we need to clear off the couch over there and get Pam to lie down." Ruth seemed deaf to all sound, unresponsive, so Dina began clearing manuscripts, books and magazines from the tired brown couch at the far end of Pam's office. She moved Pam slowly, helping her lie down. A folded, well-worn afghan hung over the back of the couch, and Dina opened it, sneezing a little from the dust its disuse had accumulated, and lay it across Pam, tucking it around her shoulders.

"Ruth, I'm going to get a wet towel of some sort to clean her up." Ruth turned slightly as if she'd understood. Dina grabbed a small teapot on her way out. She would fill it with water to heat on the hot plate and make tea.

When she returned, Ruth had moved away from the window and pulled a chair next to the couch. She and Pam were talking quietly but stopped when Dina arrived. Dina put the pot of water on the hot plate and turned it on. Then she walked over to Pam and kneeled down next to the couch, wiping the dust from her face and hair with damp paper towels.

"Would someone tell me what happened?"

Pam closed her eyes and sighed. Dina looked Ruth in the eye and waited.

"My friend, the nurse, is on her way over here to check on Pam. She said terrorists flew two jet airliners into the World Trade Center this morning," Ruth said. "Pam was on her way to work and she saw it. There was lots of falling debris and white dust. She was that close..."

Dina jumped up and walked over to the small television on the built-in shelves behind Pam's desk and turned it on. The reporter was speaking in stunned tones, his face alarmed, voice hesitant as he relayed more bad news. Two more planes he said. One flew into the Pentagon, another went down in a field in Pennsylvania. Had the world come to an end, Dina wondered, just as she was starting to revel in her new life? Mankind had simply gone mad while she remained oblivious.

Looking over at Pam and Ruth, slumped and immobile as she took charge, she found herself in a role so foreign to her being that she felt like Alice after she walked through the looking glass to a new world turned backwards and inside out where nothing was as it had been or perhaps as it seemed. The manuscripts from earlier that morning now lay, harbingers of another lifetime, in a quixotic melee across the floor. The water for tea was boiling. Dina turned off the hot plate, dropped tea bags into three sturdy mugs, and poured the steamy water over them.

"Are you okay?"

She heard Michael before she saw him. He didn't look as if he'd arrived from anywhere near the World Trade Center. The newscaster was saying public transportation had stopped and people were walking home, some back over the Brooklyn Bridge, others wondering how to get from Manhattan to their loved ones in New Jersey and elsewhere. Perhaps Michael walked from his office. She knew he worked in business development he had said, for a large company. But he hadn't been more forthcoming and she hadn't asked. They'd known each other such a short time and were only slowly starting to move from friends to dating.

"Oh, Michael." Pam finally sat up. "It's awful out there. Have you heard? Have you seen?"

Dina looked from Pam to Michael and back.

"Are you alright?" Michael gently touched Dina's shoulder, drawing her toward him and hugging her tightly.

"I'm fine," Dina said. "I came in early. How did you get here so quickly?" She stepped back and looked him up and down. "You don't even look as if you've been outside at all."

"Don't be ridiculous, Dina." Pam's voice was laced with annoyance. "Of course he's been outside. He works at Simon & Schuster, not far from here. You knew that. Don't tell me you didn't know I hired you on the spot on his reference?"

Pam lay back down. Dina felt her anger shifting from the atrocity at the World Trade Center to Michael. It was singularly ridiculous of her and yet her anxiety took aim and she could not seem to stop it. "I thought you hired me because I was the best qualified person for the job," Dina said coldly.

She set the mugs of tea carefully on three coasters lined up on the coffee table and left the room, glaring at Michael. She was angry on so many levels for so many things happening now that she could not control. She wanted to spill that anger out on the floor, to scream her denial that terrorists had attacked her country, that innocent people had died and were dying right now, jumping out of windows, unable to make it out of a collapsing building. Michael was standing right in front of her and Dina could feel herself erupting on him, his very accessibility and guilt an easy target.

"You didn't think I could get the job on my own, Michael?" Dina crossed her arms over her chest to somehow contain the stone-cold feeling inside her.

"Of course I did, Dina," he said. "But I selfishly wanted to be sure you stayed in New York." He shifted uneasily from one foot to the other then reached behind him and shut Pam's door. "I'm sorry I didn't tell you." Michael met her stare steadily. "But I wanted you to feel confident. I was sure all you needed was a reference and you could go from there on your own."

"And when were you going to tell me that you worked in publishing, that you knew my boss and probably everyone else I work with?" Dina snapped. "Let me guess...you have some really big title and they think I only got this job because you want to get in my pants? Or, hey, maybe the whole company thinks I slept my way into this job, huh?"

"Dina, stop, no one thinks that...no one but Pam knows that I referred you. It was an omission on my part, a mistake, I'm sorry."

"You know, Michael, I dated a guy named Liam who always called a lie an 'omission.' A lie is a lie is a lie and the person who tells it is a liar. I don't date liars."

"Dina...look, not today. Let it go, would you? Please, I really need you."

His voice and face were so sad. She wanted to feel something but he kept disappearing and all she could see was Luke with his humiliating, endless lying, like Liam before him. She hugged herself tighter within her own crossed arms.

"Leave me alone and let me try to salvage some dignity here."

He just stood there not moving. Then he began taking steps toward her. She knew in some small, tightly closed part of her brain that she was lashing out at the wrong person, lashing out about something that was really nothing instead of grieving for the very real pain and loss she was suffering for things that could not be retrieved or undone. She clutched herself harder and felt a hollow space open like a cavern inside, a place where she could not generate any emotions except this pounding, irrational anger that pervaded everything.

"Forgive me." He was so close she could see his eyes were moist as if with tears.

"Get out," she whispered.

Dina felt ashamed the minute the door closed behind him, but she stood rooted, unable to chase after him, unable to cry until she opened Pam's door and walked to the window just as the North Tower collapsed. Then she cried for the horror before her and all the victims who would not go home tonight, for their families who would never see them again. But she could not cry for herself or for the collapsed and broken parts of her that might never be whole enough to move forward in trust and love with another human being.

"His brother worked in that building, Dina," Pam called from the couch.

"What? Whose brother?"

"Michael's brother."

Pam was upright now, with Ruth next to her, drinking tea as if, somehow, she could relax and the world would relax with her.

"Michael's brother was in...he was in...there?" Dina gestured toward the window where billows of black smoke filled the air above a hole where the Twin Towers had been. Dina felt dizzy, like she had after chemo. She was having trouble breathing now and finally realized she was sobbing so hard she couldn't catch her breath. Ruth was handing her water, rubbing her back.

"I don't know, Dina. All I know is Michael told me once, over lunch, that his brother worked at the World Trade Center. Whether he was there today or not..." Her voice trailed away. "Go ask Michael. His office is on the fourth floor at Simon & Schuster. You've been there before. Now is not the time for petty anger and grudges. Just forgive him and be glad he was in his own building this morning and not across town."

Dina got up, wiping her eyes and steadying herself on the corner of Pam's desk. She was halfway through the door when Pam called to her, softly. "I would have hired you anyway, Dina. I liked your honesty and your enthusiasm. The rest you had enough of and I could teach you what you didn't know."

Dina headed for the elevators. She wanted to run, but she felt shaky. There was a sign in front of the elevators asking people to use the stairs. Dina descended slowly. She was on the second floor, not so far away, but it seemed a long walk. She didn't feel well. All this stress was probably not good for her immune system or her remission. She felt horrified by the people, some frantically running everywhere, some walking dazed, crying, trying to head home or trying to find news on loved ones. Some people were just standing still, staring, shocked and unable to move. Dina headed southwest on Park Avenue as quickly as she could manage, turning right onto East 47th Street and swimming like a salmon upstream through people heading in the opposite direction. She reached 6th Avenue and turned right, scanning the landscape of skyscraping buildings until she saw the one she remembered as home to Simon & Schuster. She had delivered a package there once for Pam, now she hoped she could get in the building and find Michael's office.

She slid through the lobby easily and took the stairs. She felt leaden, her muscles aching when she left the stairwell on the fourth floor. Dina found Michael's office at the far end of the hallway. No one stopped her or stood in her way. People were trying to leave, or simply staring out windows. She was invisible to them. The gold-plated sign said "Michael Mann, Vice President – Business Development." Dina knocked, softly at first, then harder. She turned the knob and the door opened.

"Michael?" She stepped onto the deep maroon carpet. There was no answer. She looked around the office with its dark, cherry-wood desk and leather office chair that perfectly matched the leather couch, chairs, and coffee table in the sitting area across from it. The plants, the books, everything was immaculate, professional, impersonal. Not like the Michael she knew. One lone picture of he and his brother sat on the shelves behind his desk. Even the ghost of Aleta did not invade this almost sterile environment. He was obviously not here.

She felt utterly and deeply exhausted from it all, the emotions, the trauma of what she had seen through Pam's window and, perhaps, the long hours of work so soon after surviving cancer. She sat down on the couch. It was surprisingly forgiving, with an equally soft maroon throw pillow in the corner. Dina did not know what Michael would say or think, but she desperately needed to lie down. The leather smelled new and felt smooth and cool against her cheek. She pulled the small throw pillow under her head. She was thirsty and hungry, but the exhaustion was so deep it was moving over her in waves, drowning everything else. She would rest for a few minutes, just until Michael returned. It was the last thought she remembered.

***

When she awoke, Michael was shaking her and a security guard was standing behind him. Except for the glare of a flashlight focused directly on her, the room was dark and a wall of darkness lay outside the windows where much of the city was without power and enveloped in shadows as well.

"Dina." The flashlight distorted Michael's face. "What are you doing here?"

"I wanted to tell you I'm sorry," Dina mumbled. "I was so exhausted. I just wanted to rest for a minute until you got back." She tried to sit up but she felt heavy, lethargic. Her mouth was so dry it was hard to speak.

"You've been here for eight hours, Dina. No one knew where you were. The security guard found you when he was making his rounds." Michael gently moved her to a sitting position. She clutched his arms and back tightly. She felt dizzy. "We need to get you to a hospital. I think you're dehydrated and something is very wrong."

She could feel him lifting her as if she were a rag doll and she realized she felt incredibly light, as if she'd lost a lot of weight. Perhaps she had. She'd been so absorbed in work and so inattentive to herself.

"You need to take me to Sloane-Kettering," she whispered.

He stopped and stared down at her. She wanted to explain but the words wouldn't come. Then she felt a roar in her ears and she passed out.

CHAPTER 34

Soft dancing streamers of light filtered through sheer curtains to move across the walls and the chocolate-colored, satin bedspread like swirling ribbons from a Maypole dance. Dina moved no muscle in her body except her eyelids, which opened and closed, drinking in her elegant surroundings in minute freeze-frames. There was a creak and a shuffle to her left, then the window and the sunlight disappeared, its framework filled by Michael, his face exhausted, concerned, looking down at her. Still, she could not move.

"Are you alright?" he asked.

Dina blinked, nodded, and then licked her lips. Her mouth was so dry she felt her tongue pushing words to form but she could not roll them out. Michael's hand reached for hers. It looked like coffee with cream on the warm, chocolate bedspread. She tried to smile.

"Water?" Her voice was raspy, harsh amid all this softness.

He disappeared. She closed her eyes. She could hear water running somewhere. When he returned, he held her up while she drank slowly. She was tired and weak, but the deep waves of exhaustion were gone. When she finished drinking, Michael set the glass on the nightstand and eased her back onto the pillow, gently, tenderly.

"Where am I?" Dina asked.

"You're at my house, in my bedroom," Michael answered.

"How did I get here?" She glanced at the window again. "Shouldn't I be at work?"

"Dina, you've been sleeping for over twenty-four hours. I was beginning to worry that you were in a coma."

Dina focused on Michael. He looked ragged, the lines furrowing between his brows, circles forming under his eyes. He pushed up the sleeves on an old sweatshirt then rubbed his temples.

"And how much sleep have you had?" she asked.

He didn't answer. He picked up the glass and left. She could hear water running again. She tried to remember where she had been before she woke up here, but it was fuzzy. She remembered falling asleep in Michael's office and she had some limited recall of him waking her up there. After that, all she could conjure was a deep sense of exhaustion and an all-pervasive need to sleep overwhelming and overtaking her. "I can't remember how I ended up here, Michael," Dina whispered when he returned. "I'm sorry if you were worried. The last thing I remember is waking up on the couch in your office. I went there to tell you how sorry I was...about being selfishly angry...about your brother..."

Michael was quiet for a moment. He turned his face away from her and pulled a coaster out of the nightstand drawer, setting the water glass on it. Then he walked across the room and grabbed a chair, pulling it to the bedside, close to her. Dina thought he looked angry.

"We came here from Sloane-Kettering...after you told me to take you there," he said.

She felt a rolling sensation of nausea in her stomach, followed by panic, fear.

"Am I...am I sick...again?" Her voice was shaky. Her eyes felt moist.

"No, you're not," Michael answered. "The doctor said you are very lucky for someone who has only been in remission for five months, but you were overdoing it and you need to slow down or you will be sick again."

She sighed, closing her eyes and exhaling. "I should call my sister. She's probably worried sick after what happened at the World Trade Center if she hasn't been able to reach me for two days."

"It's okay," he said. "I called her and we had a very nice conversation. She's very angry with you for pushing yourself too hard and she agrees with me that you need to take it easy."

"You can't tell people at your job that you just beat cancer," Dina said. "It's a dog-eat-dog world. They'll think you're the weak link, or the expensive health hazard...that maybe you can't keep up or worse—that you'll fall off the remission wagon and cost the company a lot of money. I wanted to prove myself and keep my job."

"And when were you going to tell me, Dina?" Michael asked.

There was calmness and an edge to his voice. She tried to gauge what he was feeling.

"I've known you for three months, Michael," Dina said. "Cancer isn't exactly an upbeat conversation to launch on a dinner date with a new guy that you really like."

"You knew I loved someone and she died," he said, his voice a low growl.

"Oh, you mean I should have told you right away so you could opt out before you got in too deep...before you really liked me? Wow! I missed that in the survivor's handbook. The part where it says we give you a head's up so, if we relapse, it doesn't blow up your world."

Dina yanked the covers back and tried to sit up. She was still wearing the clothes she'd had on at the office. "Where are my shoes and purse? I'm going home." She stood up and a rush of blood went to her face. The room spun and she leaned into the bed to steady herself.

"Dina, the doctor said you're supposed to rest for several days." Michael rose from the chair, reaching over to help her stand.

"I can rest in my little apartment in Brooklyn. You can have your bed back."

"Dina, don't...don't do this."

She caught herself, remembering that it was he who needed comfort now, not her. Dina put her arms around Michael, steadying herself and pulling him into a hug.

"I'm sorry," Michael said. "In the last two days I lost my brother, I thought I was losing you, I haven't had any sleep...really...please, get back in bed."

Janet Roberts

"No, Michael," she said. "*I'm* sorry. My body and my emotions feel like they are all over the place. I'm so, so sorry about your brother."

Tired and wobbly, she climbed back into bed, sitting upright this time, propped against the pillows and headboard. Everything felt surreal, as though life had frozen in a moment of terror and they were here, she and Michael, caught in the tension and pain and anger of it all.

"Shouldn't you be with your family right now?" Dina asked. "They must be frantic over your brother and need you there with them."

"My father was out looking for my brother...until I called the headquarters of my brother's company and they said no one survived." His voice cracked. "They were on the top floors. It was impossible."

Dina watched this strong, quiet man, struggling to put her needs before the terrible tragedy that enveloped him. "Lay down here with me, Michael, and get some sleep."

Gently, Michael crawled onto the bedspread next to her and kissed her softly. Dina wrapped her arms around him and pulled his head into her lap. He began to cry, softly, as she stroked his hair and face. Eventually, he fell asleep, rolling onto his side away from her. She curled up behind him, fitting her small frame into his back, and put her arm across his chest. It felt incredibly good to give back, to nurture someone. But this time it was different. She was giving and receiving. They were breathing in cadence, as one, and just before Dina fell back asleep she had a quiet, profound sense of coming home after a long journey.

She dreamed the familiar old dream again. She was lost in a dark forest. But this time the trees were lush and green. When she shivered it was

267

because the enormous pools of shade they created were cold. Despite the beauty around her, she felt fear. Something was still hunting her and she could hear it coming. She began running, looking for a way out. Up ahead she saw a sliver of light and the ground beneath her turned to green grass. The faster she ran, the closer the light of the sun came, but whoever was chasing her was still there and they were not deterred by the goodness of the light or the depth of the cool, green grass. She sensed her pursuer was close by. Then she heard a loud creaking sound and she turned to look back.

He was outlined in the shadows and she was about to call to him, to confront him and tell him there was no place for him in the light, but she woke up.

It was dark outside. She could see a figure in a rocking chair near the window that creaked each time it moved. It was a woman partially outlined by the streetlamp that poured yellowish light in through the sheer curtains, but her features remained darkened. Dina sat up, curious. She slid her arm quickly to her right to wake Michael, but he was no longer there.

"Hello?" she called out softly.

The woman rose slowly. She looked solid, slightly heavyset. She moved carefully until she reached the bedside lamp and turned it on. Dina looked up into a world-weary face nearly identical to Michael's, her kinky hair still pitch-black and pulled into a bun with one shocking, artistically arranged streak of white hair. She went back to the window and pulled the chair closer to the bed.

"How are you feeling?" The voice was melodic, soothing; it could sing her hymns and rock her to sleep.

"I feel a lot better," Dina said. "I have no sense of time or days though."

"It's Friday night, and I'm Michael's mother, by the way. Sophia Mann."

"I've been asleep off and on for three days? And you had to sit here with me when you just lost your other son?" Dina was shocked. "I'm so sorry."

Sophia Mann seemed to hum a bit, almost as if she were alone in the room, the notes chiming bell-like up and down as she did so, the sound more prayer than song. Her ample frame rocked and moved a little as if with the beat of a softly strumming guitar. Dina wasn't sure if she was responding or grieving aloud.

"Mrs. Mann?"

"Sophia, please. Yes, it's so terrible. But Michael is my only child," she said. "He's beside himself with grief and trying to hide it. I feel awful for him, but it was his half-brother who died. Michael's father and I have been divorced for many years."

"Where is Michael?" Dina asked.

"He's with his father and his aunts. They are trying to sort out the arrangements for his brother, but he'll be back soon. Are you hungry?"

The digital clock on the dresser across the room glowed ten o'clock. "I'm not sure how long it's been since I ate anything. I would love to take a shower first but, unfortunately, I don't have a change of clothes with me."

"Oh, don't worry, baby." Sophia smiled. "Michael sent me out to get you a few things." She reached around the chair toward the floor at the end of the bed and produced several bags, extracting underwear, socks, jeans, a warm-up suit, a couple T-shirts, and what looked like rugby shirts in the half-light. From a second bag she pulled out deodorant, shampoo and conditioner, and lotions. "Sorry, honey, I didn't know your bra size." Sophia chuckled.

"That's okay, this is enough...more than enough." Dina felt as though she might cry. "I don't know how to thank you and Michael for taking such good care of me...a stranger."

"Well, now, Dina, you make Michael very happy and I have a feeling you and I will not be strangers for long," Sophia said. "Let's get you up and into the bathroom. Then, if you can handle it from there, I'll go downstairs and make us some food."

Sophia's big, meaty arm slipped around Dina's waist and helped her stand up. Dina felt better this time, less shaky and not at all dizzy. Sophia had scooped the clothing and toiletries back into a bag and carried it in one hand, the other holding onto Dina as they walked to the bathroom. Sophia smelled like lilacs, comforting and stable like Maeve, but softer, fleshier, and exuding some sort of soulful mirth that was contagious. Dina wanted to stay connected to her but the shower beckoned.

Sophia had started the water and Dina could see the blessed steam rising over the plexi-glass doors. She began peeling the clothing away from her thin frame. Everything was loose and practically slid off with barely a tug or a push, even the underwear. She wondered how much weight she'd lost over the past few months. She stepped into the shower, the power of the water nearly knocking her off balance and inhaled the steam and moisture. She loved Michael's world. It made her feel so safe.

Twenty minutes later she sat at his kitchen table as Sophia moved agilely between two pans, one with a huge omelet bubbling and browning and another with bacon and potatoes frying away in it. Toast popped up to be buttered and the aroma was so exquisite as to be nearly painful. Dina sipped orange juice slowly so as not to pass out from hunger as she waited. She'd found her purse in Michael's room after leaving the shower and combed her short hair back off her face in a sixties-greaser style. Then she'd dropped her cell phone in the pocket of the warm-up suit she'd chosen to wear and followed the incredible smells coming from the kitchen until she was downstairs and sitting like a five-year-old on Christmas morning waiting for Sophia's meal.

Dina devoured everything on her plate and Sophia joined her with a heaping plate of her own. For the last fifteen minutes, they drank coffee and chatted companionably as if they'd known each other for years. Sophia invoked the oddest sensation in Dina. Every time she laughed or even just smiled, something unlocked deep within Dina and she wanted to hug the older woman. Instead, she smiled back and felt the wonder of relaxation and easy friendship.

Sophia wanted to know all about Dina but she was careful, leaving out Luke and skimming over her days in Ireland. She would tell Michael the whole truth, but she was not ready to share much with others yet. She would, she knew, just give it to him, lay the story of her life at his feet and see how he handled it, see whether he would stay or go. But only if he was ready. That, on top of the situation with his brother, might be too much right now.

It was close to midnight when he returned, the circles under his eyes belying his assertion that he was fine. He poured himself a cup of coffee and set it down on the table. Walking behind Sophia, he began rubbing his mother's neck. She closed her eyes, her face a seamless tableau of gratitude and relaxation.

"Did you get any sleep at your father's house?"

"I grabbed a little sleep in between all the commotion."

"Are you hungry, Michael?"

"No, I'm fine, Mom. You must be pretty tired. The extra bedroom is ready and waiting for you."

It was a cue, Dina knew, to leave them alone, and Sophia responded as graciously as she had with everything else that evening. Kissing Dina on the top of her head, Sophia stretched and issued a rather overdramatized yawn, then headed through the doorway with a wave, a smile, and not a word to either of them.

Michael pulled his chair close to Dina's, sliding his coffee cup along with him. He touched her hair, almost dry but still with some damp patches, and smiled. For the first time in a very long time, before illness and chemo and betrayal, before the struggle to survive on every level she knew of had taken over her life, Dina felt herself wanting a man. Not just any man; she wanted Michael right then and there. To take him upstairs, make love to him and forget all about the last three days, the last three years. Maybe she'd just forget about the fragility of her life up to this point and feel whole. Time would tell after she told him all about the parts of her own life she wanted to sweep under the rug right now. If he didn't kick her out or run away, then they would see what the future held.

"So, let's talk about us and whatever happened to you that brought us to this place," Michael said.

"Are you sure you want to talk about us...about me and my past...right now? You've had enough stress over the past few days to last a lifetime I would think."

"For some reason, maybe because I've been catching sleep at crazy hours or maybe because I'm drinking coffee at midnight, I'm wide awake. I want to clear things up with us. I can't clear up the situation with my brother. Not now."

"But you think you can clear up the situation with me?" Dina sighed. She wanted to savor the feelings of desire mixed with her sated belly and the freshness of soap, shampoo, and lotion that still oozed from her body for a little while longer. "So where do you want me to start?"

"Usually, the best place to start is at the beginning."

"Hmm. I'm still a work in progress. I wonder what constitutes the beginning," Dina joked.

He smiled without laughing and waited. He would let her decide what constituted the beginning and how much she would tell. Michael shared his mother's patience and kindness, although his was imbued with far more intensity, and sexually charged to boot.

"Well, Michael, all stories good and bad begin with 'once upon a time,'" Dina said. "Usually I only tell this particular story if I'm drinking something stronger than coffee, but here is how it goes."

Then Dina poured it all out. She told him about her mother's death, about Maeve raising she and Celia, about Liam and Ireland. When she got to the part about Katie, her long-lost baby, she stopped. Dina had never told anyone about Katie, not even Celia. It was so painful and yet, he was still there, in front of her, listening, rubbing her shoulder and holding her hand. So she told him about Katie, afraid to look him in the eye, wondering what this kind, wonderful man would think of a woman who gave her child away. When she finished, she hung her head.

"If you want leave now, I'll understand," Dina said. "I can't imagine what you think of me."

Michael moved his chair as close to hers as possible. Then she felt his arms wrap around her as he pulled her head to his shoulder.

"I think you're incredibly brave and strong. That must have been a very difficult thing to do," he said. "One of the most difficult imaginable."

Dina wanted to cry but she knew if she let go she would not finish the story she had begun to tell and now she wanted it all out, every last dark and damaging detail.

"There's more, Michael."

"I'm still here."

She lifted her head from his shoulder and, looking him in the eye, Dina explained how, after giving up Katie, she'd returned home but was barely able to put together a decent job or stable life. She told him about Luke and Josh, the cancer, and finally discovering him with Amber. She smiled when she described the houseboat where Luke could not find her and her recovery in that beautiful, peaceful place.

"I found my writing again on that houseboat," Dina said.

"So, medically, you were still recovering when you showed up in New York," Michael said. "I'm glad you showed up, but you really should have been taking it easy for another three or four months, don't you think?"

"Yes, but I needed to get out of Erie," Dina said. "I never want to see Luke again. I want a new life. When Pam gave me a chance I was determined to prove myself and make it work."

"So you told no one about your condition except the docs at Sloane-Kettering and you worked way too hard and way too many hours for a person in early remission," Michael said. "And you just about relapsed."

Dina stared at him for several seconds. "Didn't you hear anything I said?" she whispered. "Isn't this the part where you realize that if you stay you are saddled with a woman who could relapse at any time, who has more baggage than anyone you've ever met, and who may not be able to emotionally commit in a sustainable way...ever?"

"That's not really how I see you."

"I've never succeeded at anything and with this illness...well, it's unlikely I'll ever be able to have children again. I may or may not stay in remission. It's not fair to you."

"Oh, I think you are exactly what I deserve. You're a strong, self-aware survivor, who also happens to be a beautiful, independent woman. I'm not going anywhere...unless, of course, you're kicking me out of my own house." He smirked.

"I don't think you know what you're in for."

"Oh, I think I know exactly what I'm in for, and I can't wait."

He scooped her up in his arms and headed for the stairs. Dina pulled his head down toward her and began kissing him, slowly and tenderly at first, but by the time they had reached his bedroom door she was out of his arms and they were both nearly naked. Sophia found a closed door with a pile of clothing outside the next morning and she smiled. She could go home now. Michael would be fine.

CHAPTER 35

CELIA

C elia watched the steady streams of traffic and people moving outside through the gently falling snow as J.D. lay in her arms vigorously drinking juice from a small plastic bottle. There were so many people here. It was overwhelming to her, but she could see why Dina felt safe in the anonymity of it all. No one would ever find her if they didn't know where to look, especially in that rundown dump in Red Hook. Celia couldn't understand why her sister didn't just move in with Michael. Finally, she'd found someone really great and Celia was worried Dina would ruin it all. But Dina did not seem worried. In fact she seemed supremely self-confident and happy in a way Celia had never seen before. Dina said she wouldn't move in without a commitment from Michael. She wanted to be sure. She wanted no more tragedy and hurt in her life.

Celia, Dave, and the baby were staying with Michael. There was no room at Dina's apartment and even Dina conceded that it wasn't the best place for J.D. Since her sister never seemed to want to come back to Erie, Celia had suggested they come to New York for Christmas and Dina was thrilled. She'd called back an hour later to tell Celia not to book a hotel because Michael would put them up in his townhouse. They'd arrived two days ago and all her fears about Michael, all her fears for Dina, had disappeared. Then she'd met Sophia and for the first time Celia felt she could relax, she could let go and let Dina be. These people loved her and they would take care of her. It was as if a lifetime of heaviness now lifted. She had never known it was a burden until it no longer existed and she could finally breathe without worry.

"Dina... Dave and I lived together for a long time before we got married," Celia had told Dina earlier that day as they sat in the kitchen talking, Celia feeding J.D. "Your arguments about why you won't move in with Michael are a load of crap. You're still thinking about Luke, harboring some issues with him, and you're putting up walls."

"I don't love Luke, anymore," Dina said. "I love Michael."

"That's not what I said. I didn't say you loved Luke, I said you still have issues where he is concerned."

"I'll always have issues where he is concerned. That's why I'm being careful this time. Isn't that what you always told me to do?"

"I said be careful who you pick," Celia retorted. "You picked a good one this time, so don't lose him by hedging and shutting him out. Luke was a bad pick from the get-go. You should have seen him one more time, had it out, made closure. Not that I ever wanted you to speak to him again, but you were in pain and you ran off before you were healthy enough or ready. And you ran off to get away from him, not to come here."

"So what if I did?" Dina said. "I ran right into the arms of a wonderful man."

"Without resolving all your issues with Luke."

"What do you want me to do, CeCe? Go back to Erie and confront Luke?"

"No, it's too late for that. I want you to let it go and give in to this new life one hundred percent, no holds barred. Luke will dissolve after that. In time, he'll just fade away."

"It's a fine line between love and hate. One or the other has always been on fire inside of me when I think of Luke." J.D. had finished eating. Dina reached her arms out to him. The baby gurgled with delight as Dina lifted him up and held him close to her.

"Dina, you never listen to me but I'm going to give you some advice anyway," Celia said. "You never loved Luke, you just wanted him to love you so badly that a stubborn part of you hates that you lost that battle and wants satisfaction of some sort. If you want that satisfaction, that resolution, if you keep wanting to see him hurt as much as he hurt you, you'll wake up with nothing. Michael is not stupid you know."

"I went through so much with Luke, with the cancer and all," Dina said. "And then he betrayed me, broke his promises, ruined what could have been."

"Don't you understand, Dina? It never could have been. And maybe he tried to keep his promises, but he's weak. In the end you went through that cancer on your own while he moved his life in a different direction without you." Celia stood up and began moving around the kitchen, putting a kettle on to boil then dropping a tea bag into a mug and rinsing J.D.'s dishes in the sink.

"Is he still seeing her? That Amber person?"

"Yes, I think he is, pretty openly too. I've seen them once and Dave has seen them out a couple times when he's stopped for beers with the guys."

Celia could see Dina struggling with the pain of rejection. Then Michael had arrived, and he and Dina left to pick up dinner for all of them. Now Celia sat in a chair by the front window, watching happy strangers walk by laughing and smiling, and wondered if perhaps Dina was not ready for a permanent relationship with Michael, or anyone else for that matter. It was Christmas Eve and she was no longer worried about Michael's intentions. She knew, because Michael had confided in Dave and then asked for her blessing, that later that night he was taking Dina for a carriage ride in Central Park and he was going to ask her to marry him. It was a perfect, beautiful night for it, with light, powdery flakes that gave the ethereal effect of living in a snow globe and the expectation that people might burst into Christmas carols and song at any moment. She wanted Dina to say yes and move forward. She wanted her to leave Luke behind for good. So she had given Michael her blessing and hugged him, wishing him luck and welcoming him into what there was of their little family.

Celia could hear them coming in through the front door now, stomping off snow, laughing and kissing and juggling plastic bags filled with white Styrofoam containers that were emitting wonderful smells. She looked at Dina's face. It was shining, glistening, as melted flakes dotted her cheeks and brow, sporting a wide smile. She was happier than Celia had ever seen her. This man was the right thing for her and even if Dina did not go into this relationship with a clean slate, it would all work out for the best in the end. Celia would make sure of that. She'd hated to hurt Dina earlier, but she hoped it was the nudge Dina needed to launch forward.

"I know Dina and commitment," she'd told Dave earlier. "If she marries him she will not turn back unless he does something awful and I'm as sure as I can be that he's the kind of guy who will love her and only her."

"He's a good guy," Dave acknowledged, "but I don't think Dina is ready. She's still raw in many ways. She left without letting all that anger out and someday, it's going to have to come out."

"No, I don't think so," Celia said. "Dina told Michael everything, about Luke and the cancer...all of it. We know Luke will never contact her again. Hell, he'll probably never think of her again. So if he doesn't contact her, she'll just go forward into what I think will be a happy life."

"She deserves to be as happy as we are." Dave wrapped little J.D. and his wife in a hug, the baby giggling in the middle of his parents.

"Yes, she does, and she will be."

"I don't think she's heard the last of him though."

"Luke? Why do you say that?" Celia's voice was sharp, her brows furrowed.

"Because a guy like that...she didn't leave on his terms, he didn't get to break if off or get the last word," Dave answered. "That will eat at him. One day he'll want to prove to himself that she still wants him, even if he dumps her immediately afterward. It's who he is. And his reputation took a beating after you told the world what he did to Dina."

"He got what he deserved," Celia had said confidently. "I have no regrets."

She followed the smells of the carry-out into the kitchen. Dina and Sophia were unpacking the food and putting it on plates, giving it a quick warm-up in the microwave. Dave was uncorking a bottle of wine and Michael was reaching for J.D. Celia handed him over gladly. He was fighting sleep and fussy. Ten minutes later, his head on Michael's shoulder and his chubby fist wrapped around Michael's fuzzy locks, and he was sound asleep. Michael took J.D. upstairs and put him in the crib he'd borrowed from neighbors whose children outgrew it several years earlier, returning with the baby monitor to find them all eating.

"Sorry, honey, we're starved," Dina said.

They all laughed and he with them as he shrugged amiably and sat down. Celia felt warm from the wine and the strange sensation of belonging with these people in this room at this moment in her life. Sometimes she felt this way with Dave's family and other times she did not. It was a feeling she and Dina had only known in spurts—when Maeve was alive. She could sense everything changing for the better and she smiled. If only she could control this moment, keeping all of them frozen in this space and time.

CHAPTER 36

DINA

It was dusk and big, white flakes shimmered in the muted glow of the streetlights as Dina and Michael slid into the back seat of a cab waiting in front of his house. Celia stood at the window waving good-bye. The scene felt dreamlike, odd, much as it had felt all week with all of them piled in Michael's townhouse as if they'd been a family for years, as if it was her home as well as Michael's. She'd gone back to her apartment one night and felt so lonely in what had once been her refuge, her place to think and write, that she'd packed enough clothing for a week and just stayed with the rest of them.

Michael took the week off but Dina didn't have that much vacation time. So each morning she left for work while the rest of the group spent the day together, seeing the city or just staying in and decorating for Christmas. She had never seen Celia so relaxed or so warm and accepting of someone as she was of Michael. For this odd and isolated week they were all living like one big happy family, but Dina had no experience with this and she couldn't determine whether she loved it or it scared her to death. It was what she had wanted so desperately with Luke, what she had watched Luke share with his parents, sisters, and his son while she hovered just outside the circle, longing to be invited in. Now she was inside a family circle with Michael, Sophia, Celia, Dave, and J.D., and angry. Angry with herself that any thought of Luke would surface to torment these moments with the memory of the painful, angry longing she had experienced then.

"Central Park," Michael said to the cab driver.

"Oh, I bet it's beautiful tonight," Dina said. "Don't you think it'll be packed with people on Christmas Eve?"

"It's alright, they know we're coming." Michael smiled.

He's smiling but he's nervous, Dina thought, watching him shift in his seat and tug at his coat, putting his gloved hand in his pocket and pulling it back out repeatedly. She'd come to know him so well in such a short time. He had this open, genuine, welcoming quality. She must have liked the challenge of taming a wayward guy with Luke. None of those stresses existed with Michael and, to top it off, he was amazingly hot. Everywhere they went, women were looking at him and Dina often wondered how and why he had chosen her. She knew this was something special, something wonderful, and she wished on every star tonight to let her fear move aside so that Michael's goodness would be all that remained. Yet something gnawed at her, some twinge of pain and doubt, unfinished business that her mind told her was best left undone and her heart longed to put to rest.

They hopped out of the cab at the entrance to Strawberry Fields and walked forward. A carriage with a beautiful black horse sat up on the main path. Snow shimmered on the horse's back and a green garland with red bows decorated the sides of the carriage. Dina watched as Michael spoke to the driver, then handed him some money.

"Dina?" Michael held his hand out.

"Are we taking a carriage ride? Is this my Christmas surprise?" Dina felt tingly with excitement, as if she were a small child on Christmas morning. She had often watched couples in these carriages and longed to take a ride. Now, on Christmas Eve, with the blanket over their knees, a little flurry of white falling around them and on them, she held Michael's hand and shivered with happiness. "It's like we're in a snow globe, don't you think? Or on the front of a Christmas card?"

There were people everywhere, but it felt as if they were alone, just the two of them, moving slowly through such breathtaking beauty. She wanted to inhale the full experience silently.

"Dina?"

"I'm sorry, it's just so wonderful I didn't want to talk, just to enjoy it."

"In silence? You don't want me to talk?" He seemed disappointed.

"No, no, we can talk. Just that first moment, I wanted to breathe it in...to appreciate it fully."

He nodded, distracted, one hand holding hers on the blanket, the other in his right pocket. It was so peaceful. She felt such a deep healing in this moment, in this place, with this man.

"I love you, Dina," Michael said.

She looked at him for a long moment. It was torturous for him, she knew, that she had never uttered those words. She felt them, often, but she blocked and tackled them as quickly as they surfaced. Now Dina wondered what her life would be like without Michael, because how she answered now might determine that. She believed she was not ready for him but she did not want to let him go, to live without him. She loved him and he was way ahead of her in time and space, in need and readiness.

"I love you too, Michael," Dina said.

He wrapped his arms around her in a bear hug and she knew it was decided, ready or not. When he released her, a small box was in his right hand. She had that unreal feeling again, as though she were somehow watching from afar, not part of this experience that was determining the course of her life. Dina opened the box slowly, knowing she would see the sparkle of the diamond against the blanket and the snow, lighting up the peaceful surroundings, demanding in its own right an answer of her.

"Will you marry me, Dina Benet?" Michael asked.

Dina heard the word "yes" echoing down a long tunnel, reverberating through her as Michael put the ring on her finger and began kissing her. She closed her eyes and hoped she had done the right thing. She loved this man. She wanted this peace and security. She could not lose him. She would banish Luke to the farthest reaches of her mind where she had once put Liam and eventually, as the years went by, he would disappear altogether. Dina was sure of it.

When they returned to Michael's townhouse, Celia grabbed her left hand, took one look, and wrapped her in a hug. Dina felt herself passed from Celia to Sophia to Dave and back, finally landing with J.D., awakened by all the happy, congratulatory noise, in her arms. She closed her eyes and willed herself to believe.

"So you'll be getting married in St. Patrick's...in Erie, right?" Celia said.

"No, I'm not going back there," Dina shot back. There was silence. Everyone stared at her. She looked down at J.D. "CeCe, can we work this out later? I just got engaged. Who cares where I get married?"

"It's tradition, Dina. Granny was married there and so were Dave and I."

"Well, yours seems to have turned out well and we all know how Granny's turned out," Dina said. "That's 50-50 odds that tradition may or may not be in my favor. Maybe I'll just find a place to get married here."

"I say Dina and I talk about it later, and we'll let all of you know what we decide," Michael said.

Dina smiled at him, grateful. He could handle Celia's persistent need to control everything without offending her. Dina relaxed, walking into the living room with J.D., cooing and talking to him, leaving them all behind to think what they would. She wasn't ready to plan a wedding yet, especially not one that would send her back to the very place where so many of her demons lay waiting.

CHAPTER 37

Dina sat on what she had come to think of as her bench in Central Park, the one on which she'd been seated when she first met Michael and to which she gravitated instinctively when she wanted to think. She looked at the green buds gracing the stark, barren trees overhead, some flowers emerging from the ground here and there. It was late March and still cold, but the crisp air felt good today as it mingled with the noon sunshine. She was supposed to be writing, but she'd struggled for hours to maintain her focus without success.

She and Michael had attended a candlelight service for his brother last night at a small church in Harlem where his father lived and Michael's deep sorrow still resonated with her. It had taken all this time to have a service because Michael had waited for some shred of his brother to bury, but it seemed there would be nothing. Every physical part of him, every cell, every fragment, had vanished in a moment. So Michael finally agreed they all needed closure and a service would help put the tragedy to rest for his father's family.

Even though Dina and Michael had helped with fundraising for survivors, it hadn't hit home for her the way the service for his brother did. Michael asked her to move in with him as soon as they were engaged, but she'd balked, insisting she would move in after they were married. It didn't make sense to him and it made perfect sense to Dina. She wanted that last stretch of time alone and single. But when she saw how much Michael missed his brother, how sad and alone he felt at times, she'd agreed to move in next weekend. Her lease was almost up and her landlord had another tenant who was interested in the place. So she sat here now, wanting to write about Michael's sorrow, about her need to be alone and yet to be with him as well, about moving forward with her life. The feelings were all there, rambling around inside of her, but the words would not come.

Over the past six months her writing had grown deeper and more profound. She'd been publishing short stories and poems here and there, in small literary magazines, with Michael rather persistently urging her to put a collection together for publication.

Dina wasn't sure why she always felt excited yet fearful about her writing and not quite ready to turn it into a larger project. She should jump at each new chance and become a mountain of frenzied energy instead of a big lump of dreamy, motionless contemplation. She looked from the blank page up to the buds on the massive oak tree above her. Soon, soft, new green leaves would emerge. Soon she would marry Michael in St. Patrick's Church in Erie, in June, because she had finally relented and let Celia take over. Her only request was that the wedding be small, private, and in the evening, and that no notice be published in the paper. Celia was tackling the project with zest, especially enjoying keeping it a secret of sorts. Dina was afraid she would see actual bodyguards there, but so far it sounded like Dave's friends would watch the door.

There were few real secrets in a community like Erie where people grew up and stayed for life, where the warmth of the small town mingled with some of the attributes of a larger city. For a moment she missed the beach, the vast waters of Lake Erie, the rocking, womblike security of the houseboat. She wanted to get married on the beach, but Celia wouldn't hear of it, as though only a church could seal Dina and Michael together in some sort of eternal permanence.

"Don't you think it's a little egotistical of you to think Luke would even care or show up?" Celia had asked.

"I know him better than you do, Celia," Dina said.

"That's debatable," Celia snorted. "I know his kind."

"Is he still seeing Amber?" Dina asked.

"I don't know why you care, but no, he is not. My sources say he's not seeing anyone."

"Not a chance. He never goes without. There is someone and she, whoever she is, came into the picture before he let Amber go."

"Well, you shouldn't even be thinking about that anymore. Did you find a dress?"

Dina laughed to herself now as she tapped the blank page with her pen again. An elderly couple sat down on the bench across the pathway from her. They were holding hands and she smiled and waved, hoping this was what she and Michael would look like one day.

Celia sent her a list of chores for the wedding each week and she complied. Getting engaged to Michael had moved some part of her forward and she couldn't imagine not having him in her life now. Luke's life held some morbid fascination for her but no pain, no hurt, nothing more. It was a relief. Perhaps another year and even that would dissipate in the mists of her past. Everything was packed to move to Michael's house, and in a small box shoved back in the shadowed recesses of her closet she'd found her journals from Ireland and begun reading them. Tonight she would finish them, even if she stayed up all night to do it.

Dina found it hard to imagine she'd had the feelings for Liam she'd written about, and she'd laughed when she skimmed through the first journal. Hard to imagine she'd ever felt that way about anyone but Michael. She needed to be completely alone to read the journal about Katie. It would be like a rite of passage that finally, all these years later, she was somehow getting it right in this life of hers. But the cost she had paid for the ticket to take the journey to this moment, this marriage, had been high.

Dina uncapped her pen and wrote "moving forward" on the page. It was coming to her now. She wrote "the line of demarcation" below it. She looked at the two lines. Michael was that line of demarcation: the line that separated her from her past and her future. Dina knew what she wanted to write about now. She wanted to help others put their mistakes and all the pain associated with them on the other side of that line, creating a fog where they could neither see nor experience them anymore. She wanted to help others move forward. The words were clamoring for release now, flooding her consciousness. She jumped up and began running, looking for the first warm coffee shop where she could work, dialing Pam's number as she went. Dina knew she would not return to the office. Pent up emotions were rolling forth the words she so passionately needed to set free and she could not wait another day to bring it all together on paper.

***

"Could you check out my scribbles?" Dina asked, handing Pam a thin manuscript.

"Your scribbles?" Pam reached out for the document.

"Remember when I called in about a month ago and said I couldn't come back after lunch? Well, this is the result. It's been worked over a little since I scribbled it out onto paper, but it's still rough. I call it my scribbles."

Pam laughed, flipping through the pages quickly at first, and then slowing down. "It looks like your scribbles have a name—'Moving Forward.' You know I usually only handle novels and large works of fiction, Dina."

"I know, I know," Dina said hurriedly. "I'm not *asking* you for anything, I just want your opinion and feedback."

"Hmm, alright then, give me a couple days." Pam dropped the manuscript into her briefcase as she spoke.

Dina headed back to her desk with a lightness in her toes that tingled up through her legs and spine, filling all of her. Anything Pam put in her briefcase was there because she intended to take it home and read it. Everything else went into a huge stack on her desk where it might take weeks or months before anyone looked at it unless a persistent agent or some gentle prodding from Dina moved it from stack to briefcase at a faster pace.

That happy feeling was long gone two weeks later and Dina was alternately depressed and irritable because Pam seemed to have forgotten her manuscript. They worked side by side and she made no mention of it, no word as to whether she thought Dina had done well or whether it was publishable. Dina feared the worst, that Pam had hated it and didn't know how to tell her. Yet, Pam didn't seem to be avoiding her at all or to be in any way uncomfortable. She wanted to march in and ask her, but Pam had been on one conference call after another with the door shut all morning. Dina sighed and bent over a particularly difficult novel she was trying to edit.

"What's wrong with you, Dina?" Pam seemed to appear next to her desk magically, arms folded across her chest, crazy-colored cat-eye glasses hanging from their multi-colored chain to rest on her forearms. "You've been in a bad mood for two days and, frankly, it's ruining my week and everyone else's around here. So out with it...what's wrong?"

"Did you read my manuscript?" Dina blurted out. "I've been waiting to hear from you and not a word for weeks...no feedback, no opinion."

"Well, yes, not only did I read it," Pam said. "But I sent it over to a friend at *The New Yorker*. He called yesterday. They love it and want to publish one of the poems and talk to you about a few of the stories. I was planning on telling you as soon as I had a free moment."

"Pam! That was a rough draft!" Dina didn't know whether her voice had risen to a rather loud decibel out of fear and anger or astonishment that they wanted to publish her work. "It wasn't ready yet!"

"Well, obviously I thought it was ready and my friend at *The New Yorker* thinks it's pretty close to ready," Pam said. "So, that leaves only you with the problem of whether it is ready or not." Pam disappeared into her office and returned with a slip of paper, which she dropped on Dina's desk. "Here's his name and number. Call him and please, go see him today and come back in a better mood."

"Pam, some of that stuff was personal and, well, Michael hasn't seen it yet." Dina fingered the slip of paper tentatively.

"He should see it, Dina. It is deep and intense and moving. That's what happens when you write from your soul. Don't ever be ashamed of taking what you know and using it in fiction to deepen the story. That's what a really good storyteller does and you, my dear, are a very good storyteller."

"Thanks, Pam." Dina could feel her eyes welling up with tears. "Thank you so much."

"My pleasure," Pam said, walking back to her office. "Oh, and Dina? Drop the silly leprechauns, fairies, and Irish folklore from the last story. Where did you get that stuff?"

Dina smiled a secretive smile with no answer. The leprechauns could go but never the fairies of Maeve O'Malley's lore. They were the metaphor that wove her lifeline back to a time when she first knew love and security, could travel with fairies on the backs of fireflies, and snuggled under a quilt with her sister while the wind howled with the voices of a million banshees.

CHAPTER 38

CELIA

Candles flickered everywhere in St. Patrick's. Their muted light touched the life-size statues, highlighting each station of the cross, and skimmed lightly over the stained glass windows and polished wood pews. Celia handed J.D., well-fed and fast asleep, to Sophia. There were only a handful of people there, mainly Michael's friends and cousins from New York and Celia and Dave's friends from Erie Insurance. Dina had invited Kathleen to come from Ireland as well as a few of her students and the women she'd taught with at the community college in Erie, but only the students were in the church waiting for the service to begin. Kathleen sent a lovely gift and card, but she had two little children now and it was a long trip to make.

Celia made her way back toward the bride's room where she herself had stood only a few short years before. What incredible changes had come and gone during that time. She and Dina would walk down the aisle together again, Celia holding her sister's hand and then passing her over to Michael. It had been Dina's idea, surprising her, but it seemed fitting and symbolic. *Just don't let Luke show up.*

"He's not the type to risk making a fool out of himself," Dave said when she voiced her concerns over breakfast. "Besides, he was over Dina long before the whole thing actually ended."

"It's not about *feelings*, Dave...it's about control."

"No, he's moved on. He could care less."

"Dina said women don't break up with him. She was worried that her leaving town without talking to him and me badmouthing him would make him want to prove something."

"Prove what? I think you need to stop worrying. This is a great day for Dina. Be happy."

But then, just fifteen minutes earlier, while she finished feeding J.D., Dave had told her he'd seen what he thought was Luke's car in a parking lot across the street. Then Luke had passed under the streetlights, crossing over and appearing at the bottom of the stone steps leading up to the church doors.

"I thought Dina was crazy when she told me she didn't want to get married here because he would show up," Celia had said.

"I thought you were both crazy for worrying about a guy that's old news," Dave said. "Anyway, I told him he wasn't welcome and to keep moving along."

"What did he say?"

"He claimed he wanted to see Dina one more time and wish her well, but I told him no. Tony and Jim were with me and saw him so I left them to guard the front door and made sure all the other entrances were locked. He can't get in."

"That rat bastard! He doesn't want to wish her well, he wants to twist her all up inside and prove to himself she still has feelings for him," Celia said bitterly. "He wants to ruin this for her."

"I have to tell Michael," Dave said.

"Why? I think that is a big mistake."

"How will I explain why they need to go out the side door and into a waiting car after the reception downstairs, rather than walk out the front doors?"

"Okay, I can go along with that but do *not* tell Dina. Maybe we'll tell her later and maybe we'll never tell her. But not a word to her today. Make sure Michael understands that too."

"How did he find out, Celia?"

"I don't know. We were so careful, no announcements, inviting only close friends and co-workers. I'll figure it out later, when the wedding's over and they're long gone on their honeymoon." Dave had nodded in agreement and left to talk to Michael while Celia headed for the bride's room. She wanted to get it all over with quickly, before anything else happened. "Ready, Dina?" Celia asked. She'd reached the top of the aisle, near the front door, and was knocking lightly on the bride room's door.

The organ was beginning to play in the distance. Dina opened the door. Her eyes held that faraway dreamy look that, to Celia, spelled danger.

"CeCe?" Dina's voice held a thousand questions.

"Dina, Granny is here with you. She would love Michael and she would know, like I do, that he will always be there for you." Dina smiled softly at her. "He loves you, Dina, and you love him. We didn't learn much about that kind of love from Justine or from Granny. That's why you picked so many bad guys. You didn't know what to look for. Then you found Michael or he found you, and now he's teaching you what love between a man and a woman is supposed to be. Just like Dave taught me."

Celia could see Dina snap back into the moment and she sighed with relief. Picking up her flowers, she handed Dina the bouquet of white roses and forget-me-nots then offered her arm.

"Ready to give me away, CeCe?" Dina winked, looping her arm through Celia's.

"I never thought I would...or that I could. I've taken care of you for so long. But I can give you to Michael and I know, Dina, you will be alright."

"I can take care of myself, you know," Dina retorted with a laugh.

Celia opened the door to the entryway and they both stepped to the top of the aisle.

"Dina," Celia said, the candles blurring as tears filled her eyes. "I believe you can take care of yourself."

"Just trust me."

"I trust you." Celia looked down the aisle. Candles burned in holders attached to each pew and flickered all over the church. She'd come in early to light candles for Maeve and Dina, and then ended up lighting one for her mother too. Perhaps she could finally forgive Justine after all these years. Straight ahead, Michael stood waiting, so tall in his suit, with Dave beside him. People were on their feet now, waiting for Dina. The music was playing.

"Let's go, CeCe," Dina said. "I'm ready."

Celia looked at her sister whose eyes were locked on Michael and she believed Dina was ready, that the worst was behind both of them now. They moved forward together as if they were slowly gliding and when she put Dina's hand in Michael's and stepped aside, she felt a sense of weightlessness. She prayed silently for Dina as the priest took them through their vows and J.D. slept soundly on the pew behind her.

CHAPTER 39

LUKE

L uke had stood in the shadows of a parking lot across the street from St. Patrick's Church and pondered what he should do. He and Stacy had had the mother of all fights last night when she told him Dina was getting married the next day at St. Patrick's to "some black guy from New York City," as Stacy put it. He didn't care about that, he said, he just couldn't believe that she had never answered his letter, that she wouldn't at least talk to him while she was back in town.

"I sent a letter to her at Crown Publishing last fall, after the attack on the World Trade Center, to see if she was alright," Luke said. "I asked her to contact me so we could talk and she never did."

Stacy looked uncomfortable. She stood up from where she'd been sitting next to him on the couch and walked to the other side of the room, looking out of the window. Luke had been seeing her for about nine months now and he really liked her. Not only was she great in bed and great to look at, she was a lot like him in ways that made him uncomfortable—but also happy he didn't have to hide the darker, weaker sides of himself. He could be who he was, warts and all, with Stacy. It was a relief of sorts and he'd not strayed or cheated on her since their first date.

"I have a confession to make," Stacy said. "I'm sure you'll be furious, but you would've done the same thing if you were me. I saw the letter you addressed to Dina on the counter one morning and I took it out of your mailbox. She never got it."

"You fucking bitch!" Luke said, coldly, as he stood up. "Did you read it? Did you?"

She nodded, panic on her face.

"Get out!"

She stood there frozen.

"I said, get out," Luke repeated. "Get the fuck out! And no, I would not have done that to you. I don't own you and you don't own me."

"You told her you wanted her forgiveness, that you cared for her but you would never be in love with her," Stacy said. "I was afraid I'd lose you."

"Get this through your head, Stacy," Luke said. "I may not ever be in love with anyone. It may not be who I am or who I'm capable of being. But I'm more honest and more of a real person with you than with anyone I've ever dated. But no one, not even you, sneaks around behind my back and invades my privacy. Get out before I throw you out."

"What are you going to do?" Stacy asked. "About Dina and her wedding, I mean?"

"None of your goddamn business." Luke grabbed her purse in one hand and her arm in the other and shoved her out the door into the garage. He could hear her crying but he couldn't feel anything but rage. It was a rage he did not understand because with Stacy he was as close as he could come to being in love. And yet Dina continued to evoke these feelings of guilt and need, of wanting forgiveness, and of fury at being unappreciated and misunderstood.

So he'd found himself standing in the shadows across from the church, composing his thoughts and deciding what he would say to Dina when he saw her again for the first time in nearly two years. Then he'd crossed the street from the parking lot, intent on entering the church. The black jacket and jeans helped to partially hide him, but the streetlamp shone off his gray and silver hair. Suddenly the church doors had opened and Dave came down the steps with lightning speed until he was in front of Luke. Two men stood at the doors like sentries in the night, arms crossed over their chests, as though posing as the Secret Service.

"What's up Luke?" Dave said. "Where do you think you're going?"

Dave's voice was amiable but his eyes were hard and his mouth was set in a tight, pinched line across his face.

"I just need a couple of minutes with Dina," Luke said. "To explain, to talk...some closure and forgiveness. And to wish her well, of course."

"Well, that's not what Dina needs, right now," Dave said. "She needs you to stay away from her and let her go, in peace, into what will be a wonderful future for her, I'm sure."

"Come on, Dave," Luke cajoled. "You and I know she's still in love with me and it's not fair to her or that guy if she marries him."

"She's not in love with you, Luke, and you are not going to play mind games with her just to satisfy your own ego," Dave said. "Besides, it's a rehearsal, not the actual wedding. Tomorrow is the wedding."

Luke hesitated. Maybe he had twenty-four hours to find her and talk to her. But something was wrong. Dave wouldn't wear a tuxedo for a rehearsal dinner. He must be lying.

"So you're not going to let me in there?" Luke asked.

"No, I'm not," Dave said. "I don't know who told you about the wedding, but Dina deserves better than this. She deserves better than you, and that is what she's going to do. Marry someone better." They stood in a silent impasse for moment. "Get lost, Luke. No one wants you here. Have some pride and leave."

Luke had shrugged nonchalantly and walked back to his car. Dave stood on the steps of the church talking to the other men, watching him, and then he went back inside. Luke had pulled out and drove around the block to a nearby restaurant, where he'd been sitting at the bar for an hour, drinking Jack and Coke, wondering why he didn't just go home and forget about it. Forget about her. He knew they were lying, that Dina was getting married tonight, but it made no difference to him. Dave was right, he needed to get lost, move on. He *had* moved on, for Christ's sake, but he wanted to see her. Luke paid his tab and left.

His head was buzzing from the whiskey as he pulled the car around the block and parked it on Holland Street, out of sight. He walked around to the back parking lot behind the church and boldly sat on the hood of a parked car. The liquor made him feel warm and cocky. A long black limousine was parked next to the side door of the ancient stone church, its shiny chrome winking in the headlights of passing cars and the security lights amidst the shadows cast by the eaves of the church's roof.

He reached into his breast pocket for the cigarette he'd bummed off a guy at the bar and the bar matches he'd grabbed to light it with. Luke didn't smoke anymore, but he was half-drunk and the nicotine tasted good. It had a calming effect, mixing with the whiskey in an easy, familiar way he'd forgotten he liked. He began blowing silly smoke rings into the air until he realized the limo driver might see him. Then he hopped off the car and crushed the cigarette onto the pavement, watching as it flickered red briefly then went black and cold. It seemed as though he'd leaned against the car for a long time, his leg and back muscles getting stiff, but when Luke looked at his watch, its glowing digital face showed it had only been thirty-five minutes since he arrived.

The side door to the church opened and Luke crouched down quickly. Dave appeared, glancing around the parking lot before speaking to the limo driver. Luke peered around the front of a small, white Toyota. Even if Dave saw his car he had no idea where Luke was. He heard the driver start the limo's engine and he peeked over the car's hood. Dave was gone.

Luke rushed across the parking lot at a crouched run, stopping beside another car several yards away from the limousine, but firmly in the shadows of a neighboring building. The church door opened again and a small crowd of people poured out. He could see the priest and Celia captured in the light from the open doorway. Dave came out holding a small child, followed by a tall, well-built guy with dreadlocks tied back in some sort of ponytail.

Surely that was not Dina's husband, Luke thought. That guy wouldn't fit in here at all, in Luke's opinion. Then he realized Dina would not be living her married life here. She would be gone to New York for good. He'd read that she had a book coming out next year, a collection of short stories and poems. It was a new life for her.

A burst of white appeared in the doorway and there was Dina. The car door opened for her and for several seconds she was caught in the car's interior lights glowing outward from the open door of the limo. Her hair had grown back and her veil lifted on a small breeze, causing her to pause. She looked directly at him as he stood slowly and leaned against the car, arms crossed. She looked breathtakingly vulnerable. Luke raised his hand to wave but he was seconds too late. She disappeared into the vehicle, the tall, brown man following behind her, and then it pulled away and she was gone.

He began walking from the church parking lot back to the street, where he crossed and was nearly to his car when he heard Celia calling his name. Luke wondered if Dina had seen him, if she had thought, for a moment, about coming over to speak to him. He would enjoy pissing Celia off. It would be a good way to blow off steam before he headed home. Dina was married and gone. Yet, it felt as unfinished between them as it

ever had. He was sure that it was not over yet, just as he was sure it
would be a long time before they met again.

CHAPTER 40

CELIA

"So why are we leaving out the side door?" Dina had asked suspiciously. "Tell me again."

The pictures were over and the champagne drunk. The cake was cut and partially eaten.

"The neighborhood isn't all that safe, Dina," Dave had said. "The priests lock the front doors when no one is upstairs to make sure there isn't a break-in. All the doors are locked by eight o'clock except one side door if people are still here."

Celia fussed over cleaning up, trying not to make eye contact with Dina. She wasn't sure Dina wouldn't see through her nervousness and ferret out the lie.

"The car is right outside the door," Michael said. "And I don't know about you, Mrs. Mann, but I'm ready to go on our honeymoon."

Celia had watched him kiss Dina and saw her sister smile and visibly relax. They were heading straight to the airport and flying to Toronto for the night. In the morning they would head for Ireland and a three-week tour of the British Isles. Their suitcases were loaded in the trunk of the limousine. Dina had wanted to change from her wedding gown into a pair of jeans and a short-sleeved shirt, but Michael insisted it would be even more fun to fly in full wedding attire. Since Dina's wedding dress was a fairly simply, comfortable gown, more like a long summer dress with a jacket, he said they could have a bit of fun on the plane without feeling uncomfortable. Celia knew Dina put the change of clothes in her carry-on. Celia thought the whole idea sounded more comfortable for Michael than for Dina, but she agreed with him just to get her sister out of the church and out of Erie quickly. In a couple hours, she could slip into a bathroom at the Toronto airport before boarding for Ireland, put on casual clothes and relax. When they went downstairs for the reception Dave had reported that Luke's car was gone. There had been no sign of him, but still she sensed he was there, somewhere nearby.

Outside, the limousine driver had opened the back door and waited. As Dina walked forward, her veil lifted slightly on a breeze and she paused, staring into the seeming darkness of the huge parking lot behind the church for a moment, then one hand on her veil and the other lifting her skirt, she ducked into the car with Michael close behind her. They waved good-bye as the car drove away.

Celia saw him, leaning against a car, half in the shadows, wearing jeans and a black leather jacket. Dave was holding J.D. and everyone was filing back into the church to help clean up or just gather their things and head to hotels and homes. Celia scanned the parking lot again but he was gone. She stayed outside and headed for the front of the church, where she found him, keys in hand, walking to his car, which he'd parked on a side street.

"Luke," Celia called to him, lifting her long dress, crossing the street in several easy strides.

He stopped without speaking and waited for her to reach him. When she did, she wished she had not called out to him. She wished she could not see the smirk on his face, the arrogant glare in his eyes.

"Celia, how nice to see you again," Luke said. "Miss me?"

"What the hell did you think you were doing, lurking around here?" Celia said. "You sick son-of-a-bitch! Trying to ruin her wedding after all you've done to her."

"Done *for* her you mean, don't you?" Luke said sarcastically. "I was the one that stuck by her during cancer, remember? I just wanted to wish her well is all."

"You mean cheated on her during cancer and broke her heart? You were here to prove to yourself that she couldn't marry or love some other guy. You just can't stand it, can you?"

"She doesn't love some other guy and she never will. If I called, she would come back. But I won't do that to her. I care about her too much."

"Bastard!" Celia cried. "She loves Michael and you can think otherwise all you like. But if you ever call her to come back, you'll deal with me. I won't have you ruining the best thing that ever happened to her."

"Ahh, big sister Celia to the rescue." Luke laughed. "But even you just admitted that I could ruin things. Because you know she would come back. It's my call and I'm letting this guy have her."

Celia could hear Dina asking to be trusted. What she had blurted out was not honoring her sister's request. "Why don't you just try calling her to come back, Luke? I'm absolutely sure you'll be in for a big surprise. And no one will enjoy watching the results more than me."

She turned to go, leaving him standing there, praying under her breath that he would not take her up on the dare. She wanted to trust Dina, but she did not. Not yet.

CHAPTER 41

DINA

The flight from Erie to Toronto was the last one of the night and it was packed with people ready to hit the Toronto nightlife for a weekend of musical theater, drinking and dancing. They whooped and hollered when Dina entered the plane in a wedding dress, Michael in his tuxedo close behind.

"Just married!" Michael called to the other passengers. They all cheered, alternately yelling "kiss" and "champagne." Dina and Michael complied with a big kiss for their new audience. A happy, easygoing flight attendant took the microphone and announced there were a few bottles of champagne and, once they took off, she would pour a glass for everyone to toast the new couple. Another round of cheers was followed by the sound of seat belts buckling as the engines roared and the plane began to taxi toward the runway. "Today Toronto, tomorrow Ireland," Michael said.

Dina touched the wedding band over and over, turning it on her finger. She had been surprised, from the moment he looked into her eyes and put it on her finger, by how she felt. It was a good feeling of coming home, a feeling of beginning something solid and wonderful together. All the months and weeks of planning had not erased her doubt and worries or dreams plagued with past loves and mistakes, the way that one moment had. As Michael, with the love in his eyes, the words rolling off his lips, slid a ring onto her finger, she became part of something permanent with him. She knew, in that second, that she had made the right decision, that he was the right man. She should have known before with absolute certainty that she was in love with him, but she had not. She had doubted herself.

"Dina?" Michael looked at her with concern. "Are you okay?"

"Yes, I'm better than okay." She smiled at him. "I love you and I'm so happy to be your wife. It's the first thing I think I've ever really done right in my life."

"No regrets?" He laughed.

"None, except perhaps that I didn't hear another word of what I'm sure was a lovely ceremony after you put this ring on my finger."

He held her hand and leaned back into the seat, closing his eyes, his face peaceful. She would never tell him that she had doubted the depth of her love for him or that she had worried she was too damaged by her past to be his wife. She would never tell him that, for a second before she dove into the waiting limousine, she was sure she'd seen Luke, and she'd felt no more, no less than relief that Luke was her past, and Michael her future. Dina should have known all of this before she'd said she would marry him. Some things, Dina decided, were better left unsaid.

She looked at their hands resting together, light brown on soft, freckled white, clasped but relaxed, the twin gold circles shining. Ireland would be green with leaves and flowers just starting to bloom in earnest. Everything was beginning anew with them. She hoped her past in Ireland would not rear its head in an ugly way. Kathleen was meeting them and Dina was anxious to hear about Katie, to hopefully see pictures that would let her know that, like marrying Michael, giving Katie up had also been a good decision.

***

They'd been holed up in the Conrad Hilton in Dublin making love since the previous afternoon, only taking a break to order room service and sleep. Dina was dreamy and sated, happy through and through as she now walked with Michael toward the familiar Quays pub in Temple Bar where they were meeting Kathleen and her children for lunch.

It had been so long since Dina had seen Kathleen. They swapped Christmas pictures.

"Does it bring back any bad memories, being here?" Michael asked.

"No. I admit I was a little worried but it's just been this great new adventure," Dina said. "I credit you with that!"

Michael laughed. He seemed a bit nervous, like he had that night in the carriage in Central Park when he'd proposed to her. "Dina...Kathleen has a surprise for you, but I'm thinking perhaps it shouldn't be a surprise." Michael paused. "Maybe I should tell you."

He stopped on the sidewalk, shifting from one foot to the other. He shoved his hands in his pockets and took them out again.

"Maybe you should tell me," Dina said. "I'm not big on surprises." He was so nervous she was concerned. He looked down at his feet then cleared his throat.

"For some reason, Kathleen thinks everything will just work out fine...but I tried to tell her you needed some time to absorb...to decide if you could pretend."

"Pretend what?" But in that moment, Dina knew. The entrance to the pub was no more than ten feet away. "Look at me, Michael. Look me in the eye and tell me if Katie is in that pub."

"Yes, Dina. She is."

Dina began jogging toward the door. She could hear Michael behind her. He caught up just before she yanked the door open, blocking her way. "Dina, wait."

"No! I've been waiting since the day I let her go."

"Katie doesn't know who you are."

"Kathleen wouldn't do that, Michael. Not when I've waited so long to see her."

"I tried to tell her that it wouldn't work, just springing this on you, but she seemed to think you'd be fine and she could talk with you about it later."

"I don't know how I'm going to be..."

"Well, Katie's adopted parents said she could meet you, but only on the condition that she be told you're Kathleen's American friend. They think it would be too much for her. That she's not ready. So you can't go in there unless you can abide by that."

Dina froze. All this time, since she'd handed her beautiful baby over to strangers to be raised, she'd dreamed of this moment. Now she was finally going to meet her daughter, but as a stranger, someone the girl did not associate in any way with her biological mother.

"That's why I disagreed with Kathleen," Michael said. "No one wants this sort of thing to be a surprise. I wanted you to be ready. I'm sorry, I just couldn't decide when to tell you."

"I have to pretend." Dina was near tears.

"Kathleen thought it would be better for Katie to just get to know you as a person without the stress of knowing who you really are first. If all goes well, they can tell her later. I don't think she meant to hurt you, she was just thinking about the child's feelings and assuming you could manage fine," Michael said.

"They'll tell her later...as in, when I'm gone back to America, when it's too late to touch her or hug her?"

"You don't know what she knows, what her adoptive parents have told her about you. I'm trying to protect you...Kathleen is trying to protect Katie."

He took her hand and began walking away from the pub.

"No, no Michael. We are *not* leaving. I want to see her."

"I know, we're just taking a walk around the area for a few minutes to relax, calm down, and be ready." It seemed an instant and an eternity before they were back in front of the pub. She clutched his hand and stared at the door, as people went in and out, looking at her oddly. "Remember, I'm here with you and we can leave whenever you feel the need to."

Dina nodded, then reached for the door handle and, letting go of Michael's hand, ducked through the entrance, her eyes adjusting to the dim lighting, a quick cacophony of smells assaulting her nose as she stepped inside. It was dark and woody, smelling of beer, fish, boiled potatoes and furniture polish, much as she remembered from her youthful days in Dublin. Then she would have scanned the room for Liam, invariably finding him hunched over a small round table in the farthest corner, a half empty mug of Guinness in front of him, scribbling furiously into a tattered notebook. Today her eyes searched for his daughter, her daughter— even after all this time she wanted to remove him from the equation, allow him no part of Katie.

"Dina!" Kathleen was running across the room to hug her and then dragged her back to a table where two little boys about eight and six years old were arguing over a small car. "Ronan, Patrick, stop fighting and say hello to Dina and Michael, come all the way from America to meet us."

Dina introduced Michael to Kathleen and then he slid into a seat along the wall next to the boys, distracting them as Dina stared at the beautiful girl with dark curly hair and wide blue eyes before her.

"Dina, my cousin's daughter, Katie," Kathleen said. "Katie, this is my friend, Dina, and her husband Michael...from America."

Katie held out her hand and Dina took it slowly. She was at one moment the image of Dina and, in a turn of her head and a laugh, one part Liam and three parts Maeve. Dina was entranced with her and afraid all at once. She wondered if Katie could see the resemblance between them. Dina sat down next to Katie, focusing on Kathleen's boys instead, grateful for the distraction their wiggling and fighting caused as she tried to regain some composure. Kathleen waved the waitress over and Michael, sensing Dina's struggle, ordered for them.

"So where's your husband today?" Michael asked.

"Oh, at the office as usual," Kathleen said, with a dismissive wave of her hand. "Missing all the fun again."

"Do you live in New York City?" Ronan said in his loud, little-boy voice.

"Yes, we do," Michael answered.

"Wow!" said Patrick. "We want to go there."

"Well, you can come visit us any time," Michael said.

"Ha! Be careful what you ask for, Michael." Kathleen chortled. "They're a handful."

"My birth mother lives in America," Katie said softly.

Her words floated above the clattering of platters and mugs of beer being placed on the table amidst the noisy arguing and jostling of Ronan and Patrick seated next to her.

"Really?" Dina asked. "In New York City?"

"I'm not sure," Katie said. "Maybe."

Dina looked into intelligent blue eyes so like her own, a mirror of freckles dancing across an identical nose and she thought maybe Katie was quietly figuring it out. She seemed so centered and thoughtful, even a bit mature when compared with the silly teenage girls Dina saw riding the New York subways, trying to dress like the latest celebrity, rambling, immature, and as yet unformed. Dina didn't know what to say or whether to acknowledge that she was, in fact, that mother in America.

"Dina, are you still writing?" Kathleen interjected.

"Yes," Michael said. "She's been published in a number of literary magazines and she has a book of stories and poems coming out in the fall."

One of those poems had been chosen by *The New Yorker* for publication and, although most of the work from her book that had been pre-published had received moderate acclaim and lukewarm reviews, that poem had created more than a little buzz. Such was work that spoke from the heart, from one's pain and experience, Dina had thought at the time of the reviews. It touched a chord in others. The poem was about giving up Katie.

"I need to find the ladies room." Dina stood up and began moving in the direction Kathleen's finger was pointing. She tried not to run. *Just walk calmly*, thought Dina, *as if everything is fine*. In the bathroom she dropped her purse on the floor between her feet and began running cold water at the tap, splashing it on her face. She heard a toilet flush and a stall door slam. The water in the sink next to her ran, but still she remained bent over her sink.

"You alright there, miss?" she heard a voice ask.

"She'll be fine, I'm with her," Kathleen responded.

Dina stood up, reaching for a paper towel to dry her face. Kathleen began to hug her, patting her shoulder, still Dina could not cry.

"She knows who I am, Kathleen," Dina said.

"No, no, she doesn't," Kathleen said. "I simply told her you were my friend from America."

"Get real, we look almost identical. Except at moments when she turns a certain way or makes a certain expression and I see Liam, even my granny."

"What do you want to do?"

"I'm not sure. I never wanted to disrupt her life. But I don't want her to think I abandoned her because I didn't care, either." Dina leaned her back against the cool tiles of the wall and crossed her arms over her chest, dropping her head. She wanted Katie to know, yet she didn't want to face her if she was angry or hurt. And what if she wanted to come and live with them? Dina had no idea how to be a mother. "You know, Kathleen, one of the prices of my cancer is that I may not be able to have any more children. Katie may be it...yet, I gave her away. She doesn't truly belong to me."

"Why don't we get through lunch, then later, when you're gone, I'll talk to Colleen and see if we should tell her," Kathleen said.

"What if she's angry with me?" Dina asked. "What if she hates me for giving her away?"

"Well, we'll cross that bridge if we have to," Kathleen said. "Right now we need to get back out there and act normally, as if nothing is wrong."

Dina nodded, checking herself in the mirror and taking a deep breath.

"I'm sorry, Dina. I shouldn't have done this without talking to you first."

"No, you did the right thing. I would have told you not to bring her. But I needed to meet her, to see that she was alright, that I made the best decision I could in giving her a better home." Dina began walking toward the exit, then turned to Kathleen and hugged her. "I could never have cared for her all these years, Kathleen. I've barely been able to care for myself."

They walked back out to the table, arm in arm, Dina pasting a smile on and trying to relax as much as possible. Michael carefully asked Katie questions about her school and her friends while Dina drank in every word, wincing when she chatted excitedly about her Mam and Dad and their plans for her thirteenth birthday party next February. She couldn't wait to be a teenager.

When they left Dina could feel herself, as if she were somehow not a part of her own body, hugging Kathleen good-bye then turning to find Katie hugging her as well. She didn't want to go through it again, holding her and letting her go into a life that Dina could not be part of. As soon as Kathleen walked away, herding the two boys and Katie toward her car, Dina began moving as fast as possible to find a taxi and get back to the hotel, Michael at a near jog trying to keep up.

"Talk to me, Dina," he said. "Slow down and talk to me."

"Can't...I can't," she said, nearly running now.

"Dina, I'm sorry, this was a mistake," he said. "Kathleen and I should have known better."

"It wasn't a mistake." Dina opened the back door of a small taxi cab. She hopped in, sliding across the seat to the window, turning her head away to look out. "Conrad Hilton, please." She could feel Michael's warmth as he slid in next to her and took her hand. The door closed and the cab pulled out into traffic. "Michael, I just think I'm going to completely lose it and I don't want people to see me."

"I ruined our honeymoon, baby. I'm so sorry."

"You didn't, you didn't. I just don't know what I think. I need to think, I need to cry, I need to just be away from all these strangers." Dina cried for a long time later, in their room, while Michael held her. She let it all out, the shock, the pain of twelve years since she'd given Katie away. She felt better—emptied, but whole. When it was over, she and Michael lay side by side on the bed facing one another. "You know I might not be able to have any other children. Because of the cancer and the chemo, it might not be possible. Katie might be the only one, and yet, she's not really mine."

"She looks so much like you." Michael touched her cheek, a gentle, reassuring caress.

"What if she wants to come and live with us? Or what if she hates me and never wants to see me again?"

"If she wants to live with us then we'll take her in," Michael said. "And I thought she seemed awfully mature and levelheaded for her age. Maybe she'll just need some time to absorb all of this."

"We're only here another week. What should I do? Maybe she shouldn't ever learn the truth. Just keep thinking of me as Kathleen's American friend."

"We'll just wait and see," Michael said. "Kathleen will call."

Michael pulled her close and Dina felt a wave of exhaustion pulling her in its undertow, drawing her down. She tried to mouth to Michael how much she loved him for being there for her. How she loved that he put her first and that he loved her so deeply too, but her mouth was as heavy as her body and her eyelids. It was her last thought before she fell asleep.

CHAPTER 42

When Dina awoke, the digital clock glowed midnight in the pitch dark of the room. She was still fully clothed and laying on top of the bedspread. Michael must have asked housekeeping for extra blankets because they were strewn haphazardly across both of them. He lay on his side, his back facing her, snoring lightly. She moved slowly, gently out of the bed so as not to wake him. She was hungry but it was too late for room service. She'd have to raid the minibar, see if there were some pretzels or crackers there to tide her over.

Dina glanced at her cell phone. A little icon above the time showed she had a voicemail. She flipped the top and dialed, hoping it was Kathleen. She opened a bag of pretzels as she listened, smiling.

"Dina, it's me...Kathleen. Well, our Katie is a smart one. She figured out on her own that you're her biological mother. She's such a sweet girl...not angry, just curious. Call me. We'll talk about it."

Dina closed the phone and watched Michael sleeping, breathing in and out, peaceful. Perhaps it was finally over, the years of anguish and insecurity. In choosing this man, Dina could feel things coming together, one step at a time. He'd lifted her out of her inner solitude, that lonely place inside she'd created as a child and populated with fairies and banshees, with leprechauns and dreamy poetry, and was building a world that she had never imagined could be possible for her. She thought of Katie and then of Liam. She had no desire to see him, no unresolved issues or closure to work through. She wondered why, when she had had a child with him, she felt nothing, yet with Luke something residual, something nagging and perpetual, remained. She pushed it down, as she always did, because it disturbed her. It made her feel a lacking in herself that translated into an inability to trust others. She knew she must always trust Michael. Dina slipped into the bathroom so she wouldn't wake him and called Kathleen.

"Kathleen, are you sure she's alright? She's not upset?"

"Well, she's a bit peeved with me for not telling her right up front, but she's not the type to stay angry or upset for long."

"Does she want to see me again?"

"Yes, but Colleen is nervous about this. Katie has reassured her that she's curious about you and wants to learn more, but she loves her parents. Colleen is the only mother she knows."

"I can tell they've been great parents to her. I don't want to cause problems." Dina felt the old twin pangs of guilt and pain. Colleen was Katie's mother, not Dina. "Will she be angry with me, Kathleen?"

"No, she's always been told she was adopted and that her mother gave her away to make sure she had a two-parent home and a better life. She's never been told anything negative about you."

Dina exhaled slowly. Relief washed over her.

"Dina, she's very curious. But remember she's young and impressionable. Her feelings are very tender."

"I would never hurt her, Kathleen!"

"No, you wouldn't. But she will want to know about Liam and that, in and of itself, may be hurtful in the telling of it."

"I'll give some thought to the best way to handle the subject of her biological father."

"Honesty would be best, just delivered gently, Dina. I'll set up a meeting for you two tomorrow. She only has two more days with me before Colleen comes in to pick her up and take her home."

"I'd like to see Colleen if she's willing. I'd like to thank her and reassure her that I'm not here to intrude."

"Alright, Dina. Let me see what I can do. I'll bring Katie by tomorrow and maybe you can take her to the hotel restaurant or just talk in your room. Does that work?"

They agreed on a time the following day. Michael would head out with Kathleen for a few hours and Katie would stay with Dina. Dina couldn't remember being this nervous before, even when she'd faced her first chemo treatment or before giving birth to Katie. She decided she would start by just giving her a hug and go from there.

It worked. Katie told her later she was always hugging her mother and her friends, but that something felt different with Dina. Strange at first, and then as if they fitted together like puzzle pieces. Dina felt as if years of pain, worry, and need for closure were lifted. Her daughter was happy, healthy, and she accepted Dina.

"My mother said you gave me up because you couldn't take care of me. Is that true? Couldn't you have taken me to America?"

Dina loved just looking at Katie, hearing her still-childlike voice with its lovely lilt. She had to steel herself to provide answers she knew could cause confusion or pain.

"I was very young. I was a graduate student with no money and I don't think, emotionally, I knew how to be a mother. I wanted you desperately, but I couldn't give you a good life."

"Didn't your mother teach you to be a mother? Do I have a grandmother or aunts and uncles?"

"My mother was a drug addict. My father, too. He abandoned us when we were young, and my mother died when I was about ten...she wasn't a very good mother. My grandmother, Maeve, took us in and she was wonderful. She emigrated to the U.S. from Ireland as a young woman. It's from her that you get your middle name. Granny Maeve died the year before you were born. And, yes, you have an aunt named Celia...I call her CeCe."

Katie was quiet. Her eyebrows were furrowed in a frown as if she were pondering the answer but it wasn't enough.

"Katie, my sister and I grew up very poor, as did our mother. There was a long history of poverty, abandonment, drugs. I would have taken you home to live with CeCe and I and you would have grown up as I did, fatherless, with very little money. I wanted you to grow up in a safe and loving home with two parents. My grandfather abandoned my mother, too, and look how she turned out. I gave you up to give you something better and to stop history from repeating itself. Does that make sense?"

Katie nodded slowly. "Yes, I think so. My parents really love me."

"And you have lots of friends, a beautiful room of your own, I'll bet, and a good school to go to?"

Katie smiled, nodding.

"Giving you away was the most painful decision I've ever made, but looking at you now, I know it was the best decision I've ever made. I could only have made a very unstable life for you."

"But things are better for you now? With Michael?"

"Yes. It took a long time, but life is very good and very stable now that I'm with Michael. And CeCe is married and has a little boy, J.D."

"So I have a cousin?" Katie grinned.

They were sitting on the edge of the hotel bed, chatting like two college girls. It seemed so surreal to Dina. She pulled out her wallet and removed a picture of J.D., Celia and Dave, handing it to Katie.

"You can keep that photo. I have more." Dina felt like she would give Katie anything at that moment. Anything she wanted if the girl would agree to stay in Dina's life somehow. "Do you want to order room service or go downstairs to the restaurant?"

Katie was quiet for a moment. Then she leaned her head onto Dina's shoulder. "No, I want to stay here with you. Do you have more pictures?"

Dina had one of she and Michael, which she promptly handed over with the promise that she would send more pictures once she was home in New York. She wrote down her address for Katie and handed it to her. The thought of leaving this beautiful girl again made her sad.

"Did my father know about me?" Katie asked. She was sitting up straight again, looking Dina in the eye.

Dina sighed. This, she knew, would be the hardest part of their conversation. "I never told him. I don't know if he ever found out about you."

"Would he have wanted me?"

"I don't know. Maybe, maybe not. I didn't give him the chance because he was so irresponsible. I didn't want him to hurt you the way he hurt me." It broke Dina's heart to see tears in Katie's eyes. "When you're older, I'll help you find Liam, your father, if you want to meet him." Dina hoped that day never came, but she could understand her daughter's curiosity and need to know her biological father.

"Liam...that's his name?"

"Yes, Liam Garrity. The last I heard, he moved to London six months before you were born. I wasn't far enough along to be showing."

"Why did you break up?"

Dina hesitated. Katie was so young. Not old enough to date or understand complex issues. She might not even know much about sex. Or maybe people her age were a lot savvier than they had been when Dina was young. The Internet had changed everything, opened up the world and any subject a child wanted to explore.

"Liam never wanted a commitment. He liked having a lot of girl-friends, not being faithful to just one girl. That didn't work for me."

Katie mulled this over for a minute. "So he cheated?"

"Yes." Dina thought it was best not to expand on the subject.

"Kathleen doesn't like him. I can tell. I asked her about him and her face looked angry."

Dina laughed and hugged Katie again. "No, Kathleen never did like Liam! She's my friend and he hurt me, so she feels just like you would feel if someone hurt one of your friends."

Katie seemed to relax. This made a lot of sense to her, evidently. "I have a lot of friends. Dina, I would like us to be friends too."

Dina could feel the tears welling up but they were good tears, tears of joy. "I'd like that too, Katie."

In the end they agreed to write letters and talk to each other on the phone once a month, if possible.

CHAPTER 43

"What did you just say? You had a baby? When?"

"Take deep breath, CeCe." Dina paused and followed her own advice, taking a deep breath. "When I was in Ireland I got pregnant. I gave the baby up for adoption to Kathleen's cousin, Colleen. It was a girl. They named her Katie...Kathleen Maeve...Maeve after Granny, you know."

"So...so I have a niece who's, what...about twelve years old, and you just decided to tell me about her after all these years? Why, Dina? Why didn't you tell me then and why tell me now?"

Dina could feel Celia's anger pulsing through the phone line as she sat on a kitchen chair in their townhouse in New York within close proximity to the bathroom, reading Katie's latest letter. Dina had been throwing up all morning. Astonished to see positive results on a home pregnancy test several days ago, she'd gone to the doctor yesterday, and this morning she'd confirmed to Michael that she was about three months pregnant.

Michael had yelled the news with delight on the phone with his mother while Dina hung over the toilet heaving up her breakfast. He insisted she stay home, as if she was an invalid, and she'd gratefully agreed. The doctor said, in light of her medical history, they would have to be cautious which, to Michael, meant she should stop working immediately. Dina had no intention of doing that, but she was grateful to be home today, nauseous and tired, but reading Katie's letter in private. That news was what she wanted to tell Celia, but she'd started with Katie, and it wasn't going well.

"I knew something went wrong in Ireland," Celia said. "It was that Liam guy, wasn't it?"

"Yes, Celia. Liam is Katie's biological father, although I never told him about her. And I'm telling you now because I met Katie on my honeymoon. It's a long story, but before that she knew she was adopted but she didn't know I was her mother."

"But *why* didn't you tell me? For twelve years you've kept this secret from me. *Why?*"

Dina was getting peeved, mostly from the nausea but a little from Celia's tone. "Let's just say that you are a little judgmental, CeCe, especially when it comes to me!"

Dina heard a click and then the dial tone. She sighed and looked at the clock. It would take her sister about fifteen minutes to call Dave screaming about Dina's news, then another thirty minutes to calm down enough that Dina could call her back and tell her about the baby. She decided to read Katie's letter again while she waited.

Dina waited, hungrily, for those letters, reading and rereading them a dozen times, working hard to answer Katie's questions about Dina's parents, her life growing up, and who she had become as honestly and kindly as possible. Now Katie wanted to put both families together on her birthday. She wanted Dina and Michael to come to Ireland for her thirteenth birthday and Dina wanted to go. Although she had mixed feelings about seeing her daughter with her adoptive parents, this pregnancy was making that prospect easier. But she'd known that Michael would never have agreed to her traveling during a high-risk pregnancy. She was torn between wanting to give in to every request from this teenage daughter who had been denied her for so long and not wanting to risk the life growing inside her, a life she would not have to give up or hand over to someone else to raise.

It had turned out to be a short debate, with the doctor deciding for them, forbidding her to go, and Michael, as usual, made it easier by suggesting they check with Katie's parents then send her a plane ticket to come and visit them in New York about six months after the baby was born. Michael was pulling the fragments of her life together once again to make something whole.

"I'm so happy I can give you a child," Dina had said. "It seems like you're always giving and I'm taking."

"You're giving a gift to both of us," Michael said.

Dina was tempted to yield to his requests and quit working. Some of her stories and poems were selling and her book would be published and out in stores in the spring. She wanted to try her hand at a novel. But she loved working for Pam and she loved the thrill of digging into a deep pile of manuscripts and wondering if the next bestseller lay there waiting for her to edit it. She didn't feel ambitious like Michael, who was now fielding offers from other publishing houses after Simon & Schuster rejected his bid to be president of his division. So she'd compromised, agreeing to work partially from home during her pregnancy and part-time after the baby was born. She secretly thought that she would know, after she held this baby in her arms, whether she wanted to simply write from home and be a mother or whether she needed to keep that time in the office. Sophia, now retired and sharing a home with her sister, couldn't wait to spend two days a week with what would, probably, be her only grandchild.

Dina sipped water slowly and laid Katie's letter down. She stood up and walked across the kitchen to get the phone. It had a way of subsiding by noon, this need to throw up, and Dina hoped that after she called Celia she could shower and eat a little toast. She didn't remember it being this bad with Katie. There had been some early morning sickness, but then she'd been able to eat and had, in fact, gained a lot of weight. She was older now and her health was not what it had been then. The doctor warned her that, in this first trimester, things were precarious and she needed to get nutrients, vitamins, food, and water to the baby. But she couldn't stand the sight of food. She tried to eat but the food just would not stay down.

Dina looked up at the clock. About forty minutes had gone by. She dialed Celia's office line. "Hello," she heard Celia say. The sounds of a busy office came through the line with her voice.

"CeCe, don't hang up on me!"

"Dina? I'm still furious so this had better be an emergency because, officially, I'm not talking to you!"

"I'm pregnant, CeCe. You're going to be an aunt sometime in March!"

"So, at least this time you decided to tell me."

"Forget it." Dina sighed. "I've been puking all morning and I don't need this. If you can't get over it, then good-bye. Call me some other time."

"No, no...Dina, I'm sorry. Really, I'm thrilled for you and Michael. But won't this be hard on your health?"

"The doctor said I have to be careful, very careful. But it's a miracle, CeCe, truly it is. I never thought this could happen after all that chemo."

"You should quit working," Celia said. "I'd love to quit today. We're short-handed here, J.D.'s sick, and Dave took off to take care of him. It should be me with him."

"That's what Michael said," Dina admitted. "But what will I do all day? I'll be bored out of my mind."

"Write...write books, write poems, do what you do best and write."

Dina could feel Celia warming up to a big lecture about her health and the baby and who knew what else and quickly changed the subject. "So why are you short-handed at work?"

"A girl in my department, Stacy, decided to get married on the spur of the moment last weekend and took off the entire week for a honeymoon somewhere in the Caribbean."

"Oh, well, you should be happy for her, Celia. Quit being so crabby."

"Well, I'm happy in one way, although I think she made a huge mistake, but not so much in another way because I just figured out how Luke knew about your wedding."

"So, you finally admit you knew he was in that parking lot. I told you I saw him just before I got in the car."

"Yeah, I knew, but what I couldn't figure out was *how* he knew."

"So are you saying this Stacy told him?"

"Dina, Stacy married Luke last weekend."

Dina felt an odd mix of emotions mingling with rising nausea that she was no longer sure was the baby. She felt a punch in the gut, followed by relief, then she dropped the phone and ran for the bathroom, struggling with dry heaves that produced nothing, as there was nothing left to expel.

"Dina, Dina, are you there? Are you okay?" She could hear Celia as she picked up the phone.

"I'm fine, sorry," Dina said. "It's the baby. All I do is throw up and I can't keep any food down."

"Try toast and crackers like I did," Celia said. "It will pass, although when you're going through this stage it seems as if it will never end. And get some prenatal vitamins. You have to keep the baby healthy."

"Michael's picking them up tonight on his way home. I hope they dissolve into my system before I throw them up too."

"Dina, go lie down and take it easy."

"Celia, don't talk about me at work anymore. Don't give her any information to take home to him."

Celia was silent. Dina meant it as an admonition rather than an accusation, but she knew it stung her sister to hear it.

"I won't, I promise," Celia said. "I have to go. I'll check up on you tomorrow."

"CeCe? Are we officially talking again?"

"What do you think? I'm still mad at you but you're my sister and you're having a baby. Now say good-bye. Don't make me hang up on you again."

"Bye, CeCe. I love you."

Dina hung up the phone. She knew her sister wanted to keep that promise, but she wouldn't. She would tell Luke's new wife that Dina was pregnant. Celia always believed she could control situations to her liking and she would think this would drive him further away. Dina knew otherwise. It would fuel his curiosity and make her an even bigger challenge and a safer mark. As a married woman, she was more intriguing and less of a threat. The chase without the danger of commitment. That would be very enticing to him.

CHAPTER 44

S
he was born on a snowy St. Patrick's Day morning after hours of exhausting labor that ended in a C-section delivery when Dina's blood pressure skyrocketed and she was too delirious with pain and exhaustion to continue. When the doctor finally handed the baby to her, clean and wrapped in a warm blanket, Dina looked down into two hazel eyes set in Michael's face. With skin the color of warm sand, she had a head full of baby hair that looked like Michael's but was softer, smoother, and fell in tiny ringlets.

"She's perfect," Michael said. "I can't believe she's ours."

"She looks just like her daddy," Dina smiled. She started to hand the baby to him and then stopped. He looked disappointed. "It's crazy, but I just can't hand her to anyone yet. I feel such fear."

Michael lifted Erin from Dina's arms, and then climbed into the hospital bed next to her. Dina put her head on his shoulder.

"Then we'll all stay here together, in bed, like a family," he said.

"Hmm, until the nurse comes and yells at us," Dina said.

But it felt good to be together, just the three of them. She wanted to wake up this way every morning and marvel at her baby, at her husband, at her life. She pinched herself under the covers, but nothing changed.

"So will we name her Erin?" Michael asked.

"Well, we made her in Ireland, I believe, and she was born on St. Patrick's Day, so I know you're not Irish but I'm both Irish and superstitious," Dina said. "I think we have no choice but to name her Erin."

"Hmm, sounds logical to me," Michael said, speaking to the baby. "And what will her middle name be?"

Dina watched Michael's mother come into the room. They all smiled as Michael leaned forward to show off Erin. Sophia dropped the packages she was carrying and put out her stout arms to hold her granddaughter.

"Her name is Erin Sophia," Dina said. "I hope you like it."

She could see their stares of concern rather than joy as she felt a slipping sensation within, then everything went very, very black and her last memory was of a roar in her ears.

***

Dina woke up the next day, sore and groggy. She kept trying to ask for Erin, but her mouth was too dry to get the words out. There were tubes running in and out of her, bags hanging overhead, monitors beeping, and the nurse was calling her name. Finally they wet her mouth slightly and she was able to say Erin's name.

"She's fine, your baby is fine," the nurse said.

"What's wrong?" Dina pushed her vocal cords but the words fell out in a whisper.

"You gave us a scare, but I'll let the doctor explain," the nurse answered. She was large and when she moved aside a small, balding man seemed to appear magically from behind her and step up to Dina's bedside. He felt for her pulse, checked the monitors, then began to speak to her.

"You had some pretty serious internal bleeding, Dina," the doctor said. "You've been unconscious for about ten hours and we weren't sure you would come out of it alright. We're going to have to keep you here."

"Erin, Erin?" Dina felt frantic.

"Your baby can go home with her father today."

"No, no, no." Dina could hear the monitors beeping and feel her face flushing. The doctor barked out an order and the nurse left, returning in seconds with a hypodermic needle. "Don't take my baby." Dina felt dizzy.

"I'm going to give you a sedative to relax you," the doctor said. "Your baby is fine, just relax."

Dina began sobbing as she felt the needle prick her arm. They were taking Erin too, just like Katie. She gasped, trying to scream words that left her mouth with no sound. Michael appeared in the doorway and she tried to call to him but her eyelids felt heavy. Then he left with the doctor and she closed her eyes, tears running down her face.

"Honey, it's okay, no one is taking your baby," the nurse said. "Your husband is terribly worried about you, and you aren't well enough yet to take care of her."

Her voice was so soothing, Dina wanted to give in to it but she fought sleep as hard as she could.

"Water," Dina whispered.

The nurse wet her lips with a sponge and gave her a few sips from a straw. It was enough, she hoped, to be able to talk when Michael returned, if she could stay awake.

"You need to rest, Dina," the nurse said. "Quit fighting it and sleep."

"Dina, I'm right here," Michael said.

She could feel his hand in hers, but opening her eyes felt like lifting ten-pound weights off her eyelids.

"Don't let them...take Erin," Dina said, pushing her voice as hard as she could.

"Dina, no one is taking Erin away from you and no one is abandoning you," Michael said. "Erin is coming home to our house where my mother will take care of her until you are better and can come home. You need to work hard to get better."

"Can I see her?" Dina asked.

She could feel tears, the fear was so raw, and she was having trouble focusing on Michael's words. She meant to call Erin's name, but she heard Katie. She didn't know what she was saying.

"I'm bringing Erin in tomorrow," Michael said. "So promise me you will sleep, get well, and get ready to see her."

"Don't leave me, Michael," Dina said.

He didn't look like Michael anymore, just a big shadow. The lights on the ceiling were moving and dancing.

"I'm not going anywhere, Dina. You're delirious and you need to rest. I'm staying right here with you."

"I can't see you. I see other people, dead people..." She began sobbing and the machines began beeping again.

"Feel my hand, Dina." She heard his voice and felt a hand holding hers.

He climbed partially into the bed with her and put his arm around her shoulder. She leaned against him. His heart was thumping loudly through his shirt, but it somehow relaxed her.

"Sir, there are rules here." The nurse sounded angry.

Dina heard arguing, but still Michael stayed.

"Fuck your rules," she heard him say, and then she fell asleep.

CHAPTER 45

Dina awoke to darkness outside her window. She could hear New York's traffic and see a small glimmer from a nightlight across the room. Her body was heavy and sluggish, but her head was clear and rational. She moved her arms and hands gradually, sliding them along the railings that were up, crib-like and holding her in, looking for the call button to summon a nurse. She felt, rather than saw, the plastic, oval device and pushed hard on the button in the center. Minutes later a nurse appeared. She was small and young, with a walk like a wiry gymnast heading for the balance beam, and Dina wondered what had happened to the larger nurse and how long she'd slept this time.

"Water...please?" Dina asked.

"Hey, you seem a lot better. How are you feeling?"

She poured some water into a cup, snapped the lid on, and put a straw in. First a crib, now a sippy cup, Dina thought with amusement. She drank a small amount, slowly, while the nurse held her head up.

"I'm not sure how I feel, but I know where I am and I don't think I'm delirious," Dina said.

"You were running a pretty big fever but it looks like it finally broke." The young nurse pulled a thermometer out of a small blue and white box. It was attached to a spiral cord and it slid easily under Dina's tongue. "Let's just make sure I'm right about that."

They waited in silence until the box beeped and the nurse pulled the thermometer out. "Not bad," she said. "No wonder you feel better. It's just a hair above normal but much, much better."

"My baby?" Dina asked.

"She's a real looker, your baby is. Beautiful and healthy. We couldn't keep her here any longer. Needed the bed for other little ones, so your husband took her home. Now that you're better she can come back for a visit."

"I want to go home." Dina tried to push herself to a sitting position. "I need to be with my baby."

"Well, you need to be able to take care of that baby, and you can't do that yet," the nurse scolded. "Listen, here, you are lucky to be alive. You had internal bleeding and an infection. I think, if you stay on the mend here, that you should be home by the end of the week, but we'll see what the doctor says."

Dina groaned. A whole week of Erin's life, her first week, and she would miss all of it. Erin was bonding with Sophia, not her. She felt such despair, such a huge feeling of loss, that rocked her to the core. When Michael brought Erin in the next morning, Dina was sitting up in bed, steadied with pillows but holding her own. Her midsection hurt a lot but, in a way, she welcomed the pain. Just feeling it, just being aware of it, made her feel alive and on the mend. Holding Erin completed her and fueled her resolve to come home.

"Oh, Michael, I'm missing the first week of her life."

"You're lucky you're alive." He sat in a chair next to her bed, his voice grave, twisting the wedding band that seemed to fit more loosely on his finger now. Erin began to cry and Dina wished she could feed her, but her breasts felt flat and dry. Michael pulled out a bottle.

"She doesn't even know me." Dina was in tears. "She probably thinks Sophia is her mother."

But once the bottle was in her mouth, Erin sucked away happily. Dina couldn't stop looking at her, crying and smiling all at once.

"Dina, the doctor said no more children," Michael said.

"Is that what's bothering you?" Dina asked. Michael shook his head quickly, decisively, from side to side. "You've been so distant. I feel like I've done something to you. She's perfect, Michael. She's enough for me. I never thought I could have children. I told you that before we were married."

"That's not it, Dina. I know you were delirious and you couldn't control what was happening, what you said..." Michael paused. "You said things in your sleep, during your fever and, well, I think we need to talk."

Dina felt a jolt of concern. *What did I say while I was disoriented that caused this tension between us and that look on his face?* She was sure she'd already told him everything from her past that could possibly roll up to damage their marriage.

"I can't remember anything, Michael. All I remember is thinking they were taking Katie again, so obviously I couldn't even differentiate between Erin and Katie."

He said nothing, hanging his head, clasping and unclasping his hands.

"You talked about men—Pierre, Liam, Luke—and other names it was hard to decipher. I think one was Henry," Michael said. "You never once said my name. Were you sure when you married me, Dina? Did you love me enough then or now?"

Dina sighed, removing Erin's bottle and smiling at her sleeping face, her tiny fist clasped around Dina's finger. She had made a mess of so many things in her life. Michael and Erin were all that she'd done right.

"Where should I start?" Dina asked. "I see I've dropped my tangled past into the best thing in my life again, so I guess I'll start with: I love you Michael. I'm more sure now than ever. You are the best thing that has ever happened to me. Well, maybe the second best." She looked down at Erin and then she and Michael both laughed a little nervously. "Pierre was my father. He was an alcoholic, a drug addict, an itinerant worker, and he just left one day and never returned. A year later, we received a call that he had died. Drowned, trying to swim drunk, I believe. I went to college on the life insurance money from his death. Liam was Katie's father. I thought you knew that. And you know about Luke. Henry is Luke's best friend, or at least he was when I dated Luke. He couldn't cross lines and be my friend, but he believed I deserved better and he never told Luke I was leaving for New York until I was gone." Dina watched Michael's face relax. Then he stood up and kissed her quietly, on the cheek first, then the mouth. She didn't want to hurt this man who had given her the first shot at the kind of real family life she'd never known before. "I don't ever want to hurt you again, Michael. Tell me what you want me to do."

"I want you to see a counselor," Michael said. "Too many people have left you in your life, especially men. You are strong in some ways, but broken in ways I can't help you mend."

"I hate shrinks, please don't make me do that."

"I don't think there is another way." He was firm. "If you won't do it for our marriage, then do it for Erin. She needs a mother who is whole and emotionally resilient."

"My writing is good therapy for me, Michael." Dina's wheedling voice tried to cajole him. "I'll quit working and write about the things that have happened to me. I'll work through it that way. We have a perfect life...why mess it up?"

"I told you if you wanted to quit your job and just write and take care of Erin, that's fine with me. But you need professional help. Hell, maybe we both need to go together. Life is messy. Life is not about neat endings in carefully wrapped packages, Dina." He reached for Erin.

Dina handed her over and kissed Michael on the cheek as he bent over her bed, then slid her arms under the blankets to hide how badly her hands were shaking. She wished desperately for Maeve, as she had so many times, with her familiar lilting voice and soft flow of stories that created dreams now lying like fine linen on the old, rotting table boards of her past life.

"Michael?" He was at the door. "I'll ask the doctor for a referral."

He nodded, mouthing a thank you so as not to wake Erin.

"Michael?" she said again. He was almost out the door. "Do you still love me?"

He turned and nodded his head, and then he was gone. Dina felt empty, bereft of that which had given her a new start and lost in the confusing wilderness of her past and her emotions. She wondered where she could plant seeds and start to grow something better that would help her let go of what had made her break and run away only to repeat the pattern over and over.

Holding her incision and leaning forward slowly, Dina reached for the rolling table with and the phone the nurse had positioned on it. There was only one person who had been where she had been and could help her. Only one person whose soul would understand the dry, brown branches of her own interior right now.

"Hello?" Dina heard the familiar voice that protected her, that saved her always.

"CeCe? I need you. I need you to come to New York."

"I'll book a flight, bring J.D., and be there by Friday night," Celia said without hesitation. "Will you be home?"

"I think so," Dina said. "No, I'll make sure of it. I'll be home."

CHAPTER 46

"Are you saying you think I need psychiatric help, too?" Dina said. "I mean, I know I make bad decisions but how do I go from babbling about old boyfriends in delirium to needing a shrink?" She was banging things around the kitchen unnecessarily. All she needed was a small frying pan and a spatula to make a couple grilled cheese sandwiches. She heard a wail, from far away at first, then loudly through the baby monitor, followed by another, deeper cry. "Shit, now I woke the baby."

"I think you woke both Erin and J.D.," Celia said, heading through the doorway. "I'll take care of it, just make lunch...quietly."

Dina buttered bread and slapped cheese between the slices. She was angry at Celia for agreeing with Michael and her incision was hurting on top of it all. She wanted to make noise. It wasn't fair. She had summoned Celia here to be her ally, to be the one who understood above all others what demons she had overcome and how hard it had been to get to this land of good choices. But Celia had accused her of believing she could live one of the fairy tales she used to submerge herself in when they were kids, of making up a piece of fiction, painting the tale, and then stepping into it and expecting to live happily ever after.

The sandwiches were done by the time Celia returned. Dina dropped a few potatoes chips onto the plate with them and poured some ice tea.

"You know, CeCe," she said as soon as Celia had taken a bite. "I believe in the fairy tale. I've been chasing it all my life and now I've found it. Going to a therapist is only going to mess me up and, in turn, make a mess of a good thing." She wanted to get her point across while Celia could not respond, struggling as she was to remove melted cheese from the roof of her mouth, chew, and wash it down with her drink. "I think Michael is overreacting. It's not like I didn't tell him everything, even things I hadn't told you, like about Katie, before we were married. Now that I'm home, he and Erin and I should just start living our family life together."

Celia continued to eat in silence, wiping her mouth and hands with the now soggy napkin every so often. Dina had slapped too much butter on the sandwiches, she could see that now.

"Aren't you going to say anything?" Dina asked.

"You put too much cheese on this sandwich." Celia popped the last bite of her sandwich in her mouth and sat back, arms folding lightly over her chest, mouth chewing slowly, staring hard at Dina. Dina's sandwich remained untouched, cold, the outer edges of the cheese hardening slightly. "You just want me to help you get out of going to therapy."

"I thought you would agree because you understood," Dina said defensively.

"It is exactly because I understand that I disagree with you and agree with Michael," Celia said. "It is because I understand you better than anyone in this world that I'm surer than he is that you need to get some help. Not because you have psychiatric issues, Dina. Because someone needs to help you sort it all out. Not me. Someone who doesn't feel the pain, who is detached and impartial, with a separate view of what happened to us as children and where that took you."

"You think that's it, don't you? You think our childhood somehow screwed me up and you came out just great, all practical and responsible, and making good choices."

"Knock it off, Dina. I think we both came out of the nightmare that was our parents and childhood screwed up. We just manifest it in different ways. You think Dave and I haven't had problems because I'm controlling, afraid of risk and change, obsessed with protecting you?" Celia said angrily. "God, I thought we were going to get divorced over you, your cancer, and your relationship with Luke, because I put all of that before my pregnancy and my marriage."

"Okay, okay...I hear you."

"You've got a beautiful, perfect life with this great guy who wants to help you and if you run away this time you might lose something worth keeping." Celia got up and poured herself a cup of cold coffee leftover from that morning then stuck the mug in the microwave to warm up.

"That's probably not going to taste good anymore." Dina tapped her fingers on the tabletop like an angry child, playing with her napkin, slouching slightly in the chair. She wouldn't quite make eye contact with Celia.

"So, why do I do it then, Dina? You tell me. Why do I take old coffee from breakfast and reheat it?"

Dina was silent, petulant at first, then she sighed and rolled her eyes. "You do it out of habit." When they were children, when Justine didn't leave any food for them, Celia would heat up old coffee and they'd dip stale bread in it. "What kind of parents let us drink coffee at that age? I'd never do that."

The bell went off on the microwave and Celia pulled the steaming mug out then crossed the room, pulling her chair closer to Dina before sitting down. She leaned forward so Dina had to make eye contact and took her hand.

"Dina, bad parents, incompetent parents, parents who care more about themselves than their kids leave those kids without food. If we hadn't had Granny to teach us and help us we might have been drinking alcohol or doing drugs instead of drinking stale coffee. Look, J.D. needs to know that Dave and I love him and are there to provide food and clean clothes and, most of all, stability and routine for him so he can feel safe. When I see what I need to give him every day to make sure he grows up to be a normal, healthy, functioning adult, I know how much we were robbed of before we were even old enough to figure out that something was wrong."

Dina nodded now, tears on her cheeks as she closed her hand around Celia's.

"Would you come with me?" Dina asked. "To counseling?"

"You know I can't do that, Dina," Celia said. "For one thing, I don't live in New York and I can't come up here every week. Besides, I think we both need to work through this on our own. We've been crutches for each other for too long."

"I can't do it alone. I need you."

"You won't be alone, you'll have Michael. And it's my fault that you need me. You ran away to your fantasies, imaginary friends, and stories. I ran away by focusing totally on you and your needs and ignoring what was happening to me."

Dina put her arms on the table and lay her head on them. Her back and shoulders began shaking first and then deep sobs rumbled up through her. Celia rubbed her shoulders and waited. The wall clocked ticked methodically, like a metronome, keeping time with the faint sounds of cars traveling the street outside to accompany Dina's sobs. After a while she slowed down, then stopped, resting her cheek on her arm and blinking away tears.

"If you go to counseling here, alone, I'll go to someone at home. We can talk each week. I'll help you, but we have to do the actual counseling part on our own."

"You don't need help, CeCe."

"Yes, I do...I just realized that I do. If I don't, I'll smother J.D. and try to control him out of my own needs the way I did to you."

"It's not fair," Dina said.

Celia put her head down on her arm on the table and they stayed that way, facing each other for what seemed an eternity, just holding hands and breathing.

"No, it's not fair," Celia said, finally. "No child should have to spend a lifetime undoing disasters like Justine and Pierre. But we can do it and succeed, Dina. We can, for our kids and our marriages, we can do it."

"If we do this, CeCe, we do it for ourselves. We make ourselves right and the rest will come, it will work out."

And Dina knew, in that moment, that she was more durable than her sister, possessing a profound sense of interior power that constant searching, writing, and journeying through failure time and again had deepened and solidified in a formidable way. Dina needed to, once again, step inside and draw upon herself, then go forward to reinvent her world in a way that moved her in a better direction. Celia had stayed in the same town, in the same universe, in the same life roles that had been so violently shoved upon her as a child. She had never reinvented herself into a whole and magically unique woman, never thought of who she could have been with different parents and then moved in that direction as Dina had done.

Dina stood up and took Celia's hand. They went upstairs and lay down to take a nap much as they had as children, when they escaped, hungry and exhausted, to the warm comfort of Maeve's house.

CHAPTER 47

Erin shrieked with glee and Dina watched with a smile from a blanket within the last tentacles of shade extended by a massive tree lining Sheep's Meadow in Central Park. Michael was teaching Erin to fly a kite and every fiber of her five-year-old body quivered with ecstasy and delight as she clutched the controls and, with ongoing help from her father, kept it airborne. Dina had been alternating between editing some poetry for a collection she hoped to publish next year and watching Michael and Erin. Now she lay her papers down and leaned back on her arms, head tipped skyward, to watch the victorious kite, swaying and dipping and jerking to the right then the left in her daughter's chubby hands. It was filled with bold, colorful fish in primary shades that seemed to swim on the air as the kite soared up and down, the bluest of July skies their ocean, the streamers trailing from the bottom of the kite their funky little fish tails. There was such an immense sense of freedom in the pleasure of one small piece of canvas stretched across a small wooden cross and attached to a string.

If Dina watched long enough the churning in her stomach would stop. Her counselor often told her to focus on something light and pleasurable when the old fears escaped to flagellate her with guilt and concern, choking the inimitable, precious present which she worked so hard to live in clearly and cleanly.

"Mommy, Mommy...look!" Erin was hanging onto the kite with one hand and pointing up to it with the other.

Dina laughed and waved, watching Michael run to the rescue as the fish began a perilous nosedive seconds after Erin's call. She was such a beautiful mix of both of them, Dina thought for the millionth time, with Michael's eyes and lips, Dina's nose and freckles, and her hair and skin a cross between them both, leaving her with a creamy tan and long, bouncing curls that were just a tad frizzy in this heat. Dina wondered if things would have turned out like this had she not agreed to go to counseling. It had been rough in the beginning. She almost quit her twice-a-month sessions many times. It had taken four years of work, although after the second year she only went once a month.

"It's like shoveling thick sludge from the bottom of a dark pit," Dina told Celia after her first six months. "I must be really screwed up because the amount of stuff we're digging through seems endless. There's always another layer and another after that."

"Keep digging," Celia said, "keep shoveling. I'm right there beside you doing the same thing."

They both agreed now that their marriages were better for going to get help. Dina had seen, with each heap of psychological muck thrown out the door, a ray of light shining brighter on her life with Michael and Erin. Her writing had deepened and grown too. Although she did some freelance work and a little editing for Pam Posey now and then, her entire existence revolved around that beautiful little girl, the man standing behind her, and the new rhythm in her personal prose. Once she finished this book of poetry about mothering and the emergence of self, she was going to try a children's book. A gift for Erin. Her writing had gone outside of her to become small gifts to those she loved and, in turn, the reviews of her work and the following of loyal readers had grown right along with her, side by side.

Michael laid the kite down gently then flopped onto the blanket next to her, sweat beading his brow, Erin tucked under his arm. She wiggled free and lay on her back between them, giggling. Dina felt happiness that was as sheer and translucent and as undulating as a diaphanous pair of curtains moving in the breeze. She lay on her side, head propped on her arm, and looked down at her daughter whose endless chatter was burbling up from her tiny rose mouth, spilling over them like a waterfall. Michael leaned over Erin to kiss Dina and she sighed.

Dina lay in-between the sunshine and the dappling of the shade, in this, her favorite and most idyllic of parks with the two people she loved most. The pull to reach for Celia and inhale strength from her solid adamant response was still there, quiet but not as insistent as it had once been. Their sisterly bond was no longer a twisted rope of codependency that hurt them both.

"You know what time it is?" Michael asked Erin.

"No." Erin giggled. "What time is it?"

"Why, it's...it's...TICKLE TIME!" Dina said, laughing herself. She began tickling her daughter, her own deeper chuckles echoing off the clear, silver-bell-like peals of joy erupting from the tiny girl's body. Dina looked up at Michael and he smiled. She wanted to freeze every moment of this new life. "Oh, I love you, my little sweetness," Dina said to Erin.

They came home, had dinner, and she wrapped Erin in a big soft towel after her bath, covering her face with kisses. Dina loved the soapy, powdery smell of her daughter as she dried her off and slipped her solid little body into her favorite Dora the Explorer pajamas.

"Is Daddy gonna read me a book?" Erin asked.

"You bet I am," Michael called from the hallway outside the bathroom. "Any book you like."

"*Where the Wild Things Are?*" Erin asked.

Michael laughed his assent.

"Can I jump on the bed for the wild rumpus?" Erin asked.

"No, that's dangerous," Dina said.

Erin pouted, ready to protest. She loved acting out her favorite part of her favorite Maurice Sendak book. Then Dina saw Michael wink at her from the doorway and Erin smiled joyous moonbeams of light at him, running from the bathroom to take his hand and walk toward her room. Dina could hear them as she cleaned up the bathroom, his deep sonorous voice resonating, followed by her high-pitched question, then giggles and whispers, followed by the creaking of the bed springs as he let her jump on the bed for a few seconds.

Dina went downstairs and poured herself a glass of wine. Then she walked out to their tiny backyard, no larger than a postage stamp but highly coveted in the congestion of Manhattan, to wait for Michael. Leaning against an ancient maple, she slipped her left foot out of its well-crafted, leather moccasin and sank it into the soft, damp moss rolling round the base of the tree. He had kissed her beneath this tree under another moon what seemed like light years ago, that man inside the house reading a book to their child. The man who taught her to love and be loved. Eyes closed, she imagined another house in another time of year, sitting on a porch swing as Maeve read poetry to her while the leaves on the big elm tree nearby turned red and gold.

It had been a long time since the rich, loamy smells of Western Pennsylvania in the fall assailed her nostrils. The half-mulched leaves and moss mingled with wet grass came back to her now through the summer air, bringing nostalgia, warm and sweet. Living in a family of three amidst nine million strangers in New York had not erased the upside down feelings of longing for the earthy sensations of her childhood. They were still there, coming over her like the soft touch of hands braiding her hair or the warmth of an ample lap and large breasts amid a fall breeze on a porch swing rocking to and fro.

Dina tipped her head back, arms crossed over her chest and watched as the stars winked at her from far above. She never wanted to leave this life she had carved out with Michael. She closed her eyes and inhaled the night air. It had been a very long time since she felt herself enveloped, cocoon-like, in such absolute stillness. Catching a firefly in her hand, she made a wish and let it go as Maeve had taught her to do so many years ago. It had been an amusing surprise for Dina when she first went to Ireland and learned that not only was this not an Irish tradition, but there were no fireflies in the country. Maeve had become fascinated with the tiny creature upon her arrival in America and had decided they must be magical, capable of granting wishes. The legend had grown, year over year in Dina's childhood, until they became fairies in disguise. Dina only loved her granny all the more for bringing yet another beautiful, creative way of looking at life to her.

"Fairies they are, in truth," Maeve lectured in her singsong intonation with a serious look followed by a wink. "They move too fast in the dark for you to see closely, but they are teeny fairies sent to snatch the wishes from your tongue and carry them to heaven." Dina could feel her grandmother's spirit now, clear and almost transparent. Like a wind it moved through her, filled her, and exited behind her.

She looked up at the moon, caught another firefly, and smiled.

Acknowledgments

hank you to all the women - friends and strangers alike - who shared their stories of love, betrayal, and resulting feelings of lack of self-esteem and self-worth; who, like Dina, had to travel a difficult journey to love and forgive themselves.

My deepest gratitude goes, always, to my family - both those who are still here with me and those who have passed away - for simply believing in me as a person and as a writer. My parents, Shirley Roberts and the late Richard S. Roberts; my brothers, Jim Roberts and Doug Roberts and sister-in-law, Kathy Roberts; and the two greatest nephews an aunt could ever hope to have, Wes Roberts and Dave Roberts.

Several wonderful people gave their time and wisdom to this book at various stages in the writing process. Remo Hammid, my friend and an excellent writer in his own right. Annie Cosby, the best developmental editor I could ever wish for. This book would not have been possible without her excellent editorial skills, her stoic reading and re-reading of the book and her infinite patience with me. And thank you to my many friends across the country for your endless loyalty, support, love, and belief in me and in this book through all the struggles, joys, ups and downs that come with the writing process. You know who you are and you know how much you mean to me. A special thanks to my friends in Erie, PA. It was fun to have a chance to weave the beauty of our home town into a novel.

ABOUT THE AUTHOR

Born and raised in Western Pennsylvania, Janet Roberts graduated from Temple University with a degree in journalism. After working as a journalist and later as a paralegal, she obtained her masters in communications from Edinboro University of Pennsylvania. Janet began writing fiction and poetry as a child and never let go of her dream of publishing a novel. Although her current job has meant moving to a variety of cities, she often returns to her Western Pennsylvania roots in her writing. To learn more, go to *www.booksbyjanetroberts.com*

Made in the USA
Charleston, SC
19 July 2016